The Gospel of Eve

Praise for Rachel Mann's *The Gospel of Eve*:

'*Donna Tartt's* The Secret History *meets A.N. Wilson's* Unguarded Hours
*in Rachel Mann's intoxicating first novel. Part murder mystery, part lesbian
romance, sprinkled with literary criticism and theological conundrums,* The
Gospel of Eve *is a challenging and rewarding read.*'

Michael Arditti

'*Rachel Mann writes with authority and warmth, exploring identity and what
it means to be human.* The Gospel of Eve *is insightful and revealing. It's also
at times good old-fashioned, slightly mischievous fun.*'

Revd Kate Bottley

'*Insightful, compelling and intensely evocative. Disappear from this place into
Rachel's charming, delicately painted world, which tells us so much about
our own. This is a book with one foot inside the church and the other on the
Booker Prize list. Rachel writes with urgency, delicacy and care. A powerful
read from a brilliant author.*'

Paul Kerensa

'*This is a witty, wise, well-informed and utterly compelling blend of thriller
and theology that entertains as it enlightens about the nature of what vocation
is and isn't and the Church's hang-ups about sex and gender.*'

Peter Stanford

'*Underneath the brilliant story, the delicious characters, the questions of
what-happened?,* The Gospel of Eve *is an extended meditation on what
happens when we get the things we ask for. Rachel Mann narrates a story
that weaves holy orders with unholy means. In it, clever people face the crisis
that cleverness won't save you from anything, and that the ache to belong can
destroy as much as it promises. Desire and Betrayal, Love and Lust, Sex and
Loneliness all meet in disturbing and brilliant prose. I read it in a day. But I
won't forget it nearly as easily.*'

Pádraig Ó Tuama

'This novel is everything Rachel Mann is: intelligent, observant, full of passions and interests, and occasionally outrageous. She comfortably establishes herself as a 21st-century successor to James, Howatch and others who examine the light and shadow of those drawn to the Church of England. She is a detective of the reverent, the rebellious and the rebarbative within the Anglican world. Her own positive creativity, wisdom and energy, visible on every page, continue to make that world easier to be part of.'

Revd Canon Mark Oakley

'In the modern Church of England, the women's ministry can be a dangerous place.

'Kitty Bolton, trainee priest at an Anglican seminary in the 1990s, is exposed to Christianity at its most sinister when she's drawn into a cluster of students for whom worship is about lust, obsession and medieval mortification.

'Trying to understand what led to the hanging of her new close friend Evie Kirkland in the seminary chapel, Kitty revisits her risky encounters with tortures both spiritual and physical and is forced to face a secret that shows there can be no real escape from the past.

'The Gospel of Eve is a dark, involving mystery about the kind of people who, if they don't already exist in the Anglican Church, soon will...'

Phil Rickman

'Many memorable fictions are born in the territory where power, religion, intelligence and sexuality intersect (think of Iris Murdoch, A.S. Byatt or Donna Tartt). Rachel Mann, in this haunting novel, brings both a poetic and a theological imagination to bear on the tangled relationships of an unusual group of students preparing for priesthood, and gives us a vividly compelling story about the dangerous games that can weave themselves around faith seeking understanding. A fine fictional debut from an exceptionally gifted writer.'

Dr Rowan Williams

The Gospel of Eve

Rachel Mann

DARTON · LONGMAN + TODD

First published in 2020 by
Darton, Longman and Todd Ltd
1 Spencer Court
140 – 142 Wandsworth High Street
London SW18 4JJ

Print book ISBN 978-0-232-53495-5
eBook ISBN: 978-0-232-53461-0

A catalogue record for this book is available from the British Library

Designed and produced by Judy Linard
Printed and bound in Great Britain by Bell & Bain, Glasgow

For Daisy, who taught me another world,
and for Michael, who allowed me to hold it.

Prologue

Evie hung from a low beam in the chapel. The weak January light bled through the East Window giving her body a ghostly-glow. She looked, I thought, suspended between worlds, almost reluctant to leave. Behind her, on the window, a conventional scene: a gathering-up of angels and patriarchs and evangelists, creating a taxonomy of salvation. Christ at the top, sat on the judgment seat, pale and European, a sombre upper-class colonial who'd gone native in robe and long hair. A nineteenth-century god dispensing judgment from on high. Below, Evie, her feet mere inches above the tiled floor.

It's attractive to imagine that when faced with situations like this, one finds profound words, either dredged up from memory or freshly coined in distress. One might even hope to pray. I remember worrying whether the beam would be able to take Evie's weight. It was only designed to hold up the second-rate rood screen. I suppose they made the world to last when the chapel was built. Her skin was ice-cold, so cold it felt damp, like fish-scales. When it was clear she'd been dead for hours I went to find someone useful.

It was only later that I found myself able to think again and ask questions. Back in my room, I felt the enormity of it all steal over me. Evie. I thought I might scream, howl even, but that would only bring the whole college down on me. A vision flashed into my mind: of me, dead too, my skin chalk-white and drained of blood. The others standing over me. Slowly, I regained my self-control. As long as I kept my eyes open, I was safe from her face: Evie's beautiful, beloved face now turned blue and swollen, her tongue protruding. I sought refuge in speculation: The beam was the boundary that separated nave and sanctuary. Had that been the point? Her death caught in the demarcation line between holy mystery and the profane?

It was only much later that I began to ask whether it really counted as a suicide at all. What we think we see can mislead us more completely than any of our other senses. If challenged about what I saw that morning, I'd repeat what I've just described. Could I swear to it, in court? That's what I did when the coroner investigated Evie's death. But now? I think the only thing I'm still sure of was the fact of Evie's dead body in the chapel. As for the rest, well …

About the months leading up to Evie's death, indeed, about the aftermath, I made a solemn vow to keep silent, and I like to think I take promises seriously. Despite what happened to Evie, I still think of those months I spent in the company of her and Richard, Ivo, Charlie and Piers as fondly as I remember anything. That we swore an oath to silence is not, necessarily, a sign of guilt. You should remember that we are the kind of people who take oaths seriously and we had more things binding us together than mere promises.

I promised never to say a word about those months, so why speak now? The easy answer would be to say that confession is compelling. *Confiteri*. It makes me think of martyrs who 'confessed' their faith as arrows pierced their flesh. It makes me think of confessionals where I've revealed my sins and in which I've heard those of others. It can be such a relief to make 'public' a private truth, indeed, in the days of Soviet Russia, even the innocent felt better when they confessed to the crime of which they were accused. To be absolved by a minister *in persona Christi* can be a beautiful and terrible thing and to absolve others takes one to the heart of the fantasies we make for ourselves – our shame, our hopes, our debased and glorious dreams. About my time with Evie and the others I promised – forgive me, 'covenanted' – to hold my tongue. Ivo was fond of quoting *The Cloud of Unknowing*: 'God, unto whom alle hertes ben open, and unto whom alle wille spekith, and unto whom no privé thing is hid.' The point being, he said, that one shouldn't go spilling one's guts all over the place: God knew, so people didn't have to.

Truth is, I'm struggling to give sufficient reason for breaking the silence and yet I think I must. Perhaps a psychologist would say that that's an indication of an unresolved sense of guilt. Well, I think Wittgenstein was right: psychology is a fake science. I do not believe I am driven by guilt, though, whenever I've thought about taking this step over the years, that image from the *Inferno* has come to mind: of the very lowest level of hell, icy and paralysed, occupied by Brutus, Cassius and Judas. In making my confession or telling the truth, whatever you want to call it, why do I feel like I'm joining them? Why do I always want to place all of us, Ivo, Charlie, Piers, and Richard, even Evie, in the betrayers' icy prison?

Part One

'…daughter, you have a haircloth on your back. I wish you to take it off, and I shall give you a haircloth in your heart…'

The Book of Margery Kempe

Chapter One

When I was younger, I could never understand why people have always believed the world is going to end in some defining catastrophe. It seemed to me, that before the Bomb, there was no realistic threat of apocalypse. Now, I am not so sure. Growing up in the shadow of the Cold War and Mutually Assured Destruction, I had a definite reference point for destruction: If the world was going to end, it would be in a mushroom cloud. As a child and as a teenager, I saw pandemic, natural disaster, even the breaking down of political systems as secondary. Personal tragedy barely seemed to register. Only in the nuclear holocaust lay the definitive end of all things. Catastrophe was a fixed point.

Now I am not so sure. When the last Roman legionary looked back on the shores of England I think he knew the end of the world. When the Marble Emperor died and Constantinople fell, it was catastrophe. Now I no longer dismiss personal tragedy as second-rate. A mother who loses her son to war or a person stripped of health knows the end of the world. The truth is, life is precarious and we construct fantasies to make us safe. I tell you this because I want you to understand who I was and what I have become. It was fear of catastrophe that motivated what we did to Evie, and (arguably) what she did to us.

My name is Catherine Bolton and I am a Church of England priest. I'm a canon of one of the ancient cathedrals, responsible for its teaching work, and my doctorate was on the Church and *The*

Canterbury Tales. I've been ordained for over twenty years and I am unmarried. Those are the facts, well, a few of them, anyway. It's hard to stick to facts and they are so easily marred. In that respect, they are like flesh. In this confession, I want to stick to the facts and when I fail – as we all do – I'm sure I shall still reveal the truth. Please remember that old joke about the Gospel according to St John: 'None of it happened, but it's all true.'

How should I start? Perhaps with my arrival at Littlemore Theological College. After all, it was there I found out about the limits of the body and the cruel byways of prayer. It was there I tasted and enjoyed things the church says are off-limits and it was there I grew up and came to terms with the grubby joys of the world. It was there I was plunged into the strange, parallel universe of Evie and my friends and, if that world ultimately turned vile, in their company I never felt more alive.

The village of Littlemore is famous for two things. First, until it was closed in 1525, for its priory church. Dating back to the twelfth century, it was home to a community of Benedictine nuns whose fate was sealed by the naughtiness of its final prioress, Katherine Wells. She'd had an illegitimate daughter with a priest from Kent and siphoned off funds to provide a decent life for her. Rumour had it that she liked to punish other nuns with severe beatings for their own sexual lassitude. Littlemore's second famous resident was John Henry Newman. Before he crossed the Tiber and became Cardinal Newman, he was its first vicar and established the attractive Gothic Revival church. As I pulled onto the College's gravel drive on a warm September day, perhaps I'd hoped for a procession of clergy, and wayward nuns, and servers flailing thuribles. Perhaps I'd hoped to see Our Lady carried high down the village's main street while a choir sang the *Regina Coeli*.

Then there's the old Asylum on Sandford Road. On one side of the road is the College, its butter-yellow buildings almost more

Oxford than the city's ancient colleges; on the other, the gothic towers of the Asylum. At its centre is that hallmark of Victorian obsessions with control, a panopticon. The first time I'd seen it – at my interview – I felt a shiver of fear. It loured over the village. As I arrived for the first day of term, the old asylum – now very desirable apartments – dominated my mind. It was so quiet that morning. There should have been dozens of other ordinands arriving, but for some inexplicable reason there was just me. I looked up at the panopticon, its forty metres of brick utterly incongruous in this picturesque village. Its single pillar, topped with a 360° observation platform, made me want to throw my bag back in the boot of my car and drive off.

Settling into college life, however, was, in many ways, hardly problematic. By the time I arrived at Littlemore, I was a hardened student. I'd taken a First in Medieval History and English at Manchester, as well as a PhD in Medieval History at Lancaster. I was 24 and – if it had not been for a crisis that had led me to faith and a call to ordained ministry – I was launched on a promising academic career. Years of study had made me almost hopelessly institutionalised, and even now, decades on from university, years do not begin in January, but September. Back then I slipped into the quiet routines of college life as readily as into an ancient pair of pyjamas, and being assigned a poky room on an anonymous corridor in Davidson House, the oldest building in college, fitted my monkish aspirations. My door had one of those old-fashioned slots for your name and some efficient administrator had already slipped my details into it, handwritten in copperplate. That door, however, never fit properly. It had a two-centimetre gap between its bottom edge and the floor and in my three years in college, despite constant complaints, the handyman never replaced it.

But that little room – with its ancient single bed, scuffed desk and squeaky Anglepoise lamp, with its far too few shelves, as if one were a child at boarding school rather than a widely-read adult – was home. I knew it the moment I stepped inside and saw the dust motes rising and falling in the light streaming through the sash window. I went and looked down into the small quad formed by the four main college buildings. At its centre, a single oak, that I later found out was older than the college. Everyone called it *Lord Quercus* and in the spring, students would touch a knot in the wood four feet up from the ground for luck, ahead of exams. When I saw it first, its leaves were already beginning to turn golden. I smiled. I might even have cried. I stood there for a long time enjoying the quiet, lost in thought, until I heard a loud rap on my door.

What should I tell you about those first magical days? Should I talk about the long bicycle rides Evie and I took out through Nuneham Courtney and Little Baldon, just to have a few hours alone? Or that time we cycled out to Garsington to gawk at Lady Ottoline Morrell's old home, and how I wittered on about how the Manor's land had once been owned by Geoffrey Chaucer's son? Should I speak of how we sat out on the lawns, under the stars, drinking ginger wine, talking about medieval attitudes to sex? I daren't. You'd only laugh at me and mistake me for some callow undergrad. Yet, of those warm days of early autumn, that's what I go back to most often now. Does it matter if memory adds layers of sentiment? As if those days carried with them their own soundtrack, supplied by Vaughan Williams or Butterworth. For me, it was a second-chance to play out a long-cherished dream – a dream I'd given up when I'd failed to get the grades to go up to Oxford – even if I was already old enough to know better and see through its frauds and charades. No, let me start in another place, with that knock on the door. After all, it was that knock which changed everything.

I opened my door and a voice said, 'Hallo!' It was bright and eager. In one word I heard a private education, money, and the south. It was a voice I would come to love and dread, the kind of voice you could hear before it ever said a thing. In the corridor stood a slim young woman, perhaps a year younger than me, in a slip dress with a pretty rose print on it. Her mid-length chestnut hair framed her face, almost making a bob with its layers. She grinned sincerely at me and her eyes were large, encouraging and green. I remember marvelling at how white and straight her teeth were. In those days, before everyone started straightening and whitening their teeth, hers seemed oddly un-English.

'Hi,' I said, non-committally.

'Catherine?'

'Kitty,' I said. My mother called me Catherine. Some friends and some lovers had tried Cathy or Cath. I'd long since settled on Kitty.

'Kitty,' replied the girl, as if checking out whether she thought the name fit what she saw before her. 'I'm Evie. Evie Kirkland. I'm new here too. I thought you might like to grab a cup of tea?'

That was how I met Evie. Evie, who was at the centre of much that was good and most of what was cruel over that year at Littlemore. Evie, who had a ridiculous, yet utterly sincere love of scratchy trad-jazz records, who liked to read the crappiest airport thrillers, and watch Australian soaps, and would sit for hours watching old Fred and Ginger musicals on worn-out videos. Evie. Infuriating, exhilarating, and needy. Who could utterly disarm you with acts of sudden generosity – a bottle of Krug or a bouquet of winter roses and anemones – and yet could draw the most positive person on the planet into hell. Evie. Who appeared on my doorstep with a single word and an invitation into her world.

Did I know then what she would become to me? It's so tempting to say, 'yes'. It would be easy to say that I saw – in the kindly tilt of her head, or her easy smile – how we would soon move from the ready friendship of new students to something more physical, more dangerous. But that would be to claim knowledge that only comes with hindsight and hurt. Right then, as she stood on my doorstep, all

I saw was another keen ordinand who just wanted to make friends. How wrong I was. Then, again, how could I foresee what we would become? We were trainee priests, for heaven's sake. Lust, obsession, sex, violence, these were precisely the things that were supposed to be off the agenda. The church can be uptight about sex and love between a married man and woman; sex between women is enough to send otherwise sensible members of the church into apoplexy. So, no, I had no idea what was to unfold between Evie and me in the weeks to come. She stood on my doorstep and invited me out for a drink. I smiled back, said, 'That would be lovely', and stepped out on the path that would ultimately lead to her death.

Chapter Two

All Anglican seminaries are small. Littlemore is smaller than most, and over the next couple of weeks Evie and I fell into the comfortable, easy friendship of those of similar age and occupation. As ordinands we were also aware that, at some almost indefinable level, tutors and chaplains were watching us. Not intrusively, of course, but we were conscious of not wanting to give the impression we were aloof and unsociable. Like prisoners under the watchful eye of guards we behaved ourselves. Not that there was any need for physical guards; the belief that we were being watched was enough for us all to regulate our behaviour. We made a point of being seen with our fellow students, especially our first-year peers. For, if the Church allows introverts, indeed encourages them, those charged with forming future vicars like to see that their charges are comfortable with a wide range of people. So, I spent a lot of time – in the common room and at dinner, in chapel and in class – speaking to freshers and old hands alike.

People like Bob Hawkins, fifty-something and constantly surprised at his good luck at being recommended for training. He claimed a special bond with me because we both hailed from Worcestershire and, as he never failed to point out, he was amazed he could hear no trace of accent in my voice. I told him it was because I'd gone to boarding school. Heaven knows why, except to shut him up. I'd gone to a bog-standard comp and the fact was that as soon I'd become aware of how horrible my accent was – half-yokel, half-

Brummie whine – I'd ruthlessly sought to eliminate it. The trigger was a visit to an Oxford Open Day in Lower Sixth. During a taster seminar with a don, I'd dared to suggest a good book for budding historians to look at. Later, in the great hall, I saw a tall blond-haired boy point me out to his friend and say, in a braying voice, 'You should have heard the hippy girl in our seminar.' He then did a fair impression of a Midlands's accent: '*The Making of the Middle Ages* is ace, ayn't it?' The other boy laughed. Then, in his usual voice, the blond-haired boy said, 'If Magdalen starts admitting the likes of her, it's time to apply to the Other Place.'

I hated the smirk on his face and the way he wanted me to hear. I hated the way he said, 'Magdalen'. Maudlin. Yet, his barb about my accent stung. Over weeks, months, years even, I tried to clean my voice up. My father – a blunt, working-class man – took every opportunity to mock me for my attempts to 'talk posh'. His friend, John, a fat and lazy labourer with whom he liked to go to the pub, egged him on at every opportunity. 'You tell her, Ronnie. Lady Muck, giving herself airs and graces.' And my dad would gulp down a mouthful of tea and tell me I should stop acting as if I was better than everyone else. My mum would stay silent and turn the telly on. By the time I'd finished my first degree, however, I'd achieved my goal. No one could tell where I came from and if I wanted to say I'd been to boarding school, people would believe it.

The college also had a whole swathe of plump, middle-aged women with undyed hair, called things like Audrey and Jeanette. We christened them the pastoral vampires because they instinctively sensed other people's vulnerabilities and fed on them in a mumsy way. Jane Sampson, perhaps, sums them up. In her late forties, with two daughters in their early twenties, Jane made a beeline for the likes of Evie and me. She felt she understood us and, as she put it, 'our struggles in the church and beyond'. She would nod like one of those toy dogs, and lurked in the computer room, waiting for victims stressed out with assignments and deadlines. I almost came to believe she lived there, as many believe that vicars live in churches and bishops in cathedrals.

Over those first two weeks I made a point of speaking to the Janes and Bobs and most of the sixty-odd souls in college. I was, I thought, ubiquitous. However, behind it all was my burgeoning friendship with Evie. It was like having a sister, and a younger one at that. At school and university, I'd got on better with men, even if that often went sour if we started sleeping together. Evie, however, was funny and smart. She had this curious habit of taking a few drags on a Marlboro Light and then letting it burn down to a pile of ash between her fingers. Somehow it summed her up: her whole existence was a balancing act in competition with gravity. She could talk with unexpected knowledge about racing cars (her father, a diplomat, apparently partly owned a famous motor racing company) or the novels of Dorothy L. Sayers, then just when you thought she didn't give a damn, she'd speak passionately about God and the medieval mystics.

Perhaps one story is sufficient to give you a sense of her magic for me in those early days. We were sat in the common room bar one evening early in Michaelmas term. The bar was full and people were still testing out their emerging friendships and rivalries. The first big essay deadlines were still a few weeks off and Bob Hawkins and his new crony, Matt Smith, a tall, bearded Geordie who liked to play the bluff northerner, had been drinking and playing pool since straight after dinner. Evie and I sat near the fire with a thin middle-aged woman called Julie Hall. She had severe eczema and unselfconsciously scratched her upper arms and shoulders from time to time, as if she were a lice-ridden soldier. We were taking books out of boxes and half-heartedly sorting them for 'Dead Vicars'. 'Dead Vicars' was the college name for those book collections donated to the ordinands by deceased clerics. Books were laid out on a large trestle table according to size and theme, and anyone in college could take what they liked.

Sorting out donations could be a dispiriting affair. It gave a sobering insight into the unimaginative interior lives of most priests. There was usually a lot of Billy Graham, his high-foreheaded face smiling winsomely out from the cover of *My Answer* or *The Jesus Generation*. Unlike most, however, I rather enjoyed the book-sorting stage. It gave you first dibs. I found a handsome copy of *Piers Plowman*, the original Skeat version, unrevised. Once, when I was struggling to sleep, I got up and quietly pocketed a First Edition of *A Tale of Two Cities* I found in a box late one night.

That night, though, Evie, Julie and I were just having fun reading out book titles or author names for comedy effect.

'How about this one?' said Evie. '*Take Me, Jesus: My Journey into Trust*.' I'd had a few tumblers of Highland Park and was ripe for silliness. Evie said, 'Take me, Jesus' in the breathy voice of a comedy debutante about to lose her virginity.

'No, wait for it,' she added, seeing I was getting a little hysterical ahead of the punchline. 'By …' She raised her eyebrows knowingly. 'Rusty Kuntz …'

Julie and I laughed uproariously. A few others in the Common Room joined in.

'Sod off!' I said.

'Seriously!' She flipped the book around to show the front cover, her hand over the name section. Her mouth twitched with a knowing smile. 'Not really.' She removed her hand. 'It's almost worse.' The name read, 'Dick Handler'.

We burst out laughing again. Evie looked at the book again with mock bewilderment. 'What was this guy thinking? I mean, look at the spine.' She held it up. It read, '*Take Me, Jesus Dick Handler*'. Our hysterics renewed themselves.

Bob Hawkins, from across the common room, said, 'For Christ's sake, will you girls stop giggling. I'm trying to take a shot.'

Like many older men, Bob was sexist in a thoughtless, paternalistic way. It wouldn't have occurred to him that 'girls' or 'giggling' might be heard as sexist. Women priests were still a relatively new thing and almost no one in the church had much experience of women wearing dog collars and exercising the authority that comes with it. Littlemore liked to see itself as a progressive place, but it still attracted one or two ordinands who couldn't accept women's priestly ministry. A couple of the senior tutors, including the ageing and famous Revd Professor Albertus Loewe, had even actively opposed the changing of church canons. Bob and Matt were not like that. They saw themselves as progressives, as good guys who supported women's ministry.

Yet, Hawkins's drunken shout was dog-whistle territory, almost worse than outright misogyny. However, I didn't want a fight, nor did Julie. Evie, however, said, in the style of Jane Austen,

'Come on, ladies. We should not disrupt the gentlemen at their billiards. Let us take a turn about the drawing room.' Julie laughed.

This only wound up Bob further.

Slowly he laid his cue down on the pool table and came around to face us. As he moved, Matt said, 'Bob', his high voice pleading. Bob, however, was set on his path. As he drew close I could smell his odour: sweat and sour beer. He was drunk, though far from paralytic. Evie stared at him.

'I don't get it,' said Bob. Suddenly the whole common room, twenty-odd people, was quiet, focussed on Bob and Evie. I saw Michael Shaw, a third-year with an obsessive devotion to the Blessèd Virgin Mary and Her Majesty the Queen, nudge his partner Christopher Eastwood, a laconic Californian, and sit forward in his seat. He tried to conceal a grin. It was as if he'd been waiting for something like this all term. On the balance of probabilities, I guess, he and the other old timers probably had. In an isolated, intense community like Littlemore, blow-ups were always on the edge of happening. We newcomers had been trying so hard to be on our best behaviour and this was a breaking point.

25

'What don't you get?' said Evie, calmly.

'Why young ladies have to show off. Do you think it's funny saying the C-word? Girls are supposed to hate that word. If I said it, you'd complain to the Principal.'

'I didn't say the C-word. I said the K-word.'

'What?' Bob was momentarily caught off balance. Evie pressed her advantage.

'Bob, I said Rusty Kuntz.' I laughed involuntarily again. Evie flashed a warning glance at me.

Bob was about to speak, when Evie added, 'Rusty Kuntz was a Major League baseball player. He played for the Detroit Tigers, Minnesota Twins and, er, was it the Boston Red Sox or the Chicago White Sox?' She smiled. When Bob said nothing, she added, 'Really. You can look him up in *Sports Illustrated*.' Seeing that Bob was not alone in being stunned, she said to me, 'Daddy used to take me to games when he was at the Embassy in Washington.'

'Daddy?' said Hawkins, mockingly. This, he clearly thought, was his way back into the argument.

'Yes, Robert, "Daddy".' I was stunned by Evie's self-possession. I hated direct confrontation, but she seemed to relish it.

'Did *Daddy* get you into Oxford, Evie? Did he pay the Bishop to have you accepted for ministry?'

'*Pacyens is more worthy than myraclys werkyng,*' said Evie, unexpectedly. I smiled. I already knew that Evie had studied hard for her degree, that she was very far from being a ditzy fool, but this quote was a sharp reminder of her theological grit.

'What?' said Bob.

'It's Margery Kempe, Robert. It's basically her way of saying don't rely on miracles, but apply yourself patiently.' She pushed a lock of hair behind her left ear, and looked kindly at him. 'You'd have hated her. She had fourteen children and would not shut up.

26

She was tried for heresy several times. Apart from the kids, she's a bit of a role model, actually.'

'Screw you,' said Bob.

'In your dreams,' Evie replied. Bob stared at her harshly, then stormed out. Matt followed him. Evie smiled to herself, then looked at me.

I think that at that moment I would have done anything she asked of me. Her self-possession made my heart sing. I'm not going to lie. Part of Evie's magic for me was that she was everything I was not. She was privileged and wealthy. She'd been born into a family that had exercised real power and she felt no need to conceal her past (or so I imagined). She'd gone to the right kind of school and the right kind of university. She seemed to me to be at ease with her story and her faith; she was a Christian and an Anglican because that is what people of her background and class were raised to be. If she was, by turns, foul-mouthed and scholarly, it was because she was herself. I suppose that's what I wanted to be: Myself. I was constantly aware of my works of invention and my dissimulations. Evie just seemed a natural.

Of course, she was not the only one I was fascinated by in those first days. If, as I've said, I'd spent the early weeks at Littlemore cultivating the acquaintance of pretty much everyone in college, there was still one group that seemed out of reach, that, really, I wanted to know. It is to them – to Ivo, Richard, Charlie and Piers – I now turn. With them my story and Evie's story – my confession – really begins.

Chapter Three

Ask your average person what comes to mind when they hear the phrase 'the Middle Ages' and they'll typically talk about Plague and Black Death and rain and misery. They'll conjure pictures of knights and peasants and scheming kings. They'll talk about a nasty persecuting church burning heretics, willy-nilly. In the popular mind, life in the Middle Ages was nasty, brutish and short. It was a world of misery and ignorance in which the only way to ease the squalor was to connive and make war on each other. It's a picture that makes for good television and films. Like all medievalists, I know this image of the Middle Ages is a parody, though – as you will see – perhaps I was more beholden to this cheap picture than I care to admit.

Ivo, Piers, Charlie, Richard, Evie and I were all curiosities because we were obsessed by and, in some cases, held genuine expertise in the Medieval. For us, this knowledge was no mere intellectual matter. For us, the enchanted realm, where ritual was a kind of magic, had never gone away. We weren't fools. We accepted that science and technology had changed reality in a thousand different ways, but for us every little bit of creation was still charged with grandeur. In the medieval era, rich and poor alike knew that the supernatural and uncanny rippled through every aspect of life. It motivated the creation of the most magnificent cathedrals, as well as the superstitions of peasants who sought to ensure a good harvest; it stirred the wealthy to have their souls prayed over for eternity. You might think all this weird and naïve, but these people knew about the urgency and importance of life. Go into any cathedral or church and you will see visions of human dignity and beauty our age can barely dream of. In the medieval age, there was no escape from the wonder and the terror of creation.

The wonder and the terror. I'm not going to lie to you, when I became friends with Ivo and the others I had no idea how deep the rabbit hole would go and how terrifying it would become. Yet, one of the fascinations of the Medieval for me is its honesty about how close glory is to terror. Consider: the most popular saint in fourteenth-century England was St Katherine, she from whom we get the Catherine Wheel. In her legend, God sets her free from a wheel of knives on which she was to be martyred. As she's set free, the faithful cheer at the miracle, and yet this miracle is predicated on a catastrophe: when God frees her from the wheel of death, it explodes and kills thousands. Glory and terror. As you will see, my friends and I did things to ourselves and each other that some would consider disgusting and unholy. Over twenty years on, it's hard to disagree and my body still bears the scars. Yet, those days were glorious too. If, ultimately, you judge me as sick, that tells you as much about the cheap morality of our present age, as about me.

Ivo Termagent, or the Honourable Ivo David Matchings Termagent to give him his full name and style, would have been striking in almost any setting. At Littlemore, he was an oddity, both magnificent and strange. He belonged to one of those faded aristocratic families that still clung to the belief that the third son should go into ordained ministry. By the time he went through selection, even the Church was disinclined to believe in *noblesse oblige*. Connections helped, but the Church was looking for something more than 'my family think this is a good thing'. As it happened, Ivo had plenty to offer. Over six foot tall, broad shouldered and square-jawed, the first impression Ivo gave was 'rugger-bugger'; indeed, when I first saw him, walking towards the common room, a little out of breath and sweating from an early morning run, that's exactly what I thought. I was sure he'd be simple and patronising and sexist in the way that sporty posh boys usually are. He spoke in that drawling, friendly accent that remains a marker of our public schools, despite the efforts of many of its products (including one or two modern royals) to affect an edge of Estuary.

Ivo was hardly my type, though to be honest I'd not really moved in a world where he might have become my type. At university, I'd been a bit of a loner and, before I'd become a Christian, the kinds of guys I'd hung out with had been lefties who wore black and wanted to talk about dialectical materialism. After my faith crisis, I'd been introduced to a lot of clean-cut Christian boys with names like Seth and Sam who thought sex was a sin outside marriage and felt it their duty to teach me the meaning of St Paul's minor epistles. Ivo and his crowd were just so different. At 24 I shouldn't have been dazzled, but, as with Evie, they embodied a world of longing for me. I'd grown up in a world of cheap clothes and possessions. For my eighteenth birthday, my mum had given me a nine-carat gold necklace with my name on it from Argos. I could have died when I'd been forced to wear it out in public to please her.

Ivo, by contrast, casually exuded tradition. I'd given my life to the study of the past and Ivo was a living example. His life had been good schools and worn-out tweeds, and large rooms filled with beautiful things that were centuries old. His shoes – handmade at Grenson – looked almost as old as him. He was rarely seen without a tie, though nothing so vulgar as an old school or college tie. His shirt sleeves were always tied by cuff links, but there was never anything bright or brazen about them. His spectacles were what I would call 'continental', made of horn in Germany. He'd moved on from school to Trinity, Cambridge where he'd taken a First in Medieval History and had been rumoured to be a leading light in the Apostles. After his undergrad studies, he'd been courted by University, the City and the Civil Service.

Is it so odd that I became fascinated by him? Or Richard or Charlie or Piers? I'd grown up in a dormitory town of twenty thousand people. All the adults who didn't work in pubs or shops or entertainment, worked in the Black Country and Birmingham. My dad was a security guard and my mum did the dinners in a local school. They, like their friends, were not interested in books or culture. The highlights of the cultural calendar were the River Carnival and the local Am-Dram production of a Ray Cooney farce. They were people whose year-end highlight was the *World Darts Championship* on TV. Ivo had gone to Eton. Piers had gone to Harrow and Richard to Repton. Charlie, like Evie, was a product of Cheltenham Ladies College. When I'd gone to Littlemore, I already knew what it represented for me: a chance to finally throw off the last vestiges of my cheap working-class upbringing and become something new. If I chose to run with Ivo's crowd it was because they were who I wanted to be.

Ivo, tall and thoughtful, his hands in his pockets as he stomped across campus. Piers Halliwell, smaller and slimmer, his features almost impossibly boyish, despite the fact he was in his mid-twenties. This, along with his floppy hair, always made me think of Rupert Brooke. Indeed, he had a tendency to cultivate the bohemian-artist image by preferring loose, linen collarless shirts, thick-cut cord trousers and, to my amusement and delight, cravats. Then there was Richard Crashaw, who claimed ancestry from an old Church and Establishment family. His ancestors included the Anglican Divine, William Crashaw, as well as the metaphysical poet, Richard, who towards the end of his life converted to Roman Catholicism.

Of all our little group of friends, I can only think of Richard with uncomplicated fondness. There was something almost clownish about him in those days. Richard never came across as arch or

31

forced. Rather, he had a kind of clumsy charm. He was under six foot tall, and yet, because of his angularity and slimness, gave the impression of being taller. He had a tendency to stoop, which made his Ralph Lauren Polo specs slide off his nose and he also had this loose forelock he repeatedly pushed back up on his forehead. His clothes – tasteful and neat – somehow never quite fitted as well as they should. I suppose he had a kind of 'preppy look' – knitwear, chinos, polo shirt – that was sufficiently English to never seem prissy or too perfect. This was the era when *Friends* was peak-time viewing and that preppy thing was on-trend. But he was no Chandler or Joey, not even Ross. He was far too self-deprecating, catching himself in a mirror or shop window and saying quite sincerely, 'Gosh, I look like a dustman at the Lord Mayor's Show.' I'll never forget his smile, slack-jawed and sloppy, his teeth slightly uneven on the left side, or his knowledge of wine. It was through him I learned to distinguish between a Pouilly-Fuissé and a Pouilly-Fumé. It was in his company that I first experienced Chateau D'Yquem. If Ivo and Piers could sometimes make one feel as if one were being interrogated for a suspected crime, Richard – at heart – always wanted you to know he was a friend.

And Charlie. Of all of us, perhaps she was the most complicated and mysterious. Odd as the boys could be, I always felt it was possible to account for their presence in a Church of England theological college. They belonged to the ready, if absurdly old-fashioned, nexus of privilege that linked the past with present, Nation with Church. Charlotte 'Charlie' Bamford was new money. Her father owned a chain of upmarket supermarkets in the north of England and she was his only girl. He had had dreams for her. After Cheltenham, she'd spent a year at Bryn Mawr before studying English at Oxford. Rumour had it that she had a trust fund the size of the national debt. Evie once showed me copies of *The Tatler* and *Vanity Fair* which had prominent photos of Charlie at Henley and Cowes with phrases like 'society beauty' underneath. If she'd wanted, Charlie could have been one of those *It-Girls* so fashionable in the Nineties, and, for a brief period, I suppose she had been. She'd had the apartment in West London, she'd been connected with eligible men, and she'd had the dubious fortune of being stalked by paparazzi as she left clubs.

She was, if this is not too old-fashioned to say, an heiress, and a beautiful one at that. At five feet ten she was hardly short for a woman, but her slimness emphasised her height. She had the pale skin tones of a late Regency beauty and her high cheekbones were in kindly proportion to her small nose and chin and her chocolate eyes matched her sleek hair. I'd like to believe that I'm not obsessed with surface image, but if I was jealous of one thing about Charlie it was the way her long, brown hair flowed from her head. She always looked like she was about to appear in an advert for hairspray or shampoo, even, dare I say it, on that night when Evie was about to die. She could wear jeans, a tie and a man's old shirt or a ball gown and look unfailingly elegant.

A woman, then, made for *Society*, but a total peculiarity in the Church. No matter where she went on campus or even in town, she attracted stares and unwanted attention. Half the men at college were in love or lust with her. She told me that at her Littlemore entrance interview the college Principal had basically drooled through their one-to-one meeting and she'd had to stop him from repeating the same question over and over. What was she doing in the Church? Evie, who'd known her at Cheltenham, explained that Charlie had had a little bit of a breakdown after university. The usual: drugs, sex, alcohol. She was more fragile than she looked. It had all been handled very discreetly, of course. It was during rehab that she'd found God. Her father was friends with the Dean of Chichester and he'd become her spiritual adviser. What her father hadn't expected was that Charlie would become so serious about her faith that she'd seek ordained ministry. The rumour was that he was beyond

33

disappointed with her, that he was convinced she was throwing her life away, and that he'd stopped talking to his old friend, the Dean.

More than twenty years on, I know full well that all of us see in others what we want to see. I was young, so perhaps I shouldn't judge myself too harshly for mistaking surface impressions for reality. Charlie and the others were, for the most part, exactly who they said they were, just as I was and Evie was too. Ivo *was* a charming aristo, and Piers *was* an arty flaneur and so on, but even in those first days it was the hint of something else that really drew me in: a sense of mystery and danger, of something risky just out of sight. To return to my earlier point, rather like the Medieval itself, there was something of the glorious and terrible about them. That much was revealed by the blood incident.

Chapter Four

The blood incident happened during one of the iconic moments of the late Nineties: Princess Diana's funeral. In those days, before the internet, it was the kind of event that brought a community like Littlemore together. On the day of the funeral, the common room was packed. Littlemore's term started weeks before the University, and the fact that this was the first week of term – effectively a theological college's version of Freshers – helped. People were still trying to find their feet or establish friendships and returning students were straggling back. Some had arrived that Saturday morning, I think, just to share in the communal atmosphere of the funeral. Mr Thatch, the handyman, had set up a TV, one of those vast mock-wood monstrosities that took its own trolley to transport. Anyone more than half a dozen yards away had a very restricted view of proceedings, but nobody seemed to care. Whatever we felt about Diana, we had to be there.

Instinctively, I'd gravitated towards the back. I sat with Evie on an old cupboard, raised up above the crowd, while Ivo sat with Richard, Charlie and Piers a couple of rows in front. Arch-Royalists, Michael Shaw and Christopher Eastwood had come down early and bagged TV-side seats. Despite never having been much of a Lady Di fan, I was fascinated by the choreographed pomp unfolding before us. It was a glimpse into another age, like seeing the faint echo of a late medieval guild procession with Diana's dead body as substitute for the consecrated Body of Christ. I remember thinking it somehow obscene that the grieving young princes were made to walk behind their dead mother in front of the vast crowds. It made me think of my sister Louise who'd died in an accident when she was thirteen and I was twelve. Seeing the princes walk quietly behind the catafalque made me think how horrifying it would have been if someone had forced me to do the same for Lou.

The blood incident happened during the National Anthem. The gun carriage had arrived at the Abbey, Diana was taken in, and the great and the good had filled the vast space. Then, the Queen arrived and the National Anthem began. The Abbey rose as one and sang. The Littlemore common room remained seated and silent, at which point a young exchange student from the States, Daniel Fischer, stood up and said, loudly and indignantly,

'Why aren't you standing? I am disgusted. How can you disrespect your Queen? Stand!'

I think the rest of us were agog. Not only was it was such a random, unexpected outburst, but for those of us new to Littlemore there was an odd sense of dislocation. Was this how it was? Did people talk to each other like that? For several beats, no one reacted. Then, slowly, as if his tall frame wasn't really made for such an extraordinary act, Ivo stood. He towered over Daniel, who must have been ten feet from him. Seeing Ivo stand, a few others began to get up, as if shamed into standing for the Anthem.

Ivo stared at Daniel from behind his horn-rimmed specs. The look was such a strange combination of fury, admiration and disgust, I wondered if he was about to shout at Daniel, or even attack him. Beneath his green tweed jacket, I sensed Ivo's upper body tense for action and yet he seemed quite calm and in control, his head quite still. Slowly, he clenched his left fist. Surely, Ivo wouldn't attack Daniel, would he? That was when it happened: Ivo who had been so still and poised, winced. The left side of his face twitched, barely perceptibly, and his left arm went into a brief spasm. It was all over

36

before most people could have noticed. Then a thin, bright line of blood leaked out from beneath his left cuff and trickled down over his clenched fist. Strangest of all, Ivo made no obvious reaction to this. He simply continued to stare at Daniel and paid no heed to the trail of blood. Rather, it was Piers who reacted. He spotted the blood oozing onto Ivo's hand and was, well, riveted by it. He stared at it with nothing short of pleasure and satisfaction, as if a point had been proven. There was a kind of hunger on his face and a delight. Then, he looked up at Ivo, nudged him and gestured towards the bloody hand. Ivo looked down quickly, almost contemptuously, sighed and left the common-room. Piers walked out after him. The people who had stood up in response to Ivo looked rather embarrassed and sat back down again.

It was a quite extraordinary moment. I wanted to nudge Evie and say, 'Hey, did you see that?', but Evie was whispering with someone next to her about the soldiers' uniforms. Later that day, when Evie and I were alone in my room, I raised the incident with her.

'Did you see that?'

'What? That American facing off with Ivo Termagent? Pair of prats, if you ask me.'

'Not that, the blood.'

'What?' Evie said this in a half-hearted way, as if she was already losing interest. She'd picked up my copy of the *Decameron*, the McWilliam translation, from my desk, and said,

'Is this translation any good? I've always preferred ...'

'No, listen, Evie.' I cut across her and she looked up at me, sharply. 'Did you see that blood trickling down Termagent's hand?'

She shook her head, and said, 'Oh, come on. You must have dreamt it.'

'I did not. His mate, that Piers, he saw it and practically dragged him out of the room.'

Evie looked at me as if I were a slightly dull, if stubborn child.

I sensed she wanted to get back to talking about the *Decameron* – a book she reckoned had more to teach the church about sex and relationships than the whole Bible – but could see that I was not to be deflected. Finally, she said, 'Look, it could have been anything, couldn't it? Maybe … maybe he cut himself …' She paused, as if struck by the absurdity of her speculation.

'What? Shaving?' I said. We both laughed.

'How hirsute,' said Evie, 'would he have to be to start shaving his arms?' She stuck her tongue out to signal how deeply unattractive she found hairy arms.

'The weird thing was,' I said, 'that just before the blood trickled down his hand, I saw his arm spasm.'

'God, Kitty, do you fancy him or something?'

'No, listen,' I said, hoping I wasn't blushing, 'it was really weird. He was staring at Daniel and I thought he was going to hit him. It was that intense. And he was so still, and then his arm just went into spasm, and his face twitched, and there was blood oozing from beneath his cuff.'

'You're making too much of this,' said Evie. 'It could be for a dozen different reasons.'

I shook my head, and she said,

'Hey, do you want me to ask him out for you?'

'I do not fancy him!' I said, and we both burst out laughing again.

* * *

Later I considered Evie's words: 'It could be for a dozen different reasons.' The blood on Ivo's hand might have issued from a half-healed wound he'd picked up on one of his runs – perhaps he'd tripped up and landed on a bit of flint – or in some accident in the kitchen. Cuts do sometimes open-up and bleed again, don't they? But these explanations struck me as inadequate. I was sure something more elusive was at stake. As I lay on my bed that night, an odd connection came to me. I thought about how, as a teenager, I would often secretly stab my arms and the palms of my hands with a protractor until they bled. When I was going through the worst of my grief at losing my older sister, I found it was a way I could relieve my pain and anger. Sometimes I'd sit in my room at night and watch the blood trail down my forearms, soothed by the flow. I still had the white scars from old puncture holes on my arms and I wondered if Ivo was doing something similar.

Of course, once Ivo and Piers had admitted me to their inner circle, I discovered that my speculation was both wider of the mark and closer to the truth than I imagined. That night, however, I was sure of one thing: I had to get to know Ivo, Piers and the others. It would be the only way to get closer to a truth I was sure they were hiding. As I replayed the day's events in my mind I fixed on the strangest moment of all: the way Piers had looked at the blood as it trailed down Ivo's hand. He'd looked rapt with delight and fascination. I hadn't told Evie about that, or about something I was sure would only freak her out: the fact that, secretly, I'd felt just like Piers. I turned off the light and lay as still as I could, until I slept and dreamt of skin and wounds, of blood and pierced bodies.

Chapter Five

As term began in earnest, I began to form my plan to penetrate Ivo's inner circle. Meanwhile, Evie started an MPhil with a view, ultimately, to a DPhil, while I was asked simply to complete a Diploma in Practical Theology. This meant that, for the most part, we were auditing courses and required to write very little. I had far too much time on my hands and this only added to the allure of Ivo's group. They were on the edge of everything and yet at the centre. It was not that they were impolite or aloof, so much as unavailable. They'd slip in late for lectures and slide out quickly at the end.

Donna Nibbs, a hippyish lay woman, who taught something called 'Mission Theology' would sigh when Ivo and the others walked in late to her class, only to be disarmed by Richard's puppyish smile. Sometimes he would leave her a white carnation on her desk before he sat down and she would slide it into her poncho-like shawl. While they were in class they were funny, warm and kind and like most clever Brits instinctively concealed their abilities with wit and self-deprecation. Yet, as soon as class ended, they'd disappear with almost ghost-like powers. On one occasion, in a History of Doctrine lecture, I decided to go up to Ivo on the vague pretext of asking his view on some obscure thinker, Eusebius or John Chrysostom, say. I waited till the end of class and, in anticipation of his ability to slip out of the door before anyone else, I was already there when Ivo got to the door. I was about to speak when, to my embarrassment, I found I could not. I just stood there as they all slid by. Worst of all Charlie gave me a little nod and smirk. Somehow, she and the others created this ineffable sense that it would be bad taste to attempt to stop one of them for a chat.

I mentioned this phenomenon to Evie and her reaction was a mixture of amusement and irritation.

'They've really got under your skin, haven't they?'

I shrugged.

'They're really not worth the effort.'

'Ivo is supposed to be a brilliant medieval scholar.'

'Is he?' Her remark was sharp, almost nasty.

'What have you got against them?'

'They're not kind,' was all she would say, and she walked off to chapel or another class.

Her claim that they were not kind, made no difference to me. In the absence of any other real demands on my life, I became obsessed. The fact that Evie – who pretty much liked to be ubiquitous on campus – affected a lack of interest in them only fed my fascination. If this seems over-the-top please remember that theological colleges can do that to people. They encourage regression, and it was hardly surprising that otherwise sensible people fell in and out of love with each other during those first weeks, including one or two otherwise happily married people. For me, it wasn't a simple matter of finding Ivo attractive. Perhaps I was a bit in love or lust with him. Certainly, he had – in the archaic sense – glamour. His friends orientated around him as their leader, around his self-possession and composure, and I was drawn too by this magic, real or imagined. But it was complicated. I also felt a spark of electric between Evie and me. In those early days, I think I really began to fall for her. I loved her energy and her smile, and the way we seemed to be able to anticipate each other's sentences. I dreamed of her, and when I masturbated it was her I fantasised about. But my obsession with Ivo, Piers and the rest would not subside, not least because I could not let the day of

Diana's funeral go. I kept coming back to the mystery of the blood.

Then I figured out my route into Ivo's circle: The Reverend Professor Albertus Loewe. Once I landed on it, it seemed obvious. Loewe was a legend far beyond the confines of Littlemore. Already past retirement age when I arrived, it was said he was unsackable. Educated at Oxford, Tübingen and Harvard, he was appointed Professor of Later Medieval Literature at Oxford at the age of 33. He'd been friends with Tolkien and Lewis, and was rumoured to have been a key advisor to several Prime Ministers. It was said that he could have been Archbishop of York at the very least, Canterbury if he'd desired, but he preferred the simple pleasures of influence over responsibility.

Loewe gave specialist tutorials and seminars to carefully selected students across Oxford. At Littlemore, he generated endless complaints to the Director of Studies and the Principal, even to bishops, because he insisted on hand-picking his students. His fame was a draw, and yet he essentially acted as he pleased. At dinner once, I heard the Principal say, when challenged by a colleague about Loewe's eccentric behaviour, 'I guess we'll just have to wait for him to die. Perhaps even then he'll continue to offer the odd seminar on William of Ockham.' Most controversial among Loewe's arcane policies was his refusal to teach any woman offering for priesthood. After the Church of England's landmark vote to allow women to be priests in 1992, Loewe had withdrawn his services from female students. The Bishop of Oxford had sought, briefly, to have him removed from Littlemore until Loewe reminded him that he was primarily responsible for getting the bishop his job.

Yet despite refusing to teach female candidates for priesthood, Loewe counted Charlie among his students. His seminar class at the start of my first year was Ivo, Piers, Richard and Charlie. Being so selective would have been, in and of itself, sufficient reason to wind up many of the students. The fact that the old misogynist counted a girl among his chosen ones was red-rag territory. Women like Jane Sampson were apoplectic. One student, Ben Sherwood, who'd come to Littlemore because Loewe only taught men, decided to leave and attend a more conservative college. He was disgusted by Loewe's hypocrisy.

One day, after Evie and I had been welcomed into his inner circle, Loewe explained his rationale for accepting Charlie into his class. We were at his house, eating crumpets in his sitting room. As he brushed crumbs from his colossal, white Nietzsche moustache he said,

'*Kinder*, how could I resist?' His voice was deep and fruity, an accent already practically dead by the end of the twentieth century. 'The way she bears herself. Like the Blessèd Virgin bestriding heaven. Magnificent. She could wear a potato sack and she'd shine. And, of course, I knew her President at Bryn Mawr. Fabulous woman. Magnificent scholar.'

Loewe was everything you'd expect from that speech: pompous, snobbish, capricious and old-fashioned. With his white hair and drooping moustache, he cultivated the genius *philosophe manqué* for all it was worth. He was tweedy and fastidious, and prissy as an old woman. He was a snob and we adored him for it. He was the most extraordinary teacher any of us ever had. I might have held a PhD in medieval literature, but compared to his grip in that area, and a dozen others, I might as well have held a Food Hygiene Certificate from Bedford Tech.

Loewe was my route into Ivo's group. It was simple: gain entry into his seminar and gain access to them. If Evie thought my fascination with Ivo and Piers idiotic, even she reckoned Loewe sounded like fun. She was sure his contacts and knowledge would be valuable for her research, or in the very least, enliven it. The problem was how to make an introduction. I was sure a direct approach would be catastrophic. Loewe would be polite, friendly, and close the door on me and never open it again. The opportunity I was looking for, however, came through a rare lecture Loewe was to give on the Medieval at Brasenose at the start of the University's term in October. Evie really didn't want to go, but I pestered her. I claimed that given it was my area of expertise, it was almost a professional requirement that I attend. I told her it would add flavour to her research.

* * *

I had expected an oversubscribed event. The title, *'Sex, Pleasure and Heresy in the High Middle Ages'* was more than appealing, yet when we entered the lecture room with five minutes to go, there were only twelve in a space that could hold a hundred. I looked around for Ivo and his friends. They were absent. Evie and I were the youngest in the room by about thirty years and there was a faint smell of cabbage, pipe tobacco and dried piss. Elderly men in grubby clothes looked at us salaciously. Evie and I looked at each other and clearly had the same thought: Can we simply turn around and leave? I could see that Evie fancied it, but I was determined on my path. I needed to meet Loewe. I whispered, 'You leave if you want to.' I took it as a measure of her fondness for me that she sat down and took out a notebook.

At the precise moment the lecture was due to start, Albertus Loewe breezily entered through a side door at the front. He dropped his notes on a lectern and looked carefully around the theatre. He spotted a couple of people he knew, nodded at them and smiled. I thought I saw, in his sharp blue eyes, a flicker of disappointment at the thin attendance, the look of a once great lecturer who has become a back number. He stared disconcertingly at Evie and me, and I even half-expected him to say, 'No women'. He stared, then looked away and began. Given the lack of a crowd, I reset my expectations of Loewe's lecturing style: In his dotage, he must have had a rude fall from grace. Then he spoke and I realised how wrong I was. His notes

44

were mere props and he spoke confidently and fluently without reference to them.

As he spoke, Loewe led me back into the strangeness of the Middle Ages, as if it were the real world, exposing ours as limited and grey. He took me back through the centuries of magic, back to when illiterate peasants were known to bore 'squints', little holes in the walls of chapels, just so that they could catch a glimpse of the priest turning bread and wine into Jesus's body and blood. One peasant was recorded as exclaiming, 'I've just seen my Lord!' That was the world of my heart and Loewe, in his rich resonant voice, took me there.

Loewe spoke about how the Plague fostered anxiety about the end of the world and how heresies flourished in its shadow. He spoke of new movements which emerged out of fear of catastrophe, including those who sought to mortify the flesh in preparation for God's judgment. He spoke of those who became hungry for the Bible to be written in the common tongue and were thereby persecuted as heretics. He reckoned that many of the most extreme heretic groups – the Bogomils, the Cathars and so on, accused of practising the most libertine sexual practices and rituals – were just projections of anxious minds. In short, like medieval Joseph McCarthys, panicky clergy and worried feudal lords saw dangerous subversive groups where there were none. It was hardly ground-breaking stuff, but it didn't need to be: Loewe had been one of those who'd propagated this view.

As his talk ended, and our polite applause finished, I saw my chance. I was shocked to realise my heart was buzzing with fear. My mouth was dry and I sensed a bead of sweat slide down the left side of my forehead. I felt as anxious as a keen undergraduate desperate to impress her tutor. Thankfully, my voice was clear and composed. Loewe saw my raised hand and said, curtly, 'Yes?'

'Professor Loewe, I wonder if I could invite you to comment

on recent developments in medieval studies of sex and heresy which treat it through a queer lens? New readings of the *Decameron*, or even speculations about apocryphal texts like *The Gospel of Philip*. The work of Carolyn Dinshaw, for example?' I heard an audible intake of breath from a couple of the old dons.

I'd gone for the jugular. Even if he hated me, I'd rather be remembered, than be ignored. Perhaps you do not appreciate what I'd done. These days every academic, even in the ancient universities, reckons with queer and feminist ideas, but back then, there was a lot of mockery. In the early Nineties, dons had protested Derrida's receipt of a Cambridge honorary doctorate. Even the work of Seventies feminists was locked away in the Women's Studies departments of arriviste universities. I wanted to bait Loewe into a response. He had a reputation as a crustacean of the crustiest kind. I hoped to dig him out of his shell.

Loewe studied me carefully for a moment. Evie perked up, suddenly alert. Loewe looked ready to rage. He took a deep intake of breath through his nose and his moustache quivered slightly.

He said, 'Miss …?'

'Doctor … Catherine Bolton, ordinand at Littlemore College.'

He smiled, then quite chattily said,

'I met Dr Dinshaw in an airport once. We had eggs benedict and drank manhattans for breakfast.'

Despite myself, I laughed. Others did too. To my surprise, he then proceeded to speak fondly of Dinshaw's work on Chaucer and how they'd had a good-natured argument about the importance of Foucault. He even did me the professional courtesy of asking me about my own research. When I explained that I'd focussed on the relationship between *Church Penitentials* – the detailed rules for what happened when people committed sexual and social sins – and *The Canterbury Tales* he said, with amusement in his voice, 'You see, gentlemen. Young women today – all they are interested in is sex!'

There was an uproar of laughter, that I attempted to speak across. He grinned at me like a great white-headed wolf. Evie placed a hand on my arm as I was about to stand up and protest. I looked at her and she shook her head. I sat down again. Loewe raised his hands to calm the laughter and said,

'Gentlemen! Please. Dr Bolton and her friend deserve better from us. This is not 1937. Forgive me, Dr Bolton, I am a dinosaur. Now, if you will all excuse me, I am getting old. I think I should call this meeting to an end. Thank you!'

Applause broke out, Loewe picked up his notes, raised a hand in acknowledgement and left the lecture theatre by the same door he'd appeared from an hour before. Just as he was about to close the door, he paused and stared at me one last time. I could swear he winked.

I was sure I'd breached the Loewe castle. Evie was less convinced. As she drove us back to college in her red Audi Cabriolet, she did her best to undermine my mood.

'What the bloody hell did you think you were playing at?'

'I was baiting him,' I said.

'He mocked you. And me. It was horrible.'

'You wait and see,' I replied. 'He'll be inviting us around for tea by the end of the week.'

'Yuck. For God's sake, Kitty. He's the sort of don who gives out firsts for fucks. Just stay away.'

I ignored her. I went to bed happy that night, convinced that my tactics would bear fruit. I was sure that I was about to enter the enchanted kingdom.

Chapter Six

As the days passed, doubt set in. There was no sign of Loewe on campus, or of Ivo and Piers. Charlie and Richard drifted in and out of classes – she sullen, he showing-off that charming, uneven smile – and I became increasingly grouchy. It didn't help that Evie's face seemed to say, 'I told you so' at every opportunity. By the fifth day of no response, I was pretty much ready to accept I'd judged my encounter with Loewe quite wrongly. After breakfast, Evie and I headed to our pigeon-holes to check our mail and notices. Evie quickly rifled through her small pile, and said,

'You know, this ordinand malarkey is duller than I expected. I thought the Archbish would have invited me to save the Church of England by now.'

I was going through my pile a little more carefully, clearly still hoping for an indication of interest from Loewe.

'Oh, give it a few weeks, Eve,' I said, absently. My mail consisted of invites to sherry parties, and circulars forwarded on from my old address in Lancaster.

I was about to shove it all back in my pigeon-hole, when I found it. It was a cream, post-card sized note in heavy paper with the faint scent of tobacco and expensive after-shave. At its top, in embossed lettering, was an address in Jericho, the then unfashionable suburb of Oxford, and a name, 'The Revd Prof. Albertus Loewe'. It had that day's date. In a beautiful, slanting hand he'd written,

'Dear Catherine (if I may),

I was delighted to make your acquaintance at Brasenose the other evening. I am on campus today. I should be pleased to get to know you a little better. Would you consent to join me in my rooms for tea at four today?

Yours, Albertus.

P.S. Please bring Miss Kirkland with you. I should like to meet her too. AL'

My hands shook as I read and re-read the card. I passed it to Evie, who read it quickly and said, 'Oh.' She stared appraisingly at me, as if she were trying to decide whether to tell me something. 'Well, are we … are you going to go?'

I looked back at her, smiled and said, 'What do you think?'

* * *

When I'd read, 'Would you consent to join me in my rooms', I'd sensed pretension. Over the previous weeks, I'd spent sufficient time in the offices of Littlemore staff to know they were not, in the Oxford sense, 'rooms'. They were cramped little offices in a new build north of the original nineteenth-century quad. There were flimsy partitions and noisy photocopiers. Furniture was cheap and functional and the mood was a kind of cheery determination to make the best of things.

Loewe, as ever, subverted expectations. Evie and I found out that his rooms were in a building called Luxford House, named after a distinguished head of Littlemore from the 1920s. As we walked up to it at ten minutes to four, Evie told me it was just that: Luxford's house, which he'd donated to the college on his death. It wasn't grand, but it was pretty, enclosed in its own small orchard of quince trees. Built near the edge of campus, in the *Arts and Crafts* style, it was everything that the new-build offices were not. As Evie and I

49

drew close to Luxford, with its high, pointed roofs and decorated gables, I felt like the decades were rolling back. We might have been heading off to collect a member of the Inklings on the way to the Bird. I laughed under my breath. We really were heading into magic land.

The front door was open and we entered a tiled, chilly vestibule, looking for a sign of Loewe. Beyond a dusty inner door, on the corridor floor were old boxes of files from the fifties and sixties with phrases like 'MS – Orthodox Pneumatology' and 'Clinical Theology – Hilary 1966' written on the spines. There was a general sense of neglect. In one room off the corridor was a pile of old canvas chairs that looked like something we'd lost the Zulu War with. There was a kitchen that, given its ancient cooker and Che Guevara poster, had clearly been last used in about 1971. Evie and I looked at each, shrugged, and decided to try upstairs. The upper level looked no more loved or cared for, but we found a door with a label reading 'Revd Prof. Albertus Loewe' in the neat copperplate hand I'd found on my own room-door on my first day. I raised my right hand to knock, paused, then rapped on the door.

We waited for what felt like an age. Finally, Evie said, 'Come on, this is clearly a set-up.' She was about to leave, when the door opened a crack. A thin plume of pipe smoke leaked out and I saw one of Loewe's eyes studying us intently. As soon as he was sure it was us, he opened the door wide and said,

'My dear Catherine! And Evie! Come in!' He was quite suddenly a hearty fellow well-met. Indeed, we might have been old friends returned from a distant war, full of adventures and tales. He was dressed like a figure out of a Richard Hannay or Sherlock Holmes adventure – a raffish older gent in plum smoking jacket and cravat. The kind of person who works in some shady and eccentric government department, who plays both ends at once and would be proud to be called a double agent.

There was much fussing about as Loewe took our coats and hung them up on an old rack. He was so ceremonial that we might as well have been wearing ermine as crusty old wax jackets. As he fussed he said,

'Now, you don't mind me using your Christian names, do you? It's one of those informalities I've picked up from my American friends.'

'No, not at all, Professor,' I said.

'Tush, none of this professor nonsense whilst you're on my turf. Call me Albertus.' Having hung up our coats, he said, 'Now, come and meet the others.'

He led us through the outer room, a cluttered front office with an old desk, filing cabinet, a few shelves of books and piles of loose papers. On one side was an elegant fireplace with an *Arts and Crafts* mantelpiece. There was no fire. The next room was more pleasantly appointed. It was four or five times the size of the first and Loewe clearly used it as his sitting-cum-tutorial room. There were tired, but well-made leather settees, country-house chairs, and a low coffee table. The walls were covered with hundreds of books. Unexpectedly, there was a ping-pong table, where in months to come we would all play interminable tournaments, in which Charlie proved she was the absolute master of all of us. There was a blue line of smoke hanging beneath the yellowed stucco ceiling. And there, like figures in a Dora Carrington or Vanessa Bell painting, were Ivo, Piers, Charlie and Richard. Charlie – wearing a grey silk sheath dress – sat, her legs draped over the arm of a deep chair, holding a small book in her left hand, a cigarette in her right. Piers and Richard were hunched over a chess set placed on a rickety old card table. It was clearly Richard's move, for he held a rook up above the board, not yet ready to commit his forces decisively. Cigarettes burned in an ashtray. Ivo stood at one of the windows, a cup and saucer in hand, staring out towards the old asylum.

I will never forget that scene. It was so perfectly composed, they might have been fixed like that for centuries, which perhaps was the point. That was their world: a world of still points, of elegant rooms lined with books. Later that evening, as we walked back to our rooms, Evie said,

'Rather stagey, don't you think?'

'What?'

'That scene as we walked into Loewe's. I can picture Ivo saying, "Right, everyone, positions please!" as we arrived.'

'You're a cynic, Evie.'

It was a warm evening and at Loewe's we'd moved on from tea and crumpets to madeira. I felt the comfortable glow of alcohol and new friendship. Evie slung an arm through one of mine and smiled at me.

'You're right,' she said. 'I should be less unkind.' Though, of course, I knew, in my heart, she had a point.

After that initial painterly moment, Loewe's students had dropped their studied stillness as he said,

'Well, friends, let me introduce Catherine and Evie to you all. Though I hear Dr Bolton prefers Kitty. Isn't that right?' I nodded. 'Well, be kind to them, *kinder*. I sense we may be seeing a lot more of them this year.'

And that was that. Evie and I were in. Though as I was to discover in coming months, in this new world I'd entered there were layers of membership that someone like me could try a lifetime to penetrate and never succeed.

Richard got up and came lolloping over to me, holding out a hand to shake. As I took it, he said, in a low, unexpectedly shy and gentle voice,

'Kitty? How d'you do? I'm Richard Crashaw. Cup of tea?' I nodded, and we walked over to a rather rococo tea trolley holding home-cooked seed cake, assorted cups and saucers, and a large pot of tea. The pot was covered with a fraying cosy that might have been knitted by someone's maiden aunt. Evie had gone over to Charlie, who stood up and hugged her. They kissed each other on the cheeks. It seemed odd to me. I knew that they'd known each other at school, but they'd shown not the slightest interest in each other since we'd arrived in college. They'd behaved as strangers towards one another and now they seemed to be chatting like old friends.

'How do you find Littlemore?' I looked blankly at Richard as he handed me a cuppa in a chipped Crown Derby cup and saucer. I realised this wasn't the first time he'd asked me this question.

'Oh, yes, Littlemore,' I said. 'Forgive me, I was miles away. It's …' I tried to think of something smart to say and failed. 'It's … great.'

'Gosh. D'you think so?' replied Richard, as if I'd just said the most surprising thing. He grinned and looked down at the faded red carpet. As I was to learn in the months to come, one of Richard's most charming habits was never quite to meet your eye when speaking to you one-to-one. He could be quite the presence in class, but privately reserved. I also came to adore his habit of saying 'gosh' or 'golly' without a hint of archness. He was just that old-fashioned. He looked up again, glanced at me out of the side of his eyes and said, 'It seems pretty bloody awful to me. Albertus here, and this lot,' he gestured to Ivo and the others, 'are the only bearable things about it.' He laughed, as if at some private joke.

'So, why did you come?'

'Well, one has to do something with one's life, don't you think?' Again, he grinned, as if there was a joke I'd missed. He scratched his nose where the frames of his spectacles touched it. I saw red marks where the frames had irritated his skin. 'Now, tell me about this thesis of yours?'

We chatted amiably until he asked about my experience of working with medieval manuscripts. They were, apparently, a passion of his. After university, he'd done several internships in major libraries, including three months with the Rare Manuscripts section of the British Library. He could barely contain his shock when I confessed I'd rarely handled early texts. He called Ivo over to share his astonishment. Ivo goggled at me. I might have been a creature landed from another star system.

'But, how can you hold a PhD on *The Canterbury Tales* without ever drawing close to the early manuscripts?' said Ivo. His voice was smoother than Richard's, cooler and assured as if he were almost as old as Albertus.

'Does one need to have touched an original copy of *The Republic* to write convincingly about Plato?' I replied.

Richard laughed. 'It couldn't do any harm,' he said. We all laughed.

The conversation began to draw the others in, including Loewe himself.

Aware that he now had an audience, Ivo said,

'The point is, Kitty, that no one is much likely to get their grubby hands on an original Plato or Aristotle, but an earlyish Geoffrey Chaucer …' He paused to place his cup and saucer on the trolley, and grinned at Richard, 'they're practically lying around on the ground.'

'Ah, but you forget, Ivo …,' I felt a secret thrill as I said his Christian name for the first time, '… that making an original contribution to knowledge isn't just about looking at old bits of parchment.'

Ivo almost bowed in acknowledgement.

'Well said,' said Loewe. Then, looking around at us in turn, he said, with a twinkle in his voice, 'However, that doesn't mean one shouldn't enjoy wonderfully old things, does it?'

'Are you talking about yourself again, Albertus?' said Charlie. Everyone, except Evie and I, laughed. Loewe laughed loudest of all.

'Always, Charlie,' said Loewe. 'Though on this occasion I was thinking of something slightly different.' He twirled the left-hand side of his moustache, an action I was later to discover was characteristic. 'I wonder ... what would you young people say to seeing something very old?'

Loewe saw that Evie was offering Piers one of her Marlboro Lights and said,

'Ah, sorry Piers, before you light up ... If I'm to show you this, there's to be no smoking.'

Piers slipped the cigarette back into the packet.

Loewe gestured for us to follow him. He unlocked the door into a small, elegantly appointed room, off the large study. It contained a strange assemblage of objects. There was a beautiful trine whisky globe and an antique leather chesterfield. On the walls were a series of prints in the style of Jacques Callot's *Miseries of War*. He gestured for us to gather around a small table.

'Now, *kinder*, I have a little treat for you. But, before I show you, I'd rather like you to agree to keep schtum about it. That shouldn't be too tricky for holy people like you, should it?'

I looked across at Evie, puzzled. She raised her eyebrows indicating her bewilderment. I saw Piers smile wryly. Ivo stared coldly into space.

'I'll take your silence as consent,' said Loewe. 'Good.' He turned away and went over to a cabinet. He took a key out of his waistcoat pocket, unlocked a padlock and removed an object, about eight inches by six and an inch thick, wrapped in a silk slip-bag.

Was it silly of me to feel a thrill of anticipation? I was no child. I saw the theatre for what it was. For as long as I knew him, Albertus had the showman's need to build tension, to misdirect to create magic. Even, then, before I knew him, I'd been around enough self-indulgent egotists to know he was just trying to draw us into his world of theatre. This was a man whose personality never switched off; he was on twenty-four hour transmit. That evening I wanted to be ravished by this oddly English burlesque. If he was a collector of people and things, I was ready to be collected.

He placed the object on the table and said,

'Now, please don't ask how this came into my hands. Let's just say, it's a rather unusual loan.' He rubbed his hands together, and said, 'Right'. Suddenly, he sounded less sure of himself. He paused. I thought I knew what he was thinking – what if his stunt failed to impress? Was he showing a weak hand too soon? Gently he removed the object from its silk bag. It was, unsurprisingly, a book. A very old book, slim and bound in brown, aged leather. What I noticed, despite the room's ambient scent of stale tobacco smoke and the trace of perfume and after-shaves, was its smell. It smelt of old gloves and autumn walks. It smelt of centuries of hands and touch. It made me think of my grandfather, who I knew only when I was a tiny girl. I remember him as reassuring and kind and safe, a twinkling man.

'Is that …?' asked Piers, his voice scratchy and subdued.

'I think it might be,' said Richard.

'You recognise it?' said Loewe, sharply.

'Well, I don't think anyone would want to be that bold,' said Ivo, coolly.

I saw Charlie look at me for the first time. Her face was angular, a series of elegant planes. It seemed almost monstrous to me in its simple, direct beauty. She smiled, but it offered no hint of a clue. It was not unkind, it was just inscrutable.

'May I?' To my surprise, it was Evie. She gestured towards the book. Loewe looked at her. I saw a flicker of coldness, of suspicion, quickly concealed by his usual warm demeanour.

'Of course, my dear,' he said. Slowly, he passed her the book. Just as she was about to take it, he said, very quietly,

'Please be gentle with it. It's six hundred years old.'

Evie took the book, as if it were a new-born. She opened its pages with a kind of reverence I should not have imagined she possessed, and began softly to turn them. As she did so, Loewe spoke. There was an extraordinary stillness in the room. We might have been in church on a high holy day.

'Yes, what Evie holds there is an original *Canterbury Tales*. Well, a section of it. Perhaps the first third. Not a copy, mind. It's … it's his hand.'

'No,' I said. It was out of my mouth before I could stop myself.

'Well, possibly,' said Albertus. He smiled at me. 'I think it older than Henwrt's manuscript, certainly.' Henwrt's copy was made just after Chaucer's death. 'This,' Loewe added, 'is unique.' Before any of us could react, he said,

'Imagine it, *kinder*. What was happening in the world as Chaucer scratched his hand across the vellum? Extraordinary things, of course. And terrible things too. Salisbury Cathedral's clock began marking time. Richard II recognised John of Gaunt's claim to the crown of Castile. In 1388, at the Battle of Otterburn, James Douglas defeated Harry Hotspur and took him prisoner. And then there was Wycliffe's Bible. Ah, Wycliffe's Bible. The year it was completed signalled the death knell for the Lollards. And in 1389 the Turks defeated the Serbs at the Battle of Kosovo and think how that has resonated down the ages.

'As Chaucer's hand scratched across the page, a century began to draw to its close. A century of so much violence, but of wonders too, like all centuries. A century of plague and new mercantile confidence; of war and new religious movements. Chaucer scratched his wit and honesty into the hide of a slain animal and revealed the venality and beauty in us all.'

There was almost complete silence in the room. The only sound was our breathing. I felt an extraordinary urge to grab the book out of Evie's hands. It was irrational and violent. I wanted that book. Not just to hold it. I only need ask Loewe and he would have asked Evie to pass it to me. No. This fierce urge within me was to possess that delicate manuscript. To not let anyone else have it. I wanted to take it, run away and find a secret place to study it alone. As quickly as the fury flared, it left. Or I mastered it. I saw it for what it was. I looked from face to face, as if to check that no one had seen my desire. All were absorbed. I wondered if I dare touch it or even ask to look at it without giving myself away. My mouth felt suddenly dry.

Without thinking I said one word, 'pergamon.' Everyone looked at me. I looked at each face in turn, suddenly nervous, as if I'd committed a solecism. Evie smiled, while the others studied me with the coolness of examiners. Ivo licked his lips. Pergamon. A word which gestures back to the very edge of antiquity. Pergamon, the name of the city in Asia Minor where the process of using animal hides for paper was first fully developed. A word redolent of monkish devotion to knowledge and learning. Pergamon. A word that, for me, makes me think of great state proclamations and laws. Pergamon – made from calf-skin. Soft, subtle and yielding, and capable of lasting forever. Pergamon, the name for the very highest quality of vellum. Before I could say anything else, Loewe chuckled softly and said, 'Yes, pergamon, Kitty. Pages cut from that which was living, to make something beautiful for all time.'

I saw Ivo and Piers exchange a glance. It was avid and hungry, a look that verged on love. I had much reason to ponder that glance over the months to come. In one sense it offered the clue to all the pain that unfolded around Evie and the rest of us, though how anyone could have worked that out on that beautiful afternoon I don't know. I only filed it away for later because it struck me as a look of a piece with the one Piers gave when he saw Ivo's blood.

'And can you read any of it, Evie?' said Loewe. It was not an unkind remark in itself, though I suspect Evie heard it that way. I think Loewe meant, 'Can you decipher Chaucer's crabbed hand?' Evie looked at him, a defiant look, ready to take up the challenge.

She looked back at the book and said,

'For if the priest be foul in whom we trust, no wonder if the layman turn to rust! And shame it is, and let priests note, to see the shepherd doused in shit, the sheep still clean.'

Evie spoke fluently. It was impressive. She was, I knew, not only deciphering the handwriting, but rendering the Middle English into a clearer, modern form. She read at random from the page that was open at the time, the part of the General Prologue which introduces the poor Parson, and yet there was an edge to that sentence. When she'd finished she stared at Loewe. I felt like she'd directed the words at him, as if he were the foul priest, the shepherd covered in shit. Did that make us the sheep, unblemished by sin? Events were to give the lie to that. As I stood in that airless room I began to process new knowledge about myself. Perhaps we're all capable of lust, I don't know. All I know is that for the first time I felt its full power. I felt lust for ancient books, well, for one ancient book, anyway. And, as I looked over at Evie, I felt the desire that would lead us, that night, to sleep together for the first time.

Chapter Seven

As we walked back from Luxford that evening, I felt the stars align. I was where I wanted to be, doing something I felt called to, and I felt that my world – so often driven by a need to prove myself – was opening up. At last, I was becoming the person I wanted to be. Evie too, seemed happy. As she slung an arm through mine I felt a warm glow of friendship and more. As she turned her head towards mine with a mischievous glint in her eye, we paused and I thought we might kiss. Then she grinned, almost sheepishly, and said,

'Coffee? At mine?'

I laughed out loud at the cliché, and said,

'We'll have to be careful.'

'I promise not to pour any over your lap.' I laughed again.

'You know what I mean. It would be a shame to be thrown out after a lovely day.'

'Oh, Kit,' she said, as she squeezed my arm, 'what better sort of day is there?'

You might imagine that the kind of people who want to become vicars are chaste and prudish. Well, a lot are, of course, but most of us have a little experience of life before we take the cloth. As a teenager, I'd had my fair share of boyfriends and, at university, I'd ended up sleeping with a few, one of whom worked in a nineteenth-century library called the Portico. I slept with him a couple of times just to get access to the books. Until Evie came along, I'd never slept with a woman. Fact is, I'd never really found a woman attractive. Generally, I think I'd seen other women as rivals, but Evie was a revelation. Equally, I'd never taken any great pleasure in sex before. I felt like it was the sort of thing I should enjoy, but it had always left me cold and awkward. Whether Evie was experienced around women or not, for perhaps the first time in my life, I had a good time. The fact that part of me felt that, as trainee vicars, we were doing something rather illicit, only added to the pleasure.

I could barely conceal my pleasure at Chapel the next morning. Evie and I deliberately sat apart, hoping not to draw attention to ourselves, but I felt connected to her by an invisible thread. Her scent – orange blossom and peach – seemed to cling to the air. Every now and then I'd look over in her direction, trying to catch her eye. I kept feeling the urge to giggle and once she looked over at me and winked. All I wanted to do was sneak out of Chapel with her and go back to bed for the rest of the day. Chapel, however, was, perhaps, the one fixed point for everyone. Students were expected to attend it every weekday morning and, on Tuesday, Wednesday and Thursday, evenings too. We were also expected to worship together on Sunday mornings. While it was possible to negotiate all sorts of exemptions – and for some, especially the married students, it became something of an art-form, much to the annoyance of us singles – our rather liberal Head of Chapel, Roddy Peplow, only ever enforced morning prayer and the Sunday Mass.

I discovered that Peplow's *laissez faire* approach had less to do with generosity and more to do with the fact that he was a lush. Like many alcoholics, he struggled to sleep and found mornings the time most conducive for action; later in the day, as the alcohol took its toll, he lost more and more focus. Even with Peplow at the helm, we all spent a lot of time in Chapel; if one went in for the extra feast-day masses or had a personal devotion to Mary, or loved the strange choreography of Solemn Benediction, one might go for days without straying far from the Altar.

Roddy Peplow had, it was whispered, once been one of the Church's brightest stars, destined for a minor diocesan bishopric at the very least. Ipswich or Derby, say. His fall from grace, as for so many before him, was the result of a fondness for rent boys. When he was a senior diocesan cleric in Southwark he'd been caught in a tabloid sting, back in the days when naughty vicars could still make the front page. The exposé drove him deeper into drink. After a couple of failed parishes, he'd ended up at Littlemore, his last-chance saloon. In his mid-fifties, the whisky had taken its toll: his slim, chiselled face was lined and there were permanent black pouches beneath his eyes. His black hair – which had earned him the nickname Black Rod – was lank and streaked with grey. Yet, it was hard not to be fond of him. When, in my second year, he died, the funeral cortege was vast, attended by the great and the good as well as a few of his glamorous ex-boyfriends from the London scene. Once I asked him how to survive in the Church. I shall never forget his answer: 'Know where the bodies are buried, darling, know where they're buried.'

Rather like Peplow, the chapel at Littlemore was something of an oddity. It had been added to and tinkered with over its one hundred-plus years, and not sensitively. From the outside the building looked consistent enough – low-key Victorian Gothic, if Gothic Revival can ever be low-key. It had a small steeple, called Brierley's Folly after the first Principal. Dr Brierley was notable for writing a dogged defence of six-day creation against what he saw as the 'foolish arrogance of Darwin and his vulgar cabal'. Inside, the building was less harmonious. The compact nave had lost most of its pews to padded chairs in the seventies, many of which had the unfortunate habit of making a farting sound when someone sat down. The more childish ordinands like Bob

Hawkins and Matt Smith took great pleasure in seeking out the noisiest seats and sitting down at the most inopportune moments. The celebrant would say, 'Let us pray', the congregation would sit and Bob or Matt would be the last. It was a joke that, for most of us, got very old very quickly.

Indeed, I remember one occasion when Ivo buttonholed Bob outside chapel after a morning of prolonged sniggering. To the casual observer, Ivo always came across as the kind of person who was most at home in elegant rooms, though he was equally at home on a horse or tramping across a field with a twelve-bore slung on his arm. That encounter with Bob was the first time I realised how frightening Ivo might be when pushed. He waited until most of the students had filed out and gone for breakfast. Very kindly, warmly even, he called Bob back. Bob, who had been whispering to a couple of women about his antics, smiled and walked towards him.

'Ivo!' he said, jauntily. He seemed delighted to have been noticed. 'Enjoy morning prayer?'

Ivo blinked, then, to Bob's complete surprise, Ivo pushed him up against the wall. It was simple, effortless and quite shocking. His voice was level, low, and still polite.

'No, Robert, I did not. And I want you to be quite clear. It has to stop.'

Bob was a gobby man and I thought he was about to say, 'Or what?' He opened his mouth and thought better of it. Instead, he nodded and Ivo removed his hand from Bob's chest. Bob looked at him, as if for the first time, and left quickly and silently. Ivo turned to look at me and said, a smile on his face,

'Breakfast, Kitty?'

It was over in seconds. Bob and Matt never attempted their feeble chair joke again.

If the chairs were monstrosities, there were a few remaining pews huddled against the windows. During the months when we were inseparable, our little group of friends practically colonised the space. However, the most offensive, jarring fixture in the chapel was the 'living font'. Installed halfway down the nave by Roddy Peplow's predecessor, essentially it was an electric water-feature that pumped water through three sections into a large wooden font-bowl. We called it the Crapper because its wood had the deep patina of those old Victorian lavatory seats. In all my time at Littlemore I remember the Crapper being switched on a total of three times, each for College baptisms. On each occasion, I wanted to go for a wee almost immediately. It was an expensive, awful folly. The Principal wanted it removed, indeed, everyone wanted it removed, even the families who'd had their infants 'done' in it. However, this proved impossible, for it was the Bishop of Oxford's folly, he having paid for it out of a family legacy. For all I know, the bloody thing sits, unloved, in Littlemore chapel still.

The only feature that sat comfortably with the Gothic vision of the building was the rood screen and the chancel area. It was modelled after the beautiful fifteenth-century screen at the chapel of St Fiacre in Brittany, though less ornate. It featured a carved and painted crucifix and the two thieves crucified with Christ. Beyond it lay the chancel, calm and undisturbed. When I found Evie hanging from the Rood's crossbeam that January morning, it struck me how she'd deserved a better appointed place to die than the Chapel of St Dismas, Littlemore. It was such a hotchpotch place to die. Not Evie at all. Is it surprising that I prefer to go back to memories of another morning in chapel, at least when Evie lets me? That one when Evie and I sat catching glances of each other, aglow with the ache of sex and a secret knowledge. I think it's the happiest memory I have, a moment of almost unalloyed innocence. Even if we'd already eaten of the Apple, the bitter price was yet to be paid and I, for one, couldn't see then what was gathering in the shadows. The older I get the more it's tempting to believe that what was about to unfold – the blood and pain, the fear – could be traced back to what Evie and I tasted together in bed the night before. Though that is probably a little absurd. The issue was never just sex. It was sex and books, which, as shall become clear, was, for my friends, essentially the same thing.

Chapter Eight

The first sign that all was not well in the state of Littlemore came one Sunday morning in late October. Mass had just finished and Roddy Peplow shambled up to us. We were sat in our usual pews and Piers and Ivo were arguing about the *Gospel of Eve*.

The *Gospel of Eve* is one of the great oddities of the Christian tradition. Some claim it is nearly as old as the *Gospel of John*, but its reputation is sordid, not least because of its supposed *laissez-faire* attitude to sex and sexuality. In the early decades of Christianity, it came in and out of favour; by the third century, when the New Testament had become fixed, the *Gospel of Eve* was definitely out. Then, it disappeared. Somewhere in the early medieval era, as the Roman Empire fell apart, all copies were lost. All that was left were a few fragments which offered tantalising details about how an obscure sect called the Borborites had supposedly used it to justify free sex. Piers and Ivo loved to argue about the implications for Christianity of its lost and apocryphal texts. At one level, this was simply good natured joshing between old friends who liked a sharp debate; at another, Piers, who'd written his university dissertation on Apocryphal Texts, had a genuine interest in books like *The Shepherd of Hermas* which had once been part of the Bible but had fallen by the wayside. Truth be told, neither of them thought these books should be part of the Christian canon, but they still enjoyed arguing over their merits.

Today's argument had been triggered by a reading of Genesis

3 at Mass that morning, the section in which Eve is punished for persuading Adam to eat the fruit of the Tree of Knowledge of Good and Evil.

'Oh, for the love of Christ, Piers, stop pratting about,' said Ivo.

'I'm not. I'm quite serious,' replied Piers. 'All I'm saying is that it would have been fascinating to have the text of the *Gospel of Eve* to read alongside Genesis. I just wonder if Eve might have been given a fairer deal.'

Ivo looked at Piers with something bordering on contempt. I struggled to suppress a laugh. This kind of academic horseplay – serious and yet affectionate – was typical of their friendship.

Piers looked at me, winked, and said, 'I'm sure you'd agree, Kitty.'

'Leave me out of it,' I said, hastily.

'Even Kitty thinks you're dodgy, Piers,' said Ivo. I laughed.

Piers was about to reply, when Peplow, dressed in a shabby cassock and stinking of communion wine, approached and said, 'Well, my old darlings, I believe congratulations are in order.'

We looked from one to the other, more than a little confused. Roddy was such an old sot that it was highly likely he'd arrived with false information. Richard looked up from the copy of Herbert's *The Temple* he'd been quietly studying, and said, feigning interest, 'I'm afraid you'll have to illuminate us, Roddy.'

'Oh,' said Peplow. He ran a hand through his lank hair, and looked around the chapel for eavesdroppers. Reassured we were alone, he said, a little less heartily, 'Well, Evie … Of course.'

We all turned to look at her. All of us, except Ivo. Evie's expression moved quickly between shock, embarrassment, anxiety and, finally, defiance. Memory tells me that she blushed a little. There was the tiniest trace of nervousness when she spoke.

'Um, thank you, Roddy.' She bit her lower lip, then looked at the rest of us. 'I was going to tell you later, over dinner.' She looked directly at me. 'Albertus has asked me to help him with a small research project.'

I saw Charlie's face. In the past few weeks, she and Evie had, I thought, become firm friends. They had put away whatever past there was between them. Now, the expression on Charlie's face – fixed, cold, statue-like – made me less sure.

'It's just a bit of cataloguing really,' Evie added. 'Something to help me get in a research frame of mind.' She paused, as if weighing up what she should say next, then said, 'The *quid pro quo* is access to Albertus's private library.' Still no one said anything. I saw Ivo clean his spectacles on the end of his neat, green tie. 'It was you, Kitty, who brokered the deal.' Now, everyone looked at me. I was puzzled and a little alarmed. Evie said, 'You know, that night we went to hear Albertus lecture. You said it would be good for my research.'

The fact is, I didn't know how to react. I was completely thrown. Since that first night in bed together, I'd thought we'd only grown closer. Certainly, we'd been extra careful, especially around the others and I don't think either of us would have said that we were 'going out' with each other. In the past few weeks, we'd only slept together a couple of times, but that wasn't the point as far as I was concerned. For the first time since childhood I felt like I had a close female friend, someone with whom I could be intimate and could trust. I'd even told her a little about the death of Lou, and how it had been the catastrophe that had defined my family's story. Christ, I'd even told her about how my sister's death and my parents' lack of love for me had ultimately led me to faith and a call to priesthood. And Evie hadn't even bothered to tell me about this?

I felt like a chump and my cheeks grew hot with jealousy. More than that, I was just plain angry that she hadn't told me first. Surely that wasn't unreasonable? As far as I could see, I was as close to her as anyone in college. Closer. And we'd gone to bed, hadn't we? And, yet she hadn't said a word, not even a hint. I was stunned. I felt like she'd gone behind the backs of the rest of us, well, of me, to get closer to Loewe. I was annoyed with her hypocrisy. Hadn't she said that he was the kind of don who gave out 'Firsts for fucks'? And I just felt left out. It was me who'd sought after Loewe, after all. Okay, that had primarily been to get to know my new friends, but now that I was in, I wanted more. I wanted to be recognised as special by Loewe. I was the one with the doctorate, for God's sake. And … a new question occurred to me. One I didn't want to admit: How could she do this when … when I loved her? Evie. Who, I thought, loved me back.

There was another reason, too. One that scared me, perhaps as much, if not more. It went back to that first encounter with the Chaucer manuscript. Since that day, it had not let me go. I brooded on and dreamt about it. I was jealous of Evie because, by working for Loewe, she'd be close to it. Closer than me. Evie had mentioned 'Albertus's private library'. What other secret treasures did Loewe have in it? And I wanted to get there before the others, especially Evie. It was irrational and ignoble, but no less real for that. That first afternoon at Loewe's had stirred something in me. A need to get ever closer to another world, another era. One solution would be to volunteer to help Loewe, but if I did so now, I'd look ridiculous. *'Oh, Albertus, can I come and help you too?'* I couldn't have stood the embarrassment.

'I don't know what you mean, Evie,' I said, coldly. 'It's not like I said anything to Albertus.' I hated the trace of petulance in my voice.

'Oh,' said Evie. 'I thought …' Unless she was a superb actor, she sounded genuinely surprised. 'When Albertus asked me, he mentioned you …', she continued.

'What?' I was stunned. I felt the others looking at me again.

This time Evie genuinely blushed. 'He said, "Kitty wants you to be happy and I think this will help."'

This only piqued my annoyance again. I was irritated with Loewe, irritated with Evie, irritated with the claustrophobic life of

Littlemore, its cramped precincts and the way I couldn't get away from the same people. I thought, again, of that damned asylum panopticon louring over the place. I felt watched and controlled.

We are all born liars. All of us. We all say make-believe things and mostly it's harmless. This felt different. I felt sure Evie was making up this account of Albertus for effect. Of course, I wanted Evie to be happy! I wanted everyone to be happy, but I'd not said anything to Albertus about her. I was about to say something to this effect, when Peplow said,

'Yes, yes! Kitty, Kitty, Kitty, Cat! Come on, me old darlings! There's a fatted calf to consume and the Principal's dreadful sherry too. It's Sunday! Come, let's feast and honour the Lord.'

It was sufficient to break up our little party. We gathered up our things and headed over towards the dining room. I walked a little behind the others. Piers and Ivo resumed their good-natured joshing. Roddy cracked jokes with Evie, and her giggle – girlish, posh – irritated me. Charlie spoke conspiratorially to Richard. I felt as alone as I had since my arrival at Littlemore. I was sure Charlie and Richard were talking about me. They must have seen how I'd flushed with anger and annoyance when Evie had told the truth about Albertus's invitation to her to work for him. They must have spotted my inability to conceal my jealousy. I felt the first crack, bleak and dark, in my relationship with Evie. As we walked along the gravel path from Chapel to dining room, I tried to get some perspective, and failed. I stared furiously at the back of Evie's head, willing her to turn and see my fury, but she did nothing of the sort, of course. She just carried on giggling with Roddy and thinking everything was all right. But it wasn't. I'd let her in, like no one else before, and I felt like she'd betrayed me. I was determined to make her pay.

Chapter Nine

I rushed my lunch and ran off to my room to sulk and wait. For, each Sunday afternoon, Evie and I had got into the habit of meeting at mine at 4pm for a cuppa, a chat and a bit of half-hearted study. As the time approached, I began to steel myself for a confrontation. Would she dare come? When 4pm came and went and she didn't appear, my anger flared again. If she was going to ignore me, I would respond in kind. Then, I heard a knock on my door.

I opened it and saw Evie on my doorstep. I was about to launch into a rant, when she picked up a large box off the floor, placed it in my hands, and said,

'I'm sorry I'm late. It was a hell of a do tracking this down on a Sunday. Practically impossible, of course, but I wanted to say sorry. Can I come in?' She was her usual breezy self. I nodded dumbly, and she entered my room. She'd changed out of her smart Sunday clothes into a sweatshirt and pyjama bottoms. She looked several years younger than usual and I wondered if this was a deliberate ploy. She had a faint smile on her face, and nodded encouragingly at the box.

'Aren't you going to open it, then?'

'Evie,' I said, warningly.

'I know,' she said, simply, holding up her hands. 'I was wrong, and I'm sorry. I'll explain, but will you open your present.' She spoke with the urgency of a giddy schoolgirl. Despite myself, I smiled, and said,

'Okay.'

She clapped her hands and said, 'Excellent.'

'I haven't forgiven you yet, Evie,' I said, though more warmly. I opened the box and found a small bouquet of late Michaelmas daisies and a dusty bottle of port, a 1960 Krohn Harvest. I sighed.

Later that evening, as we lay in bed, smoking cigarettes, I said, 'Why, Evie?'

'Shhhh,' she whispered and kissed my shoulders. It was soothing and it took a huge effort to resist her advance.

'Really, Evie. Why?'

She blinked, then said, 'Okay. It was just an error of judgment … I should have trusted you, I know that now. But it wasn't you. I didn't say anything because of the others.'

'What do you mean?'

She exhaled a lungful of smoke, and said, 'I don't know how to put it without sounding silly. I tried to keep it quiet because I reckoned Ivo or Piers would try to kibosh it. You know how they like to act as if they're Albertus's favourites. They'll hate the fact he's asked me.' Not just them, I thought. 'And … I think they're all up to something.'

'What do you mean?'

'That's just it. I don't know, exactly. I just don't trust them.'

'Oh, come on, Evie.'

'No, listen to me. The other day, I decided to go for a late-night bath in that bathroom off my corridor. It must have been 2am. I couldn't sleep, and just as I got to the door, who should come out, but Richard.'

'So?'

'It was weird, Kit. He didn't see me at first and he had this look on his face. It was intense, pained. He was chalk-white. Then he saw me, and forced his mouth into a grin. Not that sloppy smile of his, but a grimace. I asked him if he was alright and he said he had a tummy upset. But, Kit, …. the bathroom … the sink was practically pink. There was a towel in the bin I swear had been soaked with blood.'

'Blood?' She had my full-attention now. I thought again of that day of the funeral when I saw blood dribble onto Ivo's left hand. I thought of the look on his face and of that on Piers. Other-worldly. Ecstatic.

'And that's not all,' said Evie. 'One Thursday night, after midnight, I saw Ivo and Piers walking back from the village.'

'And what's odd about that?'

'Only that Piers could barely walk. Ivo was holding him up. He was limping.'

'They were probably pissed from the pub.'

'That's what Piers said when I saw him the next day. He said he'd twisted his ankle on the way back from the Green Man.'

'And?'

'Kitty, I was in the Green Man that night with Roddy. Neither of them came in … And that's not all. That limp was no twisted ankle. Piers had chinos on, Kitty, and there was a dark stain across the thigh.'

'What do you think it was?'

'I don't know. But I'd swear it was a patch of blood.'

* * *

Blood again. It was all very strange, and yet I don't want to give you the impression that that term at Littlemore turned completely bizarre or sour from then on. Far from it. It was still a miraculous, joyous season. All six of us had relatively few responsibilities, especially Evie and me. The others were out and about a bit more, on short placements and attachments, but we were all very much campus-based. If I was beginning to glimpse the lies and obsessions to come, new worlds were yet to be found before the fall. How can I convince you?

Perhaps I should tell you about Friday nights. Friday nights were a joy, almost to the end. For us, as for so many clergy and ordinands before and since, Friday was the one night we felt we could let our hair down. Charlie had managed – either through money or charm – to wangle one of the rare flats on campus, typically reserved for married ordinands and their families. Every Friday night we'd head over there, for food, vast amounts of alcohol, and games. The flat itself was in a depressing sixties development, all flat roofs and grey slabs. Half of the apartments leaked during the slightest rain shower and the stairs stank of cat, specifically a tom, Macavity, who belonged to an older couple Molly and Peter Shanks. Hailing from Yorkshire, Molly was matronly without that strain of pastoral vampirism found in her type. Her husband was a witty ex-TV producer who told hair-raising stories about the heroes of Sixties and Seventies light entertainment. We were never sure if he was telling the truth or not. One night, when exceptionally drunk in the bar, he told a monstrous abuse story about a beloved TV star. Twenty years later it proved to be true.

Charlie had done marvels with unpromising resources. If the externals of the flat were appalling, once over the threshold, one entered a different time and space. As the daughter of money you might expect her flat to be filled with items that either sought to claim an elegant, landed past she'd never known, or displayed eye-burning modern design. Rather, her style was what we might now call 'up-cycled'. Now it's a tired, mocked look – the choice of hipsters in Hoxton and Aga-bound women in Hampstead – but back then I don't think any of us had seen anything quite like it. She'd taken some decent pieces – I remember she had this old welsh dresser, God knows how she'd got it in the flat, and various tables and chests of drawers – and used something called 'chalk paint' on them. Nowadays, these quick drying paints are ubiquitous, but back then, her palette – cornflower blues, jade greens, teal and burnt umber – was fresh with the suggestion of Provence or Umbria. Hers was a sunny, highly decorated space that made me think of twenties salons typical of the Bloomsbury Set. When Evie put on her trad-jazz albums, the effect was complete.

We drank like only the young and holy can. Richard would turn up with random vintages from his father's cellar. I've never drunk so well or so strangely. One week we'd try some Left-Bank marvel, an old Chateau Palmer or Léoville-Barton, and the next we'd be messing around with some distinctly dodgy cocktails. We'd nick dregs of cheap vodka and gin from the bar and make drinks up. Ivo had this tattered copy of an American cocktail manual *Drinks For Every Occasion* he'd dug up in a bargain bin on the Charing Cross Road. It had been printed in 1927 and Ivo was determined to work through every option in its foxed and grubby pages. Charlie and Piers periodically worked on a new cocktail The Littlemore – a form of Daiquiri that included beetroot juice and lime. It made its debut during the College Christmas Review, led to a college-wide case of the trots, and was never heard of again. Our shared love, however, was whisky. A taste for it was one of the few things I held in common with my father, though he preferred the easy pleasures of blended varieties. In the company of my friends, I learned to travel very far from Speyside. To this day, I shall never forget the raisin-rich, cinder-toffee pleasures of the forty-year old Highland Park Ivo brought out a few weeks before term broke for Christmas. When I found out how much it cost – most of a year's grant – his generosity almost made me weep.

And the food. Food at Littlemore was catastrophic. It was the worst of institutional cooking and it took a focussed student not to pile on the pounds over a twelve-week term. My friends, public-school children all, knew how to negotiate a system structured around stodge – mashed potatoes, pies and steamed puddings. What Ivo called, the 'brown and white diet'. Ivo and Charlie worked off the calories by running, and Richard, Evie and Piers played squash in the college's crumbling court. They'd mastered portion discipline in a way many ordinands couldn't begin to comprehend. One student, Henry Rowbotham, a chubby Lancastrian who liked to attend college functions dressed as a woman, blew up like a balloon over his two years. As for me, I'd never really felt the pull of food. My sister was the foodie. Louise loved to slurp spaghetti or drizzle gallons of vinegar on her chips. She talked of the food she'd love to try – snails and frogs's legs and pâté. I always found it faintly disgusting. If she'd lived, Louise would have become one of those women constantly yo-yoing on a diet. No, I was no foodie, though I made an exception for the wonders Richard rustled up at our Friday parties.

I'll never know where Richard learnt it all. When I first knew him, he said he'd blagged his way into top restaurants and charmed the chefs. Even then I never quite believed him. It felt like a deflection technique to stop me prying too deeply and, anyway, he struck me as just too reserved to blag his way into Raymond Blanc's or whoever's kitchen. Later, when I knew him better, he nervously told me over supper that he cooked to cope with loneliness. His parents – who ran a firm of architects with international reach – had been absent for much of his childhood. By teaching himself to cook, first in the company of a succession of nannies and then alone, he'd coped with feelings of abandonment. Whatever was true, God, could he cook. It was at his hands that I first tasted sweetbreads. Not the floppy mess that sometimes get served in gastro pubs, but classic juicy morsels, crisp on the outside and soft in the centre, served with garlic butter and Pernod. Or braised pig's cheeks in cider, even just a simple beef bourguignon served with vin de pays d'oc. On those Friday nights, we ate well and sometimes we ate lavishly. I'd not thought I liked oysters (I'd never tried them) until

Evie turned up one evening with a large sack of what she called Mistleys and Richard made a mignonette sauce. She explained that Mistleys were oysters that came from a tiny place called Mistley Thorn on the Essex/Suffolk border and with real relish (it was near Halloween, I think), she added, 'It's notorious as the former home of Matthew Hopkins, Witchfinder-General. Apparently he liked to eat a dozen oysters before burning a witch.'

Perhaps you're surprised, even shocked, to discover that seminarians could live like this. If we were, in many ways, a group apart, our tendency to over-indulge was not exceptional. Sixty-odd people cooped up on a campus in the middle-of-nowhere united by little more than a shared commitment to God and prayer was always likely to produce extreme behaviour. In our several ways, we were all fanatics. Admittedly we had few who would count, in the popular mind, as religious fanatics. Yes, there were one or two censorious puritans, but the 'Bible and Black' crowd went, for the most part, to other places than Littlemore. Our fanaticisms were both more commonplace and – given the stereotype of the gentle, buck-toothed clergyman – more outré than many would anticipate.

Would you believe me if I told you that one of the brightest boys in our cadre – who's now a rather respectable bishop – was found one Saturday morning with a pile of servers' rope cinctures in his room? It transpired that he'd got in from a club in Oxford with a pretty, young man with whom he shared a fondness for bondage. Finding they lacked anything substantial to tie themselves up with, they raided the chapel vestry. It took me ages not to feel that those cinctures were soiled with our colleague's nocturnal emissions. Or what about William Wilson, straight out of university, who had some of his undergraduate friends down from the north one weekend? One of them was a small-time dealer and three days later the entire college stank of weed.

Then there were the various college societies, mostly a little arcane, if harmless. Michael Shaw and Chris Eastwood, the great Royalists, ran the Charles King and Martyr Society which seemed to involve mostly wearing lace cottas, drinking cheap sherry, and proposing loyal toasts to the monarch. A small group of women ran the Edmund Bertram Society. Ostensibly devoted to *Mansfield Park*'s serious clergyman, it supplied an excuse for middle-aged female ordinands to drink Pinot Grigio and watch videos of Colin Firth's chest-hair. Honourable mention should be given to the Society of Saints Bibiana and Bacchus. Named after the patron saint of hangovers, and the Greek god of wine, it was the nearest Littlemore got to a drinking society. I was even invited along once, early in my time at Littlemore, and, after one blurry night of gin cocktails, I never returned. Frankly, I was disappointed. It seemed basically to consist of thin young men, just down from Oxford, who liked Latin jokes and dressed in an over-pious sub fusc manner. Goodness, could they drink, though.

* * *

'What do you make of Evie's elevation, then?' I was around at Charlie's, the Friday after Evie's shock announcement as Loewe's research assistant. The others were yet to arrive and Charlie and I sat smoking cigarettes and drinking gin and tonics on her long, squidgy settee. We'd spent the afternoon working in a desultory manner on a pastoral theology exercise together – essentially, what resources did Latin-American liberation theology have for UK housing estates – and we'd now fallen into chit-chat and drinks.

'As long as Albertus is happy, I don't see any harm.'

'That's hardly a ringing endorsement.' She took a deep drag on her Marlboro Light and blew the smoke out with amusement.

'Evie says that Albertus is probably the sort of don with sticky paws.'

Charlie laughed out loud.

'Oh, no. Not Albertus. His tastes are quite otherwise.'

'Really?'

'I should know. I've spent the best part of a year with him. Why do you think he always works with handsome young men?'

I considered this. It made a lot of sense, of course. I was no bigot or prude and I wasn't surprised or shocked about Loewe's tastes. If there was something tasteless it came down to him being seventy-odd and making passes at twenty-something men who lacked his power and position. I wondered if he'd tried it on with Ivo, Richard or Piers. If he had, of the three, I thought it would most likely be with Richard. If, at that point in our friendships, I would have said that none of them were exactly vulnerable, it was clear that Richard was quieter and perhaps the more brittle. I thought him the one who might be flattered. I took a final drag on my cigarette, stubbed it out, and said,

'What do you think about it?'

'Evie?' said Charlie. I nodded.

She considered her answer, then said, 'She was always conniving.'

I smiled to myself. I wondered what she knew about my relationship with Evie. I wondered if she was testing how close we'd become. Well, if that was her game, I could dig too.

'What's the story between you two?' I said.

'You really want to know?'

I shrugged. She got up off the settee and went over to a neat office table, opened a drawer, and pulled out a piece of paper. She came back, passed it to me and sat down again.

It was a photograph. It showed Charlie and Evie in green school uniforms, standing on a lawn, smiling in front of a gothic-looking building. They'd slung arms around each other's shoulders. Charlie looked about 17 and Evie 16. They looked the very picture of happy, well-heeled schoolgirls – fresh-faced and jolly. Charlie's hair was tied back and Evie's cut in a neat bob. They might be celebrating a school win at hockey.

'What are you saying?' I said. 'That you were lovers?'

'I suppose I am,' she replied. She took another cigarette out of the pack and offered me one. I shook my head. I loved smoking, but my chest did not. It never ceased to amaze me how they could all smoke so much and yet seem to be immune to the kind of low-level flu that affected the rest of us. Piers put it down to a strict regime of cod-liver oil and grapefruit juice before morning prayer every day.

Charlie sparked up, and said, 'Girls' boarding schools are the weirdest places. You know how it is.' She chuckled. 'Well, you don't, but you know how girls are. All the clichés – hormones, obsessions, intrigues. Lonely too, despite rarely having a moment to yourself.

'Cheltenham gave me opportunities I never dreamt of, but God ... When it was bad ... Stand out in the wrong way and girls are ruthless.'

She paused, took a sip of gin, deciding, I thought, how far to pursue this line of thought. She'd already let me in further than I'd imagined she would.

'You probably know I'm not old money. Mum went to a secondary modern, not Roedean.' She laughed bitterly. 'But that wasn't the issue. This isn't the 1920s anymore. No. My problem was that some of the girls decided I was too pretty. Or some such crap.' She paused again, stared at her cigarette. 'Pathetic, isn't it?' I said nothing and waited for her to continue.

'Well, we all need friends. The bullying could have been much worse. I only got the occasional damp bed or hair-pulling. Evie ... the thing about Evie was that though she was younger than me, she was twice as popular. I should have been the cool one, further up

80

the food chain, but she had … magic. Dappy, yet clever. Sporty, but without trying too hard. You know what she's like.

'Girls were forever falling in and out of love. It was just crushes, a way to test out what kissing was like without the risk of actual boys, but when Evie became interested in me, can you believe I was grateful? I really fell for her. The whole thing. Love letters, secret messages, midnight assignations. I'd have shagged her brains out, if only I hadn't been so prim. I thought about her twenty-four-seven. It took me years to get over.'

She stubbed out her cigarette and said, 'Listen to me! Getting sentimental! You'll be quite a priest one day, Kitty, dragging confessions out of people.'

I said nothing. I was sure, however, that either she knew or she'd guessed about Evie and me sleeping together.

'The thing is, Kitty … don't take this wrong way, but there's stuff you should know about Evie …'

'Really?' I hated the note of defensiveness in my voice, but I sat forward a little, nonetheless. As much as I cared for Evie, I still hadn't quite got over the way she'd hidden her work offer from Loewe and I sensed Charlie wanted to help me see something I could not. Just then, though, the doorbell rang.

'Hold that thought,' she said, and got up and went to the door.

She returned with the others, Evie at the front, unwrapping her scarf and taking off her coat. Richard and Piers were having a debate about naughty medieval monks, by the sound of it. Ivo knelt down to untie his muddy boots. As Evie walked towards me she smiled and said,

'Brrr. It's colder than the hinges of hell out there.' Behind her I saw Charlie. She looked past Evie at me. Where Evie looked happy, Charlie's face carried the shadow of our previous conversation. She'd been about to reveal something to me, and the opportunity had passed. She looked annoyed. Then it was gone and she said, brightly,

'Drinks!' I looked back at Evie. I realised she looked more than happy; she looked exultant, radiant, a cat who'd got the cream. I knew her well enough by now to know that something important must have happened. I wondered if she'd found out what was behind our friends' odd behaviour. Or was it something else? As Evie passed Charlie her coat, I looked back at Charlie. Her smile was as hospitable as ever. But there was something else behind it. What was it? Malice? Not quite. Disgust? No. With a jolt, I realised it was fear, naked fear.

Chapter Ten

In those first few months, I often dreamt of my sister. We'd be playing dolls' tea parties at the beach or in our parents' garden. We'd be riding our bikes around the park. Sometimes she would suddenly become Evie or Charlie. Often she would be telling me off for not trying hard enough. Occasionally I dreamt of the time Lou and I were in our primary school's Nativity. I was five years old and I'd been asked to sing a solo verse of 'Twinkle, Twinkle, Little Star'. In rehearsal, all went well, though I remember Louise being jealous that I'd got the starring role. My mum even bought her a new dress to calm her down. On the afternoon of the show, I fell to pieces. Worse. I stuttered my lines and I wet myself, right there in front of what seemed to me hundreds of adults. In my dream version, Lou laughs nastily. It's the dream that always comes back to me when I'm stressed and under-pressure. Once, when I was a teenager and had my GCSE Maths exam, I wet the bed.

Louise made it into more common-place dreams too. I'd never quite got over my first encounter with that early Chaucer manuscript. Unbeknownst to the others, I arranged several afternoons at the New Bodleian, examining some of their oldest and best manuscripts. I'd shook as I'd held a rare *Missale Sarisburiense*, a book that includes one of the earliest records of English marriage vows. I marvelled at the real gold used in the illuminations. They shone. A librarian taught me to use touch, the brush of my fingers, to distinguish between the smooth and hairy sides of vellum. At night, I'd dream of marginal drawings and illuminations. Louise would appear, her face on a Blessèd Virgin wrestling the devil, or as a rabbit chasing a hunter. Sometimes I was the Devil. Sometimes I was the hunter.

And, of course, again and again, I journeyed with her to her death in the river. In my dream it is always raining, though, in fact, it was a bright sunny day. I think it rains in my dream because Lou's death revolves around water: the swollen, brown Severn, and a riverbank that was slippery and wet from days of rain. What on earth we thought we were doing playing down there I'll never know, but it was the summer holidays and it was the first fine day in ages. Lou wanted to see if we could capture some sticklebacks. Why we didn't go to the canal or even the Stour I forget. I just remember that she said she knew this place on the big river where the water was shallow and safe. Her friend Fiona Field had shown her.

We couldn't find the right spot. We were a few minutes out of town, past the old vinegar works, in a quiet little field, and I told her we should go home, but Lou was insistent. Then she said she'd found the spot and was clambering down. I was scared.

'Come on, Kitty!' she said in her most commanding voice. Typically bossy, older sister.

Then she slipped, and fell backwards into the water, and it wasn't as shallow as she thought. Louise was a good swimmer. However, the undercurrents in the Severn can be vicious and deceptive, especially after days of storms. That's what I remember the fireman saying to my father. She fell and then she disappeared and then reappeared again. She shouted, 'Kitty, please!' or something like that, but I was so scared. I tried to run down the side of the bank as she was pulled along and she tried to get to the shore. I ran and ran, but she kept edging further away. I watched her bob, two or three times, then disappear. In my dream, I always see her falling into the water, her feet losing grip on the muddy

84

bank and her body tipping backwards. She falls in slow motion and she says something I cannot understand. Sometimes she slips. I feel that fall, I fall with her, and then I wake.

It wouldn't take a professional psychologist to explain why Louise was so much on my mind that term. I was disrupted – I'd moved to a new place, and was working in a new role – and unsurprisingly my dreams reached into my past. I enjoyed my new life at Littlemore, but I was anxious and a bit scared. Is it surprising that my dreams were full of fear? In the scariest version of my dream, Lou doesn't fall, but I push her and I just watch her struggle and drown. But this was just because I was anxious. The Christian life entails travelling into mystery and loss. It's all about transition and, through Evie, I'd discovered new possibilities of desire and pleasure. I was also sure that slowly I was losing her. I'd lost Lou and now I was losing Evie. Is it such a surprise that in my anxious dreams they were in danger of blurring into one?

And, of course, I was processing being part of Loewe's circle. Through my friends I'd gained entry into a new, longed-for world and if I enjoyed the sense of being set apart somehow, it also generated tensions. My involvement in Loewe's 'set' annoyed people who thought I should be one of the regular gang. This came home to me when Michael Shaw joined me for coffee one morning quite soon after I'd become part of Loewe's clique. We had a shared love of John Dickson Carr detective novels and often amused ourselves by trying to come up with 'locked room' plots worthy of the master himself. However, that morning was different. Shaw came to the point.

'You want to be careful around that lot.'

'Who?' I said, pleasantly.

'Oh, come on Kitty. You know exactly who I mean.'

'They're my friends, Michael, so give them a break.'

'Are you sure, Kitty?'

'Come on. Out with it.'

'Look. I know this place is weird and intense. We're all a bit screwed up. We're all scrutinising each other and asking, "Are they priest material?" But don't blow it, Kitty … That lot. They're not right.'

He reminded me of Evie's line, 'They're not kind.' His voice softened as he said,

'Seriously. How long have you known them? Their fucking medieval ideas and obsessions. They'll be thrown out and they'll take you with them.'

'Are you jealous of Evie and me, Michael?' I meant it as a kind of joke, but I was shocked when his jaw hardened and he stood up.

'Jealous? You don't get it, do you? Evie's one of them. Toffee-nosed sods. You don't know the half of it. Hypocritical bigots.' He paused, then said, 'Anyway, don't say you haven't been warned.' He stormed off.

I knew my friends were far from perfect, of course they weren't. It was obvious that one or other of them had hurt Michael, perhaps with some reference to his sexuality. That was hardly acceptable, but it was the Nineties and most of us barely knew the word 'homophobia', especially in the Church. We all said and, sometimes, did things that would be embarrassing or even anathema now. People still made jokes about 'shirt-lifters' and 'bum-chums' and in the camper theological colleges, gay men still gave each other 'names in religion' – female names – and referred to each other as 'she'. At Littlemore those days were gone, but my friends – with their public-school backgrounds – were more likely than most to be clumsy around matters of sexuality. Their single-sex world, especially the male single-sex world, regulated 'appropriate' behaviour ruthlessly. Michael had, I guessed, been on the rough end of the attitudes that public school inculcated in its products. In telling me to be careful around my new friends, Michael was just trying to be kind. I just wasn't in a place where I could even begin to hear what he had to say.

Yet, however dimly, I sensed that there were aspects of my friends' relationships with each other that were more than elusive. What Evie had told me about Richard and Piers – all that blood – haunted me, as did what I'd seen in the Common Room on the day of Princess Diana's funeral. I sensed that there was more to what Charlie wanted to tell me about Evie than schoolgirl malice. I returned again and again to the layers of mystery that lay about them and I kept sensing, almost out of the corner of my eye, missing connections that should be obvious. If I were in a detective novel, the clues would be coming thick and fast; if I were Wimsey or Jane Marple I'd have seen the links. But, of course, life is not detective fiction. All I knew was that there was something going on. Something that I was only dimly aware of. I'd thought that by getting closer to my new friends it would make things clear. Rather, I stared into a dim looking-glass: the closer and more carefully I looked the more distorted it became.

Things came to a head one particularly odd Saturday morning at Luxford House in mid-November. It was unusual for seminars to take place on Saturday. I'd fallen into a regular routine of seeing Albertus on a Friday morning. He liked to run what he called a 'masterclass' on priesthood in its historical context. In that first term, Evie and I were permanent fixtures. We did not yet have to negotiate attachments and placements in churches, hospitals, college chapels and so on. The others were there as often as they could. Ivo was doing a short attachment at the John Radcliffe Hospital, while Piers and Richard had placements with a couple of rural priests. Charlie was shadowing the Bishop's Chaplain. Loewe didn't like to go too long without gathering us all together. He said that we would be better formed as priests if we lived a life in common; he said that the Church had never quite recovered from its medieval highpoint when the best priests were also monks, sharing a rule of life. He saw us, he said, as a kind of cell of possibility for the Church. Together we could revivify it and that Saturday morning was going to be one of our private formation days.

I was running late. After our usual Friday night gathering, I'd returned to uproar in Davidson House. Another youngish woman, Fran Whittaker, was having a crisis in the small kitchenette on our corridor. The pastoral vampires had gathered *en masse*. There was Jane Sampson and Audrey Court and Jeanette Spink, all gathered around Fran. Tall and wiry, with frizzy hair, Fran had this charming habit of cocking her head to one side when she struggled to understand something. She usually commuted to college on a weekly basis and was married to a quantity surveyor or something like that. College represented a whole new set of possibilities. In short, she was also having an affair with a middle-aged trainee Methodist minister called Tanya Mitchell. Tanya, grey-haired and sour-faced, was married herself. Heaven knows what they saw in each other except a kind of false freedom. That Friday night they'd clearly had an argument and Fran was in meltdown. I did my best not to get pulled into the pastoral crisis, but the walls in Davidson are thinner than they should be. Fran's sobs, and her repeated refrain of, 'I just don't know what to do' and Jane Sampson's 'I know, I know' were on loop until the early hours. I became so exasperated at one point that when Fran said, 'I just don't know what to do' for what seemed the millionth time, I almost shouted, 'I do. Fuck off back to High Wycombe.' I felt like I slept about two hours that night.

When I arrived at Luxford, I felt ill, tired and dehydrated. I was furious with Fran and Jane and their mates and I'd had no breakfast. I was already ten minutes late and dreading Albertus's ribbing. He could be ruthless, pointing out one's frailties and foibles for ages. He'd once ribbed Charlie for weeks for confusing some lines in Aquinas with those of Duns Scotus and seeing me in this discomposed state was likely to set off a round of roasting. As I climbed the stairs I heard raised voices, although this was not uncommon at Luxford. Passions sometimes ran high and Albertus encouraged it. The spirit of disputation was a lively one, he said, and he believed that friction kept its participants warm. This morning, however, I sensed a different mood. This was not Ivo rehearsing Aquinas's ideas about transubstantiation whilst Piers threw nominalist hand grenades. There was no hint of the dry humour and play that lay behind much of my friends' bickering. The tone of the voices was sharp and snappy. Male and female voices were talking over each other.

I'm not the sort of person who usually sneaks about or listens at doors. I prefer to deal directly with situations. However, in my tired and grumpy state, I was sure they were talking about me. In my exhaustion, I was sure – if I'm honest – that Evie was up to something, sticking the knife into me. I was sure there was something going on with the whole lot of them that I was missing out on, so how could I resist? However, one of the disadvantages of Victorian fixtures and fittings is that they are heavy and well-made. From the stair-well the voices were muffled and indistinct. I crept up the stairs while noise continued to issue from Albertus's rooms. I was surprised. If he was there, how could he allow this argument to rage? I began to tune into the voices. I heard Evie and Ivo. Ivo sounded accusatory and Evie defensive, while Richard and Charlie sounded conciliatory. As I reached the top of the stairs, I thought I heard my name.

I suppose we are all attuned at some unconscious level to hearing our name. Part of us is always listening out for it. On a busy street, amidst the hubbub of traffic, we can always hear it when it's called, even if it's not directed at us. I stopped and listened intently. It was still difficult to distinguish clear sentences and specific words, but I swear I heard Ivo say something like, 'Yes, but what will Kitty think of us?' In a film or book, I suppose this would have been my cue to step forward, open the door and say, 'Think of what, Ivo?' Or failing that to creep in closer still and tread on a fatal floorboard, the creak giving my skulking away. But I did not burst in and deliver a melodramatic line, nor did I tread on a dodgy board. Rather, I lost my nerve. I wanted to burst in, just as I wanted to have the confidence to stand on the landing and just listen, but I panicked. I thought, what if I'm caught? What if one of them opens the door for some reason and finds me? I didn't think I could handle the shame.

The situation was taken out of my control, however. In response to Ivo's question I heard Evie say, 'She'll think we're bloody mad.' Then, I heard footsteps on the stairs below. Slow and heavy. The leathery slap of a pair of Oxfords. It sounded like Albertus's footstep, his right leg stronger than his left. I realised that the argument in his rooms was predicated on his absence. One of them must have a key and they must have gone in there to wait for him. I realised if I went in now, to be followed so swiftly by Albertus, they'd know I'd been eavesdropping. I was trapped. I have never been much of an improviser, but I did my best. I sat down on the top step and feebly rubbed my right knee, as one might if one had twisted it. I heard Albertus huff and puff slowly up the stairs. He reached the stairwell below the one where I was sat and looked up. I did my best to look in pain. He looked me up and down, lingering on my legs, poking out from my tweed skirt.

'Hello, Albertus,' I said. 'Here's a scene.'

'My dearest Kitty,' he said, surprise in his voice.

'I seem to have twisted a knee.'

He looked at my legs again and chuckled. 'Lucky me.'

* * *

90

'Look what I found on the stairs,' said Albertus, as we entered his inner sitting-room. 'An injured kitty-kat ...'

I hobbled into the room and said, 'Albertus, it's nothing.'

I looked from face to face and noted the bland lack of concern about my injury. Evie's face was slightly flushed, as was Ivo's. They were stood about eight feet apart, behind the two sofas. I sensed the heat and tension between them. Charlie sat on the sofa nearest to Ivo. Her eyes were red-rimmed as if she'd been crying. Richard and Piers sat perched on the edge of the other sofa. They looked curiously uncomfortable as if they were in pain. Each turned to look at me. I thought I knew what they were each asking themselves: 'Did she overhear what we said?' I tried to keep my face bland. I was sure they knew I'd overheard at least some of it.

Loewe was fussing about, seemingly indifferent to the tensions in the room.

'Come on, Ivo, be a gentleman and find Kitty a chair.'

Ivo went and found a high-backed chair and set it down near the settees. I sat, doing my best to fake a wince.

'That looks very painful,' Albertus said. He stared at my knee again and said, 'I shouldn't wonder if it swells up now, Kitty.'

'What happened?' asked Richard.

'Oh, nothing really,' I said. 'I slipped on that bloody worn step at the bottom of the stairs.' We'd often said that someone would hurt themselves on it one day. 'I was slowly working my way up here when he found me.'

'Yes,' said Albertus. 'Sat right at the top, weren't you, Kitty?' I could have cursed him. It gave away that I was right outside his door when he found me. They'd definitely know I'd heard their argument now. Albertus looked around the room and said, 'Sorry I was running late. Use your key to get in, Evie?' She nodded. 'Good girl. Now, let's escape the troubles of the modern world. Let's go back to the birth pangs of the Church of England.'

It was an excruciating session, easily the worst we ever had with him. Usually, time spent with Albertus was exhilarating and spacious. One day he'd enable us to see the links between Orthodox theology's conceptions of personhood and the nature of priesthood; on another he'd discourse on the Corpus Christi guilds of the fifteenth century or have us in hysterics with stories from the *Decameron*. On this morning, however, the mood was tense and surly as he tried to enthuse us with an analysis of Richard Hooker's Erastian theory of Church and State.

'Oh dear, my dears,' Albertus said, after twenty dismal minutes. 'Did we all have too much sauce last night?' Loewe knew about our Friday night parties at Charlie's and approved. He'd even attended once, introducing us to a cocktail of his own devising called the *Jitterbug*. It required the strongest white spirit one could find – ideally over-proof rum – bitters, and ginger wine. It was disgusting. It had, he claimed, gone down a storm in Wartime London when the Smart Set would drink spirits distilled from anything – including rotten old potato peelings – just to forget what a total bore being bombed out was.

'Sorry, Albertus,' said Ivo. 'It all got a bit wild last night.' Loewe smiled. I was sure he didn't quite believe Ivo, but didn't want to enquire any further. I continued to feebly rub my knee. Albertus looked around at our severe, unhappy faces and clapped his hands together.

'All right,' he said. 'That's enough for today.' I saw the flicker of a smile on Ivo's face. I thought I saw Evie, who had been sat rigidly in an armchair, relax slightly. I tried and failed to catch her eye, hoping to indicate that I wanted a chat. I wanted to know what they'd all been arguing about, but she refused to look my way. We began to gather up our things, but Loewe hadn't quite finished with us yet.

'But …', he said, wagging a finger in mock chiding, 'please, don't let this happen again. Sauce, arguments, gammy knees, I don't care. I really don't. But *this* matters.' He gestured to the room and the books which lined it. 'Time is short, *kinder*. It may not feel so for green sticks like you, but it is. And I have much to say before I send you out into the big, bad world. So, next time, engage. Yes?'

'Yes, Albertus,' said Richard. Loewe seemed to think he'd spoken on behalf of all of us, for he said,

'Good. Now go.' We were heading towards the door when Albertus added, 'Oh, Evie. Not you. A word, please?'

I looked back at her. She seemed pleased to be recalled. Indeed, she looked as happy as I'd seen her all morning. I wondered what he wanted to say to her. I was so preoccupied that I almost forgot to affect my limp.

'Want to come for a drive?' I looked around. It was Piers. 'I think we could do with a talk.'

Chapter Eleven

It was one of those breezy, bright early November days that belong to what is sometimes called a St Martin's Summer. Orange and gold leaves whipped up around Piers' Mazda convertible as we skittered through the lanes of south Oxfordshire. It was a warm afternoon and the top was down. Piers loved speed and the low-slung car only added to the sense of blur and movement. The engine roared and Piers had a huge grin on his face.

'For Christ's sake,' I shouted, 'where the bloody hell are we going?'

He laughed, sensing my fear. I've never much enjoyed fast cars. 'There's something I want to show you!' he shouted back.

For the past half-hour he'd driven us deeper and deeper into the Cotswolds. Pretty villages alternated with ploughed fields and gold-flecked trees. My stomach lifted into my mouth as Piers powered into the dips and rises of the gently curving hills.

'Nearly there,' Piers shouted. He slowed the car to thirty miles an hour as we entered a town called Wallingford. The twists and turns of back roads had left me sick and bewildered and I was desperate to stop. I must have looked pretty sketchy because Piers reached over, stroked my arm and slowed even further. 'Just another minute,' he said.

Finally, he turned off the road onto a gravel track. A sign read 'Wallingford Castle'. We bumped slowly along the track for about half a mile until Piers pulled into a car-park. He then led the way on foot down a squelchy path. For a while I affected my limp, until, cheerily, Piers said, 'I think you can drop that now.'

I grinned and continued to follow him down the muddy lane. Piers whistled a loose version of the *Queen of the Night* aria to himself. He seemed relaxed and happy as he led me through a small wood of coppiced ash and beech trees. As it opened out he said, with a huge smile on his face, 'Ta da!' He gestured to the wreck of a castle. I smiled back. He laughed and said,

'Come on!' He ran off down the hill towards the broken remains. His cravat trailed after him.

When I caught up, Piers stood on a rocky outcrop that might once have been the outer wall of a defensive building.

'What's this all about, Piers?'

He grinned, and said, in the manner of a pompous tour guide, 'These are the charming ruins of Wallingford Castle, first erected in the eleventh century. To stand here is to stand in the very bosom of England. This castle's story is the story of kings and empresses and civil wars and,' he raised his eyebrows in the manner of a saucy vaudevillian, and said, 'even one or two naughty monks.'

I shook my head and laughed. 'Come on, Piers. Stop being a prat.'

'No, seriously,' he continued, resuming his usual tone. 'This place is a damned epicentre of Christian England.' He gestured to a low moss-covered ruin about twenty yards away. 'To my right, are the remains of St Nicholas's College, one of the earliest collegiate churches in England. And that's before one speaks of Richard of Wallingford. Did you know that in 1326, yes 1326, Richard wrote the *Tractatus Albionis* which described a geared astrolabe with four faces? Okay, that's not as early as Roger Bacon, but, God's teeth, why the hell is this chap not world-famous? Or what about John of Wallingford a hundred years before, whose *Chronicle* gives us Europe's earliest flood table? Christ, that bloke invented hydroponics four-hundred years before anyone else!'

I shook my head and said, 'Enough, Piers!'

He jumped down off his rock and stood a few inches away from me. He stared into my eyes and for a moment I thought he was going to make a pass at me. I said, 'Why have you brought me here?'

'Because it's one of my favourite places on earth.'

'Come on, Piers, stop messing about.'

He licked his lips and pushed his hands deep into his wax jacket. I thought how boyish he looked. Then he looked away and began to walk slowly towards the building he'd described as St Nicholas's College. I fell in step with him.

'You heard us arguing,' he said. I considered denying it, but what was the point? He'd already clocked that my limp was a put-on.

'I would have had to have been deaf to miss it.'

'I didn't have you pegged as a door listener.'

'What would you have done?'

Suddenly Piers said, 'Have you ever read Kit Marlowe's *Edward II*?'

'What?!?'

'It does such a bloody hatchet-job on my name-sake, Piers Gaveston. He was given Wallingford Castle by Edward II, you know.'

'Piers …' I was becoming a little exasperated.

'Okay.' He held his hands up. 'I'm telling you all this because everyone gets misunderstood. Or forgotten. Or remembered for the wrong thing.'

'You're saying you're Piers Gaveston? Does that make Ivo Edward II? I never thought of Charlie as Isabella, She-Wolf of France.'

Piers laughed and said, 'Of all of us, Kitty, she might be able to pull it off.'

'So, what are you trying to tell me?'

'I want to explain the argument.'

'Really, there's no need.' I don't know why I said that. Inside I thought, 'Finally!' It was perhaps a mark of my naivety that I imagined getting to the truth about my friends would be that easy.

'I know,' he replied. 'I just think you deserve an explanation.'

I remembered Evie's words. I said, 'So why would I think you're all mad?'

Piers sat down on one of the castle's foundation stones and gestured for me to join him. I sat down and he said, 'This is going to sound ridiculous, but I guess we're just scared that if we take off too many veils too soon, you won't understand us. You being a proper academic and all that.'

'Oh, I'm not all that…'

He put up a hand to quieten me. 'Hear me out. Your bona fides are different to ours. How can I explain?' He paused and put the tips of his fingers together, almost as if in prayer, then said, 'Well, take all this.' He gestured around at the castle. 'Ivo, Charlie, Richard, me, you, even Evie. We're all obsessed with it. The Medieval. Rightly, in my view. We all believe that it offers us the most elegant, most substantial shape for our faith and our culture. But you're different. You come at it with a proper scholar's eye.'

'Don't we all?' I said.

'Yes, but you're like Albertus.' I shook my head. 'Seriously, you are. You bring an analytical eye to bear. Precise … thematic. But the rest of us … Consider Ivo. He doesn't process this stuff like you.'

I attempted to interrupt again, but Piers pressed on.

'Admittedly, growing up in a bloody castle hasn't exactly helped him.' He chuckled. 'But think. I remember him telling me about his time at Eton, how he learned to love manuscripts while he was there. There was one beak who was obsessed with them and taught him to read the apostils and symbols in the margins. It became Ivo's niche at school. Whatever else you might say about Eton, Kitty, it allows its students to find their passion. It exposed Ivo to the magic of vellum and illumination and ancient ink. It showed him who he was. Leaving you aside, the rest of us are like him, only less so. We've never quite left the enchanted forest. Arguably, you've only just entered it.'

'I'm not sure you've made things any clearer,' I said.

'I just want you have the background, so you don't judge us too harshly.' He pulled out a pack of Gitanes and offered me one. I took it and we lit up and smoked in silence for a while.

Finally, I said, 'So what were you arguing about? What did you think I'd find mad?'

'I think I'm scared you'll find our seriousness silly, Kitty.'

'Surely not. I'm as serious as you.'

'Are you?' There was a hardness in his tone now. 'Do you know that once Ivo and I tried making St Paul's Potion to cure one of my headaches? Ivo found the recipe in a medieval medical text.'

'How did that work out?'

'Dreadfully. It called for cormorant's blood. Have you ever tried killing a cormorant? We were down at Ivo's parents' place in Cornwall. We had this crappy old twelve-bore, there was fucking blood everywhere.'

I coughed up smoke, laughing.

'And the potion smelt and tasted like vomit.'

'Did it work?' I asked, between laughs.

'Of course not.'

'So you think I'll laugh at you all for being ridiculously medieval?'

'Well, in a manner of speaking. That's what Evie and Charlie and I thought. Ivo and Richard thought not. That's what we were arguing about. Ivo wanted to let you in on some plans.'

'Which are?'

'Well, it's Advent soon.'

'Oh, really? What's that?' I said, a little mockingly, trying to lighten the tone.

Ignoring my joke, Piers pressed on. 'Well … Season of penitence and all that …' He looked at me steadily, before looking around, as if checking we were completely alone. Then he said, as if to himself,

'Why not?' Then, more boldly, 'It would be easiest to show you. Give you, as the *Prayer Book* has it, an ensample. A foretaste.'

To my surprise, he then took off his wax jacket and began to unbutton his shirt.

'Piers! What the hell?'

He paused, held a finger to his lips and then continued. Beneath his shirt, he revealed a white cotton vest.

'Lift it up,' he said, gently.

'Piers…' I felt my face begin to flush.

'Lift it up.' He said it quietly, but with force. I reached across and touched the hem. Piers flinched and I stopped. Then he nodded and I lifted it up from the bottom revealing milky flesh and a black band, like a belt or girdle, an inch across. The skin around its edges was red and angry. It was so raw, it looked like blood might issue forth at any moment. Quietly, I said, 'Is that…?'

'Yes,' said Piers, in a whisper. I remember his voice had a pleased, assured tone to it. 'It's an old-fashioned mark of commitment to a higher cause, Kitty.' He paused and stared at me with his sweet, amber eyes. Then, he said, 'Are you in?'

Chapter Twelve

I suppose I might have laughed. Perhaps I did. If so, it was a nervous laugh, not a mocking one. Though, as I recall it now, I don't think I did. I think I felt a mixture of relief and awe. Piers' cilice was downright weird and unexpected, but there was a huge part of me that thought, 'Oh! So that's it.' I took it as holding explanatory power: My friends had merely got into experimenting with old-school religious practices. I began to understand how the incidents I'd witnessed in the preceding weeks were connected – the blood on Ivo's hand, the look of wonder on Piers' face, and Evie's report of Richard's and Piers' injuries. These were the effects of experimentation with bodily mortification.

I was also impressed. Please don't judge me too harshly for thinking that. I was, in many ways, very young. My life had been defined by books and I knew about cilices and hair-shirts and self-flagellation from their pages. Insofar as I'd thought about them at all, I thought of cilices as either a motif of ultramontane Roman Catholic sects or as a subject for Monty Pythonesque comedy. To see one being worn by someone I admired and respected, even wanted to be like, was a revelation. Perhaps for a more mature person, Piers's revelation might have been taken as a warning sign, a signal to run away from the curious group of friends I'd made. The cilice around Piers's waist struck me as no more than a fascinating curiosity. It was a confirmation that he and the others had an unexpected depth that reached far beyond the floppy, English cool they all cultivated.

It was a token of seriousness. It was not, for me, a klaxon for the monstrous. Even now, over twenty years on, I can't read it that way. Discipline – the way of the disciple – is not necessarily a symptom of wickedness.

Yes, I was turned on, though not in some cheap, sexual way. I won't deny that touching the raw skin around Piers's belt had given me a thrill. Titillation and tickling have the same Latin root. I've always been insanely ticklish, and to see his flesh withdraw at the merest touch of my hand was exciting. I had an urge to kiss it. Something more was going on, however. It was not so much an erotic desire of the flesh, as a kind of religious awakening. I felt like my whole body had been switched on and found another level. I felt more connected-up and bound into the world. It was, then, a religious experience. When Piers asked, 'Are you in?' I felt then that he – and, by proxy, the others – was offering me a richer relationship with God.

'Kitty?'

I looked back up at Piers, blinking.

'You okay?' He looked worried.

'Fine,' I said. 'Sorry, I was ...' I removed my hand and Piers pulled down his vest and began buttoning up his shirt. He looked around, checking to see that no one else had seen anything. I said, 'Does Albertus know?' The question was instinctive. I felt the need to check out that someone older and more responsible than us knew what was going on. Piers's body visibly relaxed.

'Of course. He's the one who encouraged it.' When I said nothing, he said, 'I don't know if he knows all the details. We left it up to Ivo to tell him. But Albertus has always been the one who talks about us as the new 'old' – a vanguard of ...' He laughed to himself. 'Well, you know ...'

'You told Evie before me?' It was out of my mouth before I could stop myself. Piers sighed. I guessed he had been waiting for this reaction. He said,

'It wasn't like that.' I resisted the childish temptation to say something sharp. 'Really, it wasn't. Evie found out, a week or so after that car crash in chapel when Roddy outed her as Albertus's assistant.

'It was a Sunday, a beautiful afternoon, and Ivo and I went for a walk. He wanted to show me this field of late-flowering wild flowers up towards Iffley. Yarrow and Self-heal. Knapweed. They were rather stunning, actually. We ended up back in Ivo's room for tea, and Evie decided to drop in to see Ivo … something about swapping her place on the reading rota. It all seemed a bit fishy to me. She'd been lurking around all week.' I said nothing. Given what she'd said to me the previous Sunday evening, I was sure she'd been keeping an eye on them.

He paused, as if recalling a painful, perhaps embarrassing memory, then said,

'The fact is that Ivo had been showing me a selection of cilices and … well, a scourge.' He laughed to himself. A nervous laugh. Almost private. 'This was simply for demonstration purposes. Then, Evie decided to enter without knocking. We should have locked the door, but Ivo never does. Says he's got nothing to hide.

'I must admit, I was embarrassed. The rest of us have been talking about praying a little more vigorously for a long time now, long before you and Evie came along. Using the old ways … They have a tradition and, in my view, a dignity. You remember your Peter Damian, of course … well, I don't think I need to explain all that to you.'

Indeed, he didn't. St Peter Damian had been one of those monks who'd reformed the old monastic system in the eleventh century. He was noted for the severity of his own self-discipline. At one point, he'd nearly ruined his health through self-flagellation. Despite being forced to restrain his self-discipline in later life, he never lost a spiritual hunger for mortifying the flesh.

'Ivo really was very composed about Evie. He invited her in

and gave her a cup of tea.' He smiled to himself again. 'Oh, and a leg cilice to play with.' He paused in silent reverie, then, with renewed vigour, said, 'I expected Evie to turn it all into a bit of a joke, but to my surprise she was serious. She wanted in on our plans.'

This had all been weeks ago, I thought. 'Evie never breathed a word to me.'

'She's quite something,' said Piers.

I realised he'd heard my words in a positive way. My words – instinctive, off-the-cuff – had not been intended as praise for Evie's confidentiality. Rather, they inadvertently expressed my annoyance that, again, she'd not shared a confidence with me. First, she'd kept news of her job with Albertus from me. Now, she'd locked me out of another confidence, even bigger than the first. That night we'd slept together, she'd spoken about the strange goings on with our friends – the blood, the late-night mysteries – but as soon as she'd found out what was behind it, she'd shut her mouth again. If she really cared for me, surely she'd have told me what was going on, wouldn't she? My love for Evie – not just my *eros*, but my charity, my *agape* – had, as I felt it, already been tested. Now, I began to see what Evie was capable of. However, I had no wish for Piers to know what I was thinking, so I said,

'Yes, she is that.'

Nonetheless, Piers's revelation had stung me deeply. I wanted to lash out at Evie, gain some sort of revenge. I don't think that's so unreasonable. I'd let Evie in and a big part of me expected some sort of *quid pro quo*. Evie was my best friend. Sure, she'd also been my lover too, but – first-of-all – she was my friend. As Piers and I sat out in the late autumn sunshine, that's what I told myself. Yet, there was a pain in my chest as I thought about her. She'd shown me things in bed I'd never experienced before. She had made my body sing. Even in my anger, I wanted her.

I considered what Charlie had said to me about how she'd

fallen in love with Evie as a teenager. Yet, Charlie's words had been laced with warning. She'd been close to disclosing something of significance about Evie. Then, that moment had passed, almost, it felt, for good. Much as I'd tried since to get Charlie to disclose what she was going to say that night, she wouldn't have it. She'd closed that book, at least for now. All I was left with were Charlie's eyes looking across at me on that Friday evening – mysterious, and full of potential information, withheld. As I sat with Piers, perhaps I had found the simple answer to Charlie's warning: one should be careful around Evie simply because she was deceptive. She wasn't mean or vicious as such; rather she couldn't live up to the desires of those who desired her. She created an illusion of intimacy, but she was not intimate.

'Kitty?' said Piers.

'What?'

'Are you sure you're okay?'

'Fine. Just thinking.'

'Glad someone's doing that. Look, we should get back. Let's go and see Ivo. Tell him the news.'

Chapter Thirteen

Ou might be wondering why I so readily threw my lot in with Piers, Ivo and the others. Why didn't I get out while I still could? From the distance of twenty-plus years, it's obvious what I should have done: walk away, or report them, or just bloody run for the hills. But then? Perhaps it simply sounds too blunt to say that there is only ever one reason anyone does anything and that's because they want to. Blunt or not, I still think that assessment bears truth. No matter how we disguise our motivations or dress them up, ultimately we choose to stand with one group or another or pursue one path or another because the chosen path represents what we desire. That desire might be screwy or damaged or even under duress, but it is still our desire. Which is just one way of saying we're all mysteries to ourselves. Why did I so readily run with this particular pack of wolves? I can offer endless speculation: Because I wanted to be liked, or because I was afraid of being left alone with ordinands who I found unbearable or execrable, or because – at some level – I felt like I needed to be punished. Maybe it was because I felt called to some 'elite level' of Christian devotion or I was deeply inadequate. I don't know. I just chose my friends over everything else. There's part of me, even after everything, that would do the same again.

It also occurs to me that a reader might reasonably expect my account to become pretty lurid from this point on. All chains and whips and bondage. I'm sorry to disappoint. Becoming just a little more of an insider into my friends' lives was not about entering some second-rate dungeon fantasy. As I've already claimed, the Medieval offers a subtle discourse, dangerous and pregnant with violence, of course, but nuanced. My immersion in my friends' world was just as subtle. Ordinary. It took place over a cup of tea.

'Come,' said Ivo in his rich, cultured voice.

Piers, who'd just knocked on Ivo's door, opened it, gestured for me to enter and followed in after me. I felt like I was being taken into an inner sanctum for an interview. Ivo, his face tense, gestured for me to sit on one of the arm-chairs. Piers took the other. I realised that this was the first time I'd been in Ivo's room. It was plain and uncluttered. Masculine. The desk was standard college-issue, but the arm-chairs – simple, mid-century teak in what I think is sometimes called the Danish style – were additions. The bed was neatly made and there was a pleasing lack of mess. It was less a student's room and more like a soldier's or a monk's. There were fewer books on the shelves than I might have anticipated. They primarily consisted of hardback volumes of Aquinas's *Summa*, some works by Etienne Gilson, *The Decameron*, and a three-volume edition of Burton's *Anatomy of Melancholy*. The Burton was the only volume that genuinely surprised me. It seemed, for Ivo, such a late piece of writing. Only one artwork broke up the beige walls, a superb reproduction of Dürer's *Knight, Death and the Devil*.

Ivo, who had been sat at his desk, got up, flicked across the door-lock, and pushed a tartan draft-excluder up against the door. He returned to his seat and looked at Piers. His glance, cool and composed, seemed to say, 'Well?'

'I told her,' said Piers, simply. Ivo looked at me.

'And?' he said, quietly. His gaze was locked fiercely on mine.

'She's keen.'

Ivo's face softened into a warm grin.

'Good. Good. Never had a doubt,' he said. 'Tea?'

I nodded. Suddenly animated, he stood up again and went over to a kettle on a small side table and pressed down the boil switch. Next to it stood an ancient utility teapot and half a dozen mismatched cups and saucers.

'Mind if I smoke?' I said.

'Not at all,' said Ivo. 'There's an ashtray on the desk.'

We smoked in silence until the tea had brewed. Ivo poured out three cups, settled back in his seat and said,

'Any questions?'

I took a sip of tea and said, 'Well, isn't it all a little over-the-top?'

Piers looked from me to Ivo. Having confidently announced that I was open to becoming involved in their plans, Piers's face became worried as I departed from the authorised script. He looked braced for Ivo's anger. Then again, I remembered he was wearing a cilice. I pictured the red, raw skin of his tummy. To sit in one of these low chairs must have been hellish.

Ivo considered my question carefully, then said,

'I see your point. Why not use other resources from the tradition, yes?'

'Quite,' I replied. 'One doesn't need to scourge oneself to draw closer to God. If one wants to be grounded in the Catholic tradition rather than feeble evangelical antics, there's any number of prayer disciplines to explore. St Ignatius, Teresa of Avila, John of the Cross. Physical mortification seems so … rococo.'

'You're right,' said Ivo. 'Up to a point.' He sipped some tea then, pointing at the engraving, said, 'You know the Dürer, of course.'

'Of course.'

'Well, for me, it captures it all. Why that later stuff – Ignatius, Teresa, all the rest – never quite hits the mark, not least because they speak after the fact, as it were. They *react* to something that's already taken place. As for Dürer, consider his thesis: A knight travels resolutely on his way, either to battle or away from it. Wherever he heads there will be a fight. His world is Europe, is Christendom, the late Middle Ages. War and terror are everywhere. Behind him lies Satan. To his right is Death, sat on a pale horse. His loyal dog travels with him, and oh, the look on the knight's face. Resolute, grim, knowing. Death and Satan are near and yet the noble Ritter does not give in to them.

'Dürer created that engraving just four years before Luther nailed his famous theses on that church door at Wittenberg. Though he could barely know it, Dürer's work marked the end of an era. His knight travels towards a battle he cannot yet comprehend.'

'Your point, Ivo,' I said.

He blinked and said, 'Dürer, like all Medievals, understood that our journey towards salvation is no mere spiritual battle. It is worked out, in and through the body. It is, so often, a grim task. Even the armour of faith will not deflect every injury. It cannot protect us from violence. We need to be ready to embrace pain.'

'You know that some read this engraving as fascist?' I said.

'Because Hitler approved of it?' replied Ivo. His voice became incredulous, half-amused. 'Oh, for heaven's sake, Kitty. You're better than that. Hitler was an intellectual peasant who had an appalling grasp of history. He disguised his confusion in pseudo-academic babble. And don't even try that Sten Karling reading on me. It's execrable.'

Karling – at the height of leftish analysis of culture – suggested that Dürer's knight was no hero but a robber-baron; the engraving was not meant to lionise the knight but expose him as cruel, exploiting and treacherous. It was a problematic analysis, but not without merit. I thought it worthy of defence. Ivo saw that I was about to retort, when he put up his hands, and said,

'Okay, that was a cheap point. My point, dear Kitty, is this: What are we without the practices of medieval Christianity? Inward-looking mopers. We are holy joes, even those awesome figures like Ignatius. We are souls in decay, in thrall to individualism. We might as well be the worst sort of Western Buddhist – all meditation and inner composure. Mindful. Passive. In this respect at least, the Jews and the Muslims know what's what. Faith is not about belief or doctrine so much as the body. It is eating and fasting. It is acting in the world, in the light of faith. It is knowing God in the discipline of the flesh.'

As he finished his speech, he leant back on his chair and took a deep gulp of tea. I studied him, trying to figure out how serious he was. A trace of a smile lingered on his big, square face. He looked curiously oversized in that room, his long legs and big feet only adding to the illusion. His bulky, tweedy frame, wrapped in an old suit, the soles of his shoes worn down, was, at that moment, almost comical. He took off his horn-rimmed spectacles and checked to see if they were smudged. Satisfied, he put them back on. I was struck again by how typical he seemed. He might so easily be the kind of person who – as Austen wittily puts it – takes great pleasure in professing opinions which were not their own. A kind of aristocratic flâneur. It was, I decided, a powerful disguise, as powerful as any at Littlemore. He might dress like a shop-worn Bertie Wooster, but he was quite serious. His mind was as tough as the Ritter in Dürer's engraving.

'So where do we go from here?' I asked.

Ivo looked across at Piers, then back at me.

'Where would you like to go?'

'Piers said something about Advent.'

'Well,' said Ivo, 'the rest of us discussed it as an obvious time for prayerful discipline. If you'd like to try something before then, I can help.'

* * *

That's how it happened. As quietly and simply as that. Over a cup of tea. I suppose that's how people often enter secret worlds. Spies and priests are not so very different. There is no drama or show. The nearest we got to it on that November afternoon was when I asked Ivo to show me a cilice. He suggested that the sensible option would be one for my thigh. He reached into a drawer in his desk and took out a black velvet bag. From inside it he removed a chain, a series of interlocking metal circles with small spikes on one side and clasps at both ends.

'In case you were wondering, no, it's not been used. It's yours if you want it,' Ivo said, passing it across.

It was much lighter than I expected, made of some sort of alloy rather than iron or steel.

'Do I wear it all the time?' I asked.

Piers, who had been smoking quietly to himself, blew smoke out of his mouth with sudden violence. He said,

'God, no. No more than half an hour a day to begin with. Then up to two hours.'

'But you must have been wearing that belt for hours,' I said.

'And I must take it off,' he said. 'I've a lot of practice, Kitty, but one shouldn't overdo it. One doesn't want to end up at the quack's with an infected wound.'

I held the metal chain in my hands. I pressed down on one of the studs with my thumb. It was blunter than I expected. I suppose it tells you something about how febrile my imagination was, but I'd expected needle points, sharp and cruel. I fingered the clasp, toyed with the word in my mind. Clasp. Of course, it is an erotic word, of Middle English origin. It relates to 'enclaspe', 'to hold tightly in one's arms'. I thought of Christ, of how his arms encircle the world; clasp us and all creation. I could not wait to feel his painful embrace.

Chapter Fourteen

I have long believed that those who seek to become priests of whatever tradition are people who, consciously or unconsciously, wish to be set apart. They are hungry for some kind of distinction. In the broadest sense of the word, they want to be special and wish to be seen as such. They comprise a caste within the great mass of the world. As such, they are always susceptible to secrecy and other modes of distinction and perdition; they are alert to gradation and who is in and out of favour.

I was now party to a secret. If I'm honest I'd been party to secrets for a while before I started practising the mortification of the flesh. I, like the others, had been shown that manuscript copy of the *Canterbury Tales*. Loewe had effectively sworn us to secrecy about the fact he'd 'borrowed' it. Outside of lectures and chapel, I'd spent months hanging out, almost exclusively, with a specific group of people. I'd been in the shadows for a while. But in being initiated – there's no other word for it – into my friends' private practices, I knew I'd taken a new step, perhaps a decisive one towards holding not just a confidence, but a secret. None of us wanted the other students at Littlemore to know what we were doing. The secret we shared was a mark of our bond. What I failed to anticipate on that afternoon in Ivo's room was how much the secret would become both a source of connection as well as a new layer of isolation. We were already set apart in College. Now I discovered a new layer to that distinction. For me, it supplied both a thrill and anxiety.

An early insight into this twin truth came during one of the College's excruciating Community Meetings. They happened every couple of weeks or so, and it was an accepted rule that no ordinand should enjoy them. The exception to this rule lay in those students who were either professional gabblers or dreamt of becoming College President. Quite often both groups intersected. The meetings were a way – to use that ghastly corporate phrase – to 'cascade information' to the wider student body; quite often it was used by the Principal or the College President to pitch new initiatives. It is hard to overstate just how tiresome these encounters could be. One example, in particular, represents the very nadir of college tedium.

In my first year, the College President was Miles Goodhap. His nickname was 'Baden-Powell', primarily because he tended to come across as an overgrown Scout master. He had a fondness for khaki which, from about March onwards, manifested itself in a quite catastrophic tendency to wear high-waisted khaki shorts. He wore walking shoes all winter which in spring turned into sandals with (God preserve us) socks. He also bounced on the balls of his feet whenever he preached or addressed a crowd. He also had a reputation for sticky fingers, forever goosing women 'accidentally' as he opened doors for them. Goodhap was desperate to be married and asked every single young woman in college to go out with him. I was delighted that I was low down on his list of 'potentials'. According to Evie this was because he was intimidated both by my brains and qualifications. It took him six months of rebuffs before he finally tried me. His chat-up patter involved him telling me I was a 'very attractive female'. Turning him down was one of the least burdensome tasks of my Littlemore career. After College, he married one of the members of his first congregation, a matronly woman called Joanna, and is now an Archdeacon on the south coast with five kids.

On this particular day, Goodhap was charged with

encouraging people to form something called 'prayer triplets'. Unsurprisingly, this announcement generated a fair amount of groaning and jeering. The student body's instinct for mockery was one of the few things that made the Community Meeting bearable. Molly Shanks summed up the mood of the room when she said, in her warm northern drawl,

'Oh, for the love of God, Miles, I'm the mother of twins and that's trauma enough. Why would I want triplets?'

It wasn't hugely funny, but there were still gales of laughter. Goodhap, consistently unable to appreciate sarcasm or humour, cleared his throat and said,

'Now, Molly dearest, you know full well that prayer triplets are nothing like that.' More titters.

Goodhap raised his hands to calm the crowd and explained how, in the coming weeks, we should split into groups of three to pray for mutual support; how these groups would form the basis of cells to support us in years to come and provide space for us to care and pray for each other in the challenging world of ministry. His sincerity would have been touching in a more attractive man. He suggested that the coming season of Advent would be an admirable time to start this rigorous discipline. He concluded by saying that his door was ever open to all, both male and female, should anyone want help in setting up their triplet. Half of the women in the room looked at each other, the thought of being alone in a room with Goodhap sufficient to disabuse them of his offer.

In and of itself, I don't think there is anything especially ridiculous or dubious about the concept of a 'prayer triplet'. Jesus himself said, where two or three are gathered in prayer, 'I will be there'. Nor was it really any more tiresome or trivial than countless other things which happened in Community Meetings. Rather, this insignificant incident brought home to me just how far I'd travelled from the mainstream of college life. After the initial groans and scepticism, most of the ordinands got on board with Goodhap's idea. There were murmurs of appreciation and, after the formal meeting broke up, some went up to Goodhap thanking him for his idea. Whereas, from where I sat, the whole thing felt weightless. I felt an odd mixture of specialness – because my friends and I shared a different discipline – and loneliness. I saw the happy faces of the other ordinands and felt disconnected from their capacity to 'get involved' and 'muck in' with this prayer activity.

Did that make me a dreadful person? Perhaps, but that is how I experienced that moment. I saw these people, good people I think, partnering off to practice their prayer discipline together. They were keen and sincere. Yet, I – like my close friends – sat there, bound to a deeper, more challenging discipline. I had been wearing my cilice off and on for a week or two by then and I'd come to know its challenges and fleshly irritations. It takes a lot of self-control to sit in a room with cheery, good-natured people and maintain a level of humour and warmth whilst wearing something that digs and niggles at your skin and muscles. Back then I felt sure we were doing something deeper and richer than all these good, prayerful people.

I feel ashamed to admit that now, but I want you to understand. For me, having stepped into the harsh discipline of – well, I might as well own it – the flagellant, what I encountered in the Community Meeting had a second-rate character. I was living in technicolour, they in black and white. It was as if Goodhap – as representative of the wider Church – offered something lightweight and flimsy. Prayer triplets, for God's sake. In contrast, my friends and I had gone in search of the old ways of faith. You know, the Greek word for 'disciple' is *askesis*. It's the word used by St Antony, he who led the first monks out into the deserts of Egypt; he who knew the temptations of Satan and faced them down through his trust in Christ. *Askesis*. The word from which 'ascetic' is derived. As I saw it, on that morning, it was not through prayer triplets that Antony faced down the devil.

114

He'd conquered him through suffering. He modelled a faith that was not to be reduced to prayer in comfy common rooms. As my right thigh throbbed and itched and I prayed and prayed for the meeting to end, I felt my solidarity lay with St Antony rather than Goodhap and the rest. Goodhap seemed only to be offering what Evie called 'Caring and Sharing' with a flimsy Jesus.

You might be wondering about Evie and me. On the day Piers and Ivo admitted me into the secret, we had a titanic row. I dragged her into one of the lecture theatres after dinner, and we argued as only those who are close to each other can. I tried to keep myself under control, and failed miserably. Within seconds, I'd said, 'Why didn't you tell me? I thought I was special to you.' I sounded cheap and wheedling and I was disgusted at my lack of control. It gave Evie her opening to explain how she'd wanted to say something, but had promised Ivo and Piers to keep quiet and how she thought that, anyway, I would be too disapproving, too prim and Protestant. Too – and she said this almost pityingly – middle-class. I was so angry at this all I could do was whisper my disgust. Evie smiled, 'Oh, come on, Kit. You think you're so liberal, but you're terrified that someone will find out we've slept together.'

'That's got nothing to do with it.'

'Hasn't it? Kit, you can be so naïve.'

* * *

After that argument, things were never the same. The magic in our friendship, already fading, began to dissipate quickly, even though there were still good days to come before the poison took final hold. You might even suppose that now I'd been brought deeper into my friends' shadow world, Evie and I would have had a whole new vista of subjects to talk about, that we might have spent hours comparing 'mortification devices'. The very idea is as ludicrous as it sounds. That's the thing about sharing something as curious and odd as a medieval prayer practice: one doesn't behave like one of Miles Goodhap's prayer partners. One is initiated into something almost inexpressible. One feels part of a community that doesn't need to resolve itself into prattle about how one's relationship with God is going. One feels the truth in one's flesh. And, anyway, we were not the sort of people who 'cared' and 'shared': we were drawn to something more rigorous and austere.

Yet, despite my jealousies and anxieties about her, once we'd begun to move on, Evie and I still found echoes of what we'd had. How could we not? Evie was always a charmer, and adoration does not die so quickly. I found – a little to my surprise – that as someone who'd often struggled with friendship, once I'd committed I wanted to be loyal. If we stopped sleeping together, we settled into a companionable cycle of enjoying each other's company. We remembered that we had relatively few responsibilities and this first term was going to be a time of grace. As members of an exclusive group, who else did we have except each other? When I look back now, it's difficult not to smile when I remember how Evie inveigled me into her increasingly extravagant theories about medieval sex and sexuality. Indeed, as the autumn fell towards winter it became little less than an obsession, by turns wild, strange and troubling.

The focus for her theorising were the Lollards, those fourteenth-century Christians who were the forerunners of the Reformation. Inspired by John Wycliffe, the Oxford theologian who dared to lambast the Pope as a peddler of cant, they demanded a Bible written in English and were critical of Church hierarchy. They argued that vows of celibacy among priests and nuns only led to sexual lewdness, and they denied the power of the saints and martyrs to save and heal. Their nickname – derived from a word meaning 'mutterer' or 'ranter' – mocked their lack of education. It soon became a synonym for heretic and they were accused of the wildest sexual impropriety,

116

and persecuted ruthlessly by inquisitors. This much is well-known. Where Evie sailed ever more wildly away from orthodoxy was in her insistence that not only were the Lollards pioneers of sexual liberation and feminism – channelling long-repressed ideas from early Christianity – but Oxfordshire had been an epicentre for their libertine ways.

As the term wore on, perhaps her strangest theory was that the Lollards aimed to reform Christianity by recovering the sexual magic of early Christian sects like the Sethians and the Borborites. She reckoned that far from being proto-Puritans who wanted sex carefully controlled in marriage, they were advocates of free-love and engaged in lurid rituals which involved consuming vaginal juices and semen. It was pretty outré stuff, the kind of thing that the Inquisition accused the Lollards of, simply because they criticised clerical celibacy. She even speculated that the remarkable figure of John 'Eleanor' Rykener had been a leading Lollard whose exploits had inspired copy-cat behaviour across the Thames Valley. Rykener, a transgender prostitute, lived in late fourteenth-century London. She had sex with many priests, nuns, scholars and married women. She claimed that she'd been married to a man and used her husband's name in lawsuits. She – like her contemporary, the Venetian trans prostitute Rolandina Ranchaia – was ultimately arrested, prosecuted and killed. Evie saw them as heroines of a sexually-confident, gender-fluid Christianity critical of Papal hypocrisy.

To this day, I don't believe there is a single shred of evidence that the Lollards got up to any of the wild things she claimed, in Oxfordshire or elsewhere. Indeed, at the time when 'Eleanor' Rykener was alive, the Lollard position on sex was just as conservative as that of the Catholic Church. But that was not the point for Evie. Part of the fun was the speculation, and some of my best days at Littlemore entailed being dragged along on wild-goose chases. Evie's determination to avoid the obvious was a wonder to behold, and, at times, frankly, exasperating. As we sat, late one night, smoking and drinking in my room, I said,

'Evie, where the hell is this coming from?'

'Where do you think? Books …'

I laughed. I was rather drunk and said, 'Which ones? *The Ladybird Book of Medieval Nonsense*?'

She laughed too, but wagged her finger at me.

'Now, now, Kit. We can't all have PhDs to draw on.'

'Oh, give yourself time, Eve.'

She insisted that she was only attempting to dig up a hidden history. She reckoned the clues to this ruthlessly suppressed Christian tradition might yet be found in erased passages in famous histories and court records of the era, like Henry Knighton's *Chronicon*. She was wise enough not to mention where she hoped to find these passages: Albertus's private library. That subject and her access to it was still a sore point. Rather we went off on adventures all over Oxfordshire. I shall never forget the day we visited the famous White Horse of Uffington and Evie found a couple of large flat chunks of stone which she suggested might once have been covered with the Lollards' famous *Twelve Conclusions*, their manifesto for a holier Church. We laughed uproariously when I pointed out that some teenager had scratched an ejaculating penis on one of them, but as the laughter died, I saw a sadness, a disappointment, behind her eyes. After her death, that look was to haunt me. One of the things I underestimated about Evie was her seriousness – and scholarly skill – about recovering a repressed, radical Christian past. I'd thought she was joking.

Days like that were good ones, funny and exhilarating, as was the one when we went off to look at St Anne's, Epwell. A crisp December day, we went there because the church contains a statue of a dancing Black Madonna. Evie was sure it was evidence of early medieval goddess worship, which she insisted the Oxford Lollards (as she'd started calling them) had got into. We examined St Anne's rood screen, with its thirteenth-century painting of Mary Magdalene, her sad, pale face, in stark relief to her sumptuous red dress. In her right hand, an egg, a symbol of both life and death. She stares at the viewer and points at that egg, as if to say, none of us can escape our fate. Will it be new life or death? We also spoke to the eccentric Vicar, Mr Cole. An old Littlemore alum, Mr Cole was in his sixties, white-haired and balding, with full-on Gladstone sideboards and a tendency to say 'mmm, mmm' every time one of us spoke. When Evie claimed that the village was named after the fertility goddess Epona, Mr Cole smiled indulgently and said, 'Perhaps, perhaps' in a rich West Country drawl. He even made a pitch for Evie to serve her title with him, suggesting – in a not entirely coherent speech – that in addition to all the usual things one might hope to experience during a curacy post, he could offer extensive 'brass rubbing' opportunities. On the drive back home, we entertained ourselves by speculating what 'brass rubbing' might be a euphemism for.

At Evie's College Memorial, I told some of these stories about our adventures in Oxfordshire, carefully and suitably redacted to exclude most of her wilder theories. Both those who knew her well and those who didn't took the incident at the White Horse of Uffington as characteristic – of her eccentricity, her capacity for comedy and her kindness. Now, when I think of that trip to St Anne's all I can think of is that rood screen, and more than that, how it leads me back to Littlemore and Evie's death. All I can think of is Evie suspended above the chapel floor, hanging from Littlemore's garish, second-rate Rood. A Victorian Gothic pastiche of true medieval beauty. Evie's fate had been death rather than life. I don't think I can put it off any longer. If we still had good days after that trip to Epwell, I think it's time I told you how it all went definitively wrong. For Evie. For me. For all of us.

Chapter Fifteen

I don't know if it was the approach of Christmas – and all that can mean regarding family and home – or if it was simply the fact that my body was aching and irritable from the cilice, but I felt increasingly depressed as term drew towards its close. I caught myself thinking over and over about panopticons and asylums. I felt like I was under surveillance. That all of us at Littlemore were under surveillance. From what or whom? It would sound too febrile to say 'God', even allowing for the intensities of Littlemore. Yet, in that final week or so of term, I was haunted by a dream in which all my friends' faces, sometimes even my own, peered out from the viewing platform of an asylum tower, distorted and gaunt through stained glass.

I even began thinking about my estranged parents. I hadn't seen them since a visit home on the tenth anniversary of Louise's death, an occasion after which I'd vowed not to go back. We'd laid lilies on Lou's grave and I'd read Ecclesiastes 3. It had been going well until, over a pub lunch, my dad had started going on about how stuck up I'd become and how I never kept in touch. About how it was always me who spoiled everything and how, finally, unforgivably, he couldn't understand why I hadn't done more to save her. But, as Christmas approached, and Littlemore got to me, I started going to a phone box each night to ring my parents' number. More often than not, it would just go to their answer phone and I'd listen to my mother's voice, 'You're through to the home of Lillian and Ron,' her voice full of Midlands' whine. I never left a message. My father answered once, his voice gruff, saying only one word, 'Yes?' I hung up. Once my mother answered, and I stood there holding the receiver to my head, unable to speak. After a few seconds my mother said, 'Catherine? Is that you?' Eventually, she hung up.

I was simply feeling the strain. All of this was of a piece with wider college life. As we entered December and the final few weeks of term, ordinands and staff alike were feeling the pressure of deadlines, and the crank-up in services for Advent and Christmas. Roddy Peplow, whose drinking was always prodigious, seemed to go up a level even for him, though he thrived on the combination of gin, carols, and general liturgical excess. The college musician, a severe German Lutheran, Berthold Bittrich, handled the pressure with less aplomb. Bittrich was determined to work the college choir – a voluntary, mixed-ability group of ordinands – with all the rigour of a professional outfit. He decided that this rag-tag band could pull off sections of Britten's *Saint Nicolas* Cantata for the College Carol Service, with embarrassing results. Roddy's post-mortem of the debacle, delivered straight-faced to Bittrich – 'Darling, there are pigs squealing at their own castration that have achieved finer displays of harmony than your lot' – almost led to Bittrich's resignation.

Others were caught up in a panic about essay deadlines. Jeanette Spink and Audrey Court took to camping outside lecturers' and tutors' offices. I wish I could say my friends and I were immune to the edgy atmosphere. If we were not as oppressed by the demands of essay writing as others, we were all tired and in need of a break from each other. I, for one, was feeling the strain of our Advent prayer discipline. I know Piers was too. One evening, he told me that he and Ivo had argued and when I asked about what, he replied, 'Discipline.' Piers thought he'd been overdoing it. Ivo thought not. I asked Piers to show me his tummy. When I saw it – raw, scabbed – I know with whom I agreed. Piers then showed me his back. It had red stripes from where he'd used a scourge. His upper arms were scattered with bruises. I was shocked and told him he had to stop, that it was too much. I said I would speak to Ivo about it if it might help, but Piers said there was no need. Though he and Ivo had argued, it was all now resolved. However, it was not until an extra Saturday tutorial late in the term that I realised the depths of tension in our group.

Albertus was in full flow that day. Somehow, we'd got on to the topic of enchantment and magic in religion, and this had led to a long disquisition on Tolkien and C. S. Lewis.

'Are you all aware of the concept of thinning?' said Loewe.

'Yes,' said Richard. 'No,' said the rest of us, almost simultaneously. There was a little titter of laughter, while we looked quizzically at Richard.

'I've read a lot of fantasy fiction,' he said, somewhat guiltily.

In the beat which followed Loewe's question I studied the faces of the others. With something of a shock, I saw the strain on everyone's faces, especially Ivo and Evie's. It might have been the effect of the dank winter, but they looked sallow and edgy. One of the curious things about mortifying the body is how it can lead to times of sudden and unexpected anxiety and annoyance, a kind of rippling irritability that spreads through one's body. I suspected that was what was going on for Ivo and Evie.

'Yes, thinning,' said Loewe. 'As Richard will know it's a technical term for the fading away of the magic in a fantasy world. You know, the elves leave, children enter the exile of adulthood and the world of wonder fades. I said to Lewis once, "We cannot go back. Narnia is lost. The Lion is a mirage." D'you know what he said? "As long as we have the books, as long as we have *the* Book, we are not exiles from the magic realm."'

There was a long silence after this speech. Then Charlie said,

'Are you saying that religious people never truly grow up?' I studied her, impressed by the crispness of her question. She too looked tired. There was avidness in her beauty and I thought she looks like a saint, transfigured by glory, or like Beatrice Portinari in that painting by Holiday – self-possessed, determined, intent on business of her own. Not to be distracted by others.

'Perhaps, Charlie,' said Albertus. 'And is that such a sin? We are story-bound people, whether that be the Gospel or, heaven spare us, *Lord of the Rings*. God, Glory, Hope. The magic of prayer or the magic of the elves. So often it feels like magic is leeching out of this world, and yet we have stories. Yes, a story like Sleeping Beauty is childish, silly and lacking in nuance … It can be told to children for entertainment … But it also gestures towards truths we'd do well not to forget. Who or what is sleeping? Who is the saviour who comes and what are his motives? What does it mean to wake up and face the truth?'

Quite suddenly, Evie stood up. She looked miserable. Almost furious. I thought she was on the edge of tears. As she spoke, her voice sounded forced, on the edge of breaking,

'I'm really sorry, Albertus. I need to go and lie down. I feel awful. I think I'm going to be sick. Would you excuse me?'

Without waiting for a reply, she ran out of the room. She slammed the door behind her. I caught a glimpse of Ivo's face. I was shocked by the fury on it. At that moment, his Woosterish disguise slipped, almost definitively. One could easily believe he might kill or maim or desecrate a body. Loewe was clearly thrown by Evie's sudden exit. He lost his chain of thought and looked about. He sucked on his unlit pipe, then said, awkwardly,

'Yes, well … indeed. I think that that is as good a place to end as any.' It was unclear whether he was referring to the question which had concluded his last speech, or Evie's exit. As we began to file out, I decided to find Evie and see what was up. A painful tug on my right arm woke me from my reverie. I turned in annoyance and saw Ivo.

'Can I have a word, Kitty?'

Charlie and Richard left, chatting to each other about fantasy books. Piers glanced at Ivo with concern, then disappeared down the stairs.

'What is it?' I said, more coldly than I intended.

Ivo said, in a conciliatory tone,

'I'm sorry for grabbing your arm. I just need to ask you something.'

I waited for him to continue.

'Could you look in on Evie, please?'

'That's where I'm going.'

'Oh, good,' he said, something of his warmth and charm returning. Then, he added, 'Could you do me a favour?' His head turned away slightly, registering a note of embarrassment.

'Of course,' I said. 'What?'

'Could you look in on me afterwards?' He paused, and pushed his hair back out of his eyes. He smiled, that crooked smile I could never resist. 'Just to let me know how she is?'

Until that day, I don't think I'd ever heard or seen Evie crying. It's one of the reasons I remember it so well. As I arrived on her corridor, I could hear great sobs issuing from a dozen doors down. They were so theatrical, at first I thought that it was someone rehearsing a piece for the Christmas Review. However, as I drew closer to Evie's door, I realised these tears could only be hers.

I knocked on her door.

'Piss off!' Evie's voice was thick with tears.

'It's me, Evie.'

The sobs subsided and the corridor suddenly felt exceptionally quiet. I wondered who else was around. Had others tried before me? Or had they decided to leave Evie alone, assuming this display of tears was really none of their business? Jane Sampson, pastoral vampire-in-chief, lived on this corridor. I pictured her with her ear to her door, waiting for developments. Then Evie's door opened, and she stood there, her face smeared with tears, her hair disarranged. I realised just how young she actually was. She looked, despite or because of the emotion on her face, closer to that picture of her at school than the one I carried around in my mind.

Evie walked quietly back towards her bed and sat down. I closed the door and sat on her desk chair. I realised, to my shock, that she was clutching a dog-eared cat teddy. It was black and white and most of its fur, especially on its ears, had been rubbed off. Its whiskers were long gone too. The lack of stuffing in its neck meant that the head lolled down towards the body. It looked a good twenty years old and I wondered if it had been her childhood comforter. She held it in her lap and the gesture made me think of those paintings of the Virgin and Child, where Mary dandles the Infant Christ in her lap.

I had not seen the cat toy before. I wondered if it had been rescued from some drawer or bag especially for this occasion. Evie, like all of us, was not one given to obvious childhood sentiment. Her room, if more feminine than Ivo's – there was a large mirror on her desk and there were perfumes and make-up on a small dresser – was more Spartan than one might expect of a single woman in her early twenties. There were a couple of framed posters on her walls. Both advertised exhibitions of medieval art and religion she'd visited in London and Cambridge in the past couple of years. Evie saw me glance at the cat and said,

'Oh, this is Mr Chatalon.' There was a little embarrassed laugh in her voice as she spoke, as if she was expecting judgment. 'Um, I've had him since I was tiny. He helps me sleep.'

I was intrigued by this last sentence. I wondered if she took him out each evening and hid him away when morning came. I had not seen him when I'd slept with Evie in this room.

'I had a little blanket,' I said, feebly. We sat in silence, then I said, 'Look, Evie, what's up?'

'You wouldn't understand.'

My anger flared. I was sick to death of this answer. All of them, in different ways, had been saying this to me since the start of term, a sign – as I saw it – of the public school gift for deflection and dissembling. Since our last falling out I'd felt Evie taking this to new levels, increasingly lowering the blinds to me. However, nothing would be gained by losing my temper. The way to get Evie to talk even a little was to be patient, though I must have failed to hide my annoyance, for she said,

'Oh, don't be like that, Kitty. I just don't want to drag you in.'

'I'm already in,' I said.

She stared at me, coming to a decision, then said,

'It's just friends falling out, Kit. And tiredness. And this bloody place.'

'Charlie, you mean?'

To my surprise, she laughed, with relief. 'Oh, bloody hell. No. What on earth makes you think that?'

'Nothing', I replied, quickly.

Evie put Mr Chatalon down on her bedspread, reached across to her bedside table and picked up a soft pack of Marlboro Lights. She tapped the side and a couple of cigarettes slipped forward and she offered me one. I took it, she took the other, and we lit up. I waited for her to speak. I knew her well enough to know that by being quiet it would give her time to organise her thoughts.

Evie looked out of the window, studying the iron-grey sky.

'It's going to snow.'

I looked too and said, 'Yes. I think you're right.'

Then she said,

'You can't help who you love, can you?' There was something almost hopeless in her voice. I looked at her carefully before I spoke. Could she be speaking of me?

'I don't know,' I replied. I didn't. I'd come to realise that I'd never really been in love, except perhaps with books, or learning or ideas. The nearest I'd ever come was with Evie, and even that had cooled.

'Listen to me!' she said, chiding herself. 'I sound like a teenager. Please, Kitty, ignore me. Really, I'm fine. It's just that sometimes you love someone or something, and they can't give you what you want. I'll get over it.'

I felt a curious mix of emotions. In the first instance, I felt relieved. I thought, 'Oh, so that's it. Evie is in love with one of the boys.' I felt sure it was Ivo. That was why he was so interested in hearing what Evie had to say. Now that I thought about it, I could begin to see the dots in their relationship, simply in need of joining up. If neither Ivo nor Evie were the most demonstrative people, I could recall a dozen occasions over the past couple of months that – if I'd only known what I was looking for – might have been read 'romantically' or with 'sexual-charge' between them. As Evie and my relationship had cooled off, so theirs had gained momentum. I remembered the occasions when they'd sat huddled at lunch or dinner talking intently with each other, or the times when I'd seen them heading away from campus for a private walk. It looked now like Evie's feelings for Ivo were stronger than his for hers. If only I hadn't been so wrapped up in myself I would have spotted it sooner. Yet, behind the satisfaction of finding a conclusion which worked, there was the sting of jealousy. If I was right and Evie loved Ivo, it could only mean one thing: she definitely didn't love me. She'd never truly cared for me. I told myself it didn't matter.

Suddenly, I needed to get away. I'd come expecting … what? I guess, some sort of grand revelation. What I got was utterly conventional. Precisely the kind of news one might expect from a young woman in a rather isolated and overheated religious community. Of course, it was only later that I properly appreciated how close I'd drawn to (and, therefore, how far from) a strange and explosive truth. As so often with these things, I think I already knew that something darker was going on, but I didn't want to truly acknowledge it. I behaved like one of those evangelical Christians who claim they've never met any gay people, despite knowing 'devoted friends' in their congregations for decades. I think that's why I was keen to leave. I'd made my easy conclusion and I didn't want to look closer. I wanted to enjoy the forgiving twilight rather than stand fully in the light. I got up and walked to the door. As I turned the door handle, I turned back towards Evie and said,

'Okay. But, Eve, if I can do anything.'

She nodded, smiled weakly, then said,

'I know. Hey, Kitty ...' She paused, as if searching for the right words, then said, 'Thank you.'

'For what?'

Again, she paused then said,

'For ... for ... being kind.'

'It's ...' I began to answer and stopped. Her words – soft and sincere – struck something within me. I felt pleased, gratified even, and then just as suddenly angry. I wanted to lash out. It was stupid. Irrational. I tried to say, 'It's okay', but the words stuck in my mouth. I stared at her, and she said,

'I'm sorry, Kit. For everything.' I continued to stare, trying to figure out what she meant. I opened my mouth to speak, again, but couldn't find the right words. I left.

* * *

I suppose I might have just gone back to my room. It would have been the grown-up thing to do. Instead, I went over to Ivo's. I knocked on the door and heard his characteristic,

'Come.'

I opened the door and saw Ivo hunched over his desk writing a letter with his fat, old fountain pen. I said,

'It's okay, Ivo, it's nothing. She's fine.' It was only then I realised Charlie was in the room, sat in one of his arm-chairs, mostly obscured from view from the door.

As I spoke, Charlie sat forward, and viewed me with a mixture of amusement and interest.

Ivo looked up and said, 'Come in and tell us all about it, then.'

I felt embarrassed, as if I were a faithful retainer caught in an unnecessary act of devotion. I had thought Ivo alone and would not have sounded quite so puppyish if I'd realised someone else was in the room. I sat down next to Charlie and saw that she was nursing a tumbler of whisky in her hands. I said, 'I'll have a little of that, if I may.'

'I'll have one, too,' said Ivo, and Charlie did the honours. The whisky was warming, peaty and rich and I felt it ease the tension in my body. I looked out of Ivo's window. Evie was right. It was going to snow.

'How is she?' said Ivo. His voice sounded so tense, it might break.

'Emotional,' I replied. When he said nothing, I said, 'She's just tired.'

'But what did she say?' said Ivo.

'Nothing. She said it was just relationship problems. College love. It's nothing.' Ivo smiled. I smiled back. I felt sure we understood each other and held a secret in common. He leaned back in his chair, a little more relaxed.

I took a deep pull on my whisky, and considered Evie's curious words as I was about to leave her room. Her thanks. Her strange apology. Absently, I said, 'She said she was sorry. For everything.' I regretted my indiscretion immediately.

Charlie and Ivo shared a glance, then Charlie said, 'Well, that's about time.' There was hardness in her tone.

'What do you mean?' I said.

'Oh, come on, Kitty,' she said. 'Are you being deliberately naïve?'

'I don't know what you mean,' I said. I wish I hadn't. In my head, I sounded like a character from an Oscar Wilde play.

Ivo and Charlie glanced at each other again, then Charlie said, 'She's not who you think, Kitty.'

I smiled. I was prepared for this.

'Oh, come on yourself, Charlie. You can't see her right.' I said this so forcefully, indeed mockingly, I reckoned it might even prick Charlie's ever-cool exterior. I wanted to see behind the mask. Instead of biting back, she took a sip of whisky, put the glass down and lit a cigarette. It was only after her first drag that she said,

'You're right, Kitty. I can't see her right. But neither can you. It's time you heard some home truths about Evie.'

She stopped and tapped her cigarette on the ashtray, then said, 'Do you remember your first day here?' I nodded. 'Well, let me guess. Did you find Evie on your doorstep, beaming up at you like an excited puppy?'

I reached into my bag and pulled out a pack of Craven A and lit one. I wanted thinking time. Was this some sort of trick or game Charlie was playing? Consciously trying to keep my voice cool and even, I said, 'Yes. So what?' I tried to go on the offensive again, saying, 'Were you spying on us, Charlie?'

Charlie ignored my second question and said, 'I know because Evie came to see me that morning.'

'What?'

Charlie blew out a plume of smoke and said, 'It doesn't sound likely, does it? But the fact is, Evie knocked on my door, wanting to speak. I suppose she must have seen my name on the student list, or seen my face in the bloody college brochure. I always knew I shouldn't have agreed to it. Anyway, Evie appeared on my doorstep and I almost slammed the door in her face. Stupidly, I didn't. She'd brought roses and vanda orchids. It seemed churlish not to let her in.'

Ivo laughed and said,

'Typical Evie.'

'Quite,' said Charlie. 'Typical in more ways than one.'

'What do you mean?' I said.

'You really haven't spotted how Evie operates, have you?' said Charlie. 'It's quite sweet, really. Then, again, I was naïve enough to think Evie had come to see me to say sorry for being such a cow at school. The sort of thing one might expect from a trainee vicar. But, no. We spoke about school friends and acquaintances and so on, but what she wanted was information.'

'About what?' I asked.

Charlie considered this for a moment.

'Well, you,' she said. 'Not directly, of course. I mean, the first thing she wanted to know was who was worth knowing. Then she wanted to know who was coming up to college this year. Had I heard any rumours, that sort of thing. Who might be going places. Who might help her. So, mainly to get her out of my hair, I mentioned you.'

There was a long silence while I processed this news. Did it matter? Really? Maybe not. Yet something rankled. Not so much Charlie talking about me, as Evie's ruthlessness. I tried to tally Charlie's claims alongside what I knew. It did make some sense. In some ways, it was part of Evie's charm that she was unafraid to cultivate useful people. I recalled the occasion when our Visitor, the Bishop of London, had come to lunch and how Evie – to the amusement of the rest of us – had somehow ended up sitting next to him. But that was just Evie. It would have been a horrific trait if it hadn't been balanced with her eccentricity and sense of fun. Roddy Peplow reported how, when Evie met the Bishop, she took him to task about his recent *Times* article in which he'd said that marriage was always better for a woman than being a single mother. Apparently, she'd been so passionate in her analysis of the Blessèd Virgin as proto-single mother, that the old Bishop had promised to go off and think again.

131

Yet, for all Evie's charm, she was ambitious and had an eye for the main chance, not that that was a sin, even in our strange outfit. Indeed, the more I've seen of the back-stage manoeuvrings of ambitious clergy, I wish more people were upfront. Back then, however, I was still young and envious. Since I was four years old – when I first remember my parents' preference for my sister over me – I've known that envy is my abiding sin and it was hard to forget how quickly Evie had gone from being on the edge of our group to being Albertus's research assistant, which in my mind, basically equated to his special one. I noted again how she'd made that happen on the sly, without comment. Indeed, as I sat in Ivo's room, I realised how much Albertus had become the surrogate father-figure for my own failed and absent one. I'd wanted to be his favourite, but Evie had got in ahead of me. Indeed, perhaps ahead of the others, who had known him so much longer.

Oh, Lord. I felt sick. I looked at Ivo. His view, I thought, would be decisive.

'What do you think?'

He stubbed out a cigarette, sat back in his chair, and said,

'I'm actually very fond of Evie. I'm sure you realise that. Of course, I don't have Charlie's childhood baggage to deal with, so that makes things easier. But … and it's a big but, Kitty, I trust Charlie's judgment on this.'

'So, what are you saying?' I said, as much to Charlie as Ivo. It was Charlie who answered.

'How many degrees do you have, Kitty? Do I really need to spell it out?'

I rubbed my left temple with my free hand. I was getting a headache. I felt like the room was wobbling. It felt hot and stifling. I was sure it wasn't the result of the whisky. Finally, I said, 'You're saying I've been used?' My mouth felt dry and foul.

'My own view,' said Charlie, 'is that you were never really the target, Kitty. Evie had Albertus in her sights.'

I looked up and noticed that the air was blue with hanging smoke. It only added to my sense of nausea.

'But that's ridiculous,' I said, sarcastically. I thought of the day I'd dragged her to Brasenose and her reluctance to hear Loewe speak. I said, 'Evie didn't even want to hear Albertus's lecture. She did everything to slow me up. We nearly missed it.'

'But you didn't, did you?' said Ivo.

'No, but … you weren't there … you don't know how it was.'

'But Albertus was,' said Ivo, simply. 'I saw him for breakfast the next day. He told me about two women from Littlemore. A Dr Catherine Bolton and her friend, Evie Kirkland.'

'Oh, come on. He didn't use her name. How could he know? She didn't say a word.'

'Simple,' said Ivo. 'She'd written to him before the lecture.'

A dim memory came back to me, of how when I'd put my hand up to ask my question he'd said, 'Miss…?' At the time, I'd put it down to convention. I was young and a woman. Why wouldn't he think me 'Miss' rather than a 'Dr'? Now I saw that he might have thought me 'Miss Evie Kirkland' rather than someone else. Charlie said,

'I'm sorry, Kitty.'

'But, that can't be.'

'I assure you it can,' said Ivo. 'Speak to Albertus about it, if you like. He said he'd received a note. It said something about how much she admired his book on Dante. Even quoted a couple of lines. She told him how much she was looking forward to the lecture.'

I went over the events of that evening. The way Evie had wittered on about the boy she went dancing with as an undergrad. The way she dragged out her coffee when I'd wanted to hurry to get good seats for the lecture. Did Ivo's information tally with what I knew? Not really. And yet why would he lie? Why would he invite me to speak to Albertus if it wasn't true? In my anxiety, I'd felt like Evie was being deliberately tardy and refractory. Yet, now I began to suspect that my anxiety had messed with time. Considering the chain of events carefully I could appreciate that, for all my sense that Evie had dragged her coffee out, we were well in time. We were seated and ready to go before Albertus appeared. We had not arrived out of breath or with seconds to spare. There was also that glance Albertus gave as he left the lecture theatre, the way he stopped at the door and looked across. At the time, I'd been convinced he'd looked at me and winked. Now, as I replayed the scene, I became convinced I was wrong. He'd been looking past me at Evie.

I shivered. I really was feeling quite ropey. I was coming down with something, a fever, quite fast. Flu, perhaps. I felt chilled, almost frozen, inside. I wanted to get out of the smoky, oppressive room, but I had one more question. 'Was this what you were trying to tell me that Friday afternoon?'

'Yes,' replied Charlie. 'Evie can't help herself, I'm afraid. She uses people to get what she wants. She's ruthless, and very cunning about it. She has an instinct. She gambled on you being worth knowing and turned up at your door, with the charm at full volume. You were a ticket to more interesting company. Albertus.'

'Oh, God,' I said. I sat forward, and placed my face in my hands. I breathed out and felt like I was deflating. I felt so ill I would have been happy, in that moment, to have deflated and deflated until I was nothing but a puddle on the floor. I had to get out. I had to get away from this room and these people. And Evie. I breathed in, and stood up. I felt light-headed and clammy. I must have swayed because Charlie said,

'Kitty, are you sure you're okay?'

'I just need to go and lie down. I think I'm coming down with the flu or something.' I knew, however, that how I was feeling – confused, anxious and upset – was not simply a symptom of a fever.

Looking back now, I see that that afternoon was decisive. A Rubicon. I crossed a line that I now believe ultimately led to Evie's death. I'd like to call it a choice between stories – between what is believable and unbelievable or, perhaps better, what is plausible and implausible – but I'm not sure it had such a voluntary character. Most of what passes for 'choice' is already marked out; when St Augustine says that grace is something which goes ahead of us, he might be talking about our decisions. Most of what we choose happens at an unconscious level, recapitulated after the fact. That afternoon I became convinced that if Evie was charming, amusing and fun, she also manipulated those whom she appeared to love. This was less an intellectual 'belief' and more of a gut certainty. As I sat there, my body was convinced. I was convinced that Evie had done me wrong and was rotten. If my faith told me to resist, in my bones I wanted revenge.

I stood up and walked towards Ivo's door. I was shivering, chilled to the bone. I felt sweat trickle down my forehead and my back. I felt it trickle down my left leg, burning into the wound where I wore my cilice. I thought I heard Ivo say something and I turned back to look at him. I must have imagined it for he was looking away from me, out of his window. He was quite still, with as much repose as one might expect from a holy man. I followed the line of his gaze, studied the iron sky again. He looked out towards the panopticon. The winter's first snow was beginning to fall.

Part Two

'God seyth hym self, as wryten we fynde,
That whenne þe blynde ledeth þe blynde,
In to þe dyche þey fallen boo,
For þey ne sen whare by to go.'

John Mirk, Instructions for Parish Priests

Chapter Sixteen

It was a bleak Christmas that year. Oh, what am I saying? Christmas is always bleak for me, even allowing for the birth of the Christ-Child. It's the time of year when it's almost impossible to avoid thinking about family, home and my complicated relationship with both. I always end up thinking excessively about my sister. Christmas is never good, but that year, it was tougher than usual, primarily because, as term ended, I was ill and it took weeks for me to fully recover. As I'd suspected on that December day in Ivo's room, I had full-blown flu, and it completely wiped me out for the final week of term and the first week of the holidays.

Missing out on the last week of term proved a mixed blessing. It meant – joy of joys – I managed to avoid some of the worst inanities of student life. The day after the snow fell there was a snowball fight across college. I suspect that if I'd been well, I would have enjoyed letting off a bit of steam, but the fight got out of control. Various students used it as a cover to attack those who'd annoyed them. Never let it be said that religious people are above sneak attacks. The low-point of all this – so Richard reported – was a totally over-the-top reaction from Miles Goodhap when he received a fantastically accurate snowball in the face from Tanya Mitchell. He responded by chasing her around the quad, lifting her up in the air and then dropping her on the floor. The snow was not as deep as Miles had thought and Tanya ended up with two cracked ribs and bruises on her face. She threatened to report Miles to the Principal for actual bodily harm.

Of course, during that final week of term, my friends checked in on me at regular intervals. Piers and Charlie brought griottines and Valrhona chocolate. Piers claimed that if the griottines were not exactly loaded with Vitamin C, the sugar and alcohol would make me feel better about being ill. Ivo arrived late one afternoon with a dog-eared copy of Ellis Peters' *A Morbid Taste for Bones*, a bottle of Highland Park and a first edition of Sands' *Middle English Verse Romances*. While he thought I'd see the joins in the Peters' mystery, he reckoned it was perfect fodder for ill people. Richard, sweet Richard, brought cake. He knew I had an exceptional fondness for Lemon Drizzle and for Seed Cake and he brought two home-made slabs for me. He sat with me, sometimes for hours, and read passages from the thirteenth-century French fabliau *Bérenger of the Long Arse*, offering commentary on it, while I dozed.

'You still awake, Kit?' I nodded and took a sip from my hot toddy. 'Bérenger really is bloody marvellous, isn't it? And people think that women were oppressed in the Middle Ages.' The tale concerns a noble woman who puts her ignoble husband to shame. Having been married off to a useless knave by her Earl father, the woman discovers her husband has faked his knightly valour; she dresses as a knight herself and gives him the choice of fighting her, in the certain knowledge he'll lose, or kissing her arse. Out of cowardice, the husband chooses the latter. The woman declares she is 'Bérenger of the Long Arse, who puts to shame the chicken-hearted.' Later, when the husband returns home, she tells him that she has met Bérenger. To protect his name the husband is forced to submit to her wishes for the rest of his life.

'I think it was meant as a warning to men,' I croaked.

'I know, but one doesn't have to read it that way, does one?'

'Maybe you're becoming a feminist, Richard,' I said. I smiled weakly.

He put down his book and said, 'What are you doing for

Christmas, Kitty?' They'd all asked me this. I knew they meant well, but I was tired of being asked.

'Well, it depends. If I feel okay, I'll go to see some friends up north. Otherwise I'll hunker down here.' The first part of this was partially true. My old PhD Director of Studies had written to say I should drop in if I was in Lancaster over Christmas. In recent years, I'd often spent Christmas Day alone, something I didn't mind. Either that or I'd volunteered at a church lunch for the elderly or the homeless. What I couldn't stand was the thought of being pitied by my friends.

'That's no good, Kit. Come and stay at my parents. You won't have to do a thing. You can even stay in bed all day if you're feeling ill.' I was more than tempted. Richard would be spending Christmas at his parents' townhouse in west London with his two sisters. His parents were off on some second honeymoon thing on the QE2. We would have the run of the house and there would be more than enough room for me. Richard was sure I'd get on well with his sisters. That, however, wasn't the only offer. Piers was off to stay with family outside York. Again, Piers was quite sure there'd be plenty of space for me. His brother – a racehorse trainer and breeder – was, in Piers' opinion, 'dull as shit' and the prospect of having 'someone who's read something other than *Horse and Hound* in the house' was a boon. Charlie and Ivo were both going to be out of the country, Charlie in New York and Ivo with some cousins in Austria.

As for Evie, I suppose the good thing about being ill was that I could avoid what I'd learnt from Ivo and Charlie about her. I was too ill to begin to process it. I just wanted term to be over and to be left alone so that I could get better and begin to process the news in my own time. During that last week of term, of course, I couldn't completely hide from her. She was still my friend and, like the others, she came around to see me. Sometimes I'd pretend to be asleep. Sometimes I was asleep. When I wasn't, being ill gave me a good alibi for my awkwardness and stilted conversation. She told me she was going back to her family in Wiltshire for the holidays and was looking forward to seeing her mother, with whom she was close. She didn't invite me to spend Christmas with her, and I was glad.

On the final day of term, she must have slipped into my room while I slept, for when I woke I found a card and a small tightly-wrapped parcel. The card had an image of Our Lady of Tindari on the front, a striking medieval example of a Black Madonna dandling the Christ-Child. Inside, Evie had written, 'Dearest Kitty, Get well, sweet cat! Enjoy this marvellous image of the Black Madonna! I've missed your smile so much this week. College is a bore without you. Have a wonderful, holy Christmas! Eat many mice (!) pies, like a good Kitty Cat. I hope you like my little present. See you in the New Year! xx Evie.' Twenty years on, I still have that card. I take it out at Christmas to remind me of Evie's indisputable capacity for silliness and joy. It reminds me, perhaps more than anything else, of how much I misunderstood her and her intentions. It reminds me how people can write the jolliest things whilst being deeply miserable. The gift, too, I treasure. It exemplified Evie's capacity for reckless generosity. It was a silk Hermès scarf in red with a wild swirling motif that conjured books and library shelves. The print was called *Ex Libris*. It must have cost an eye-watering amount, but its beauty and workmanship mean less to me now than the note Evie had put in the box: 'You always look magnificent in red, Kitty, like the Magdalene herself. This pattern might have been made for you – lover of books and libraries. Thank you for all you have given me.'

'Thank you for all you have given me.' It is such an enigmatic, ambiguous statement. In the weeks to come I'd puzzle over it. Was it a simple statement of affection? Was it an acknowledgement that she had used me? Was it a little of both? Years on, I believe I know how to read it. I have placed it – rightly I think – with one other curious moment during that week of fever and sickness. When Evie

142

first came to see me, I was still very woozy, running a temperature, and I pretended to be asleep. I could hear Evie's breathing, as she sat beside me. It sounded shallow, rather faster than I would have thought. Her scent – 24 Faubourg – drifted across to me: Orange blossom, peach and gardenia. I don't know how long she sat there, a while I think. Then she stood, I heard her dress rustle, and I sensed her lean over me. Her scent rose strongly in my nostrils and I could feel her warm breath on my cheek. Then she kissed me gently on the forehead and left.

But I digress. Richard was very keen for me to come to London with him. He even offered to pack for me. When I said I was tired and could we talk another time, he said,

'Well, if you won't come to London with me …' He paused, suddenly nervous. 'Well, perhaps you should see your parents …' Of all my friends from those days, Richard was always the most sensitive and cautious, in some ways, the most enigmatic. He did not like to pry into anyone's business. I think he believed that if he was discreet about others, others would not pry into his life. There was a long pause whilst I thought of what I might say.

Sensing perhaps that he'd strayed into dangerous territory, he said, 'I'm sorry, Kitty. I shouldn't have said that. It's just that you never talk about them. If … if you hadn't mentioned them in your fever I might have thought them dead.'

This came as a shock. I had no memory of this.

'What did I say?'

'Oh, gosh. Nothing really,' he replied. 'Something about a Louise. You said, "Mummy, I'm sorry." Then something about your dad I couldn't make out.'

I said, 'Louise was my sister. She drowned. My mum and dad … they're dead too, or might as well be.' It was the first time I'd revealed my sister's name to any of them.

One of the things I adored about Richard was he instinctively

143

understood where the limit lay. It was one of the most priestly things about his character. There was a long silence, then I said, 'May I have a cigarette?'

'No, Kit, doctor's orders I'm afraid.' Suddenly he stood up and began to collect his things. Just as he was about to leave, he stopped, holding his long coat so that it folded down over his stomach towards his knees. With only my Anglepoise lamp on and the curtains half drawn, he looked a curiously shady figure, shrouded, somehow. An elegant and slim young agent of the Angel of Death. In my half-fevered mind, I thought this is how Death might look if he were to adopt the guise of a young, upper-middle-class man.

'There is one other thing.' He paused, embarrassed I thought, then continued. 'That whole scheme of Ivo and Piers this term. Bloody stupid, if you ask me. I love them to bits, but it all got a bit out of hand. I'm sorry you got dragged into it. I damn near got blood-poisoning.'

'What do you mean?' I said.

He put his coat back on my desk and began rolling his right shirt-sleeve up. His skin was pale, the skin of the dead, and the arm was surprisingly sinewy. It had the definition one sees on a long-distance runner, not muscly, but nonetheless powerful. About three inches above his elbow I saw a nasty, scabbed band of flesh about an inch across. In the half-light, it looked almost black, like a tattoo. He looked down at it as he showed it off.

'Quite something, eh?' He looked back up at me and said, 'It got infected. It took some explaining to my doctor, I can say. Luckily, I know a chap in London who's more than discreet. Looks after the bishops, you know, on a *pro bono* basis. Thinks it's going to smooth his access to heaven.' I recalled there had been a couple of days a few weeks back when Richard had gone up to town. He'd been looking pasty and said he wanted to consult his father's doctor.

Richard began to turn his sleeve back down again. He winced

slightly. The wound clearly hadn't healed fully. He buttoned the sleeve and picked up his stuff again.

'Have a good Christmas,' I said, croakily.

'You too, Kitty.' He'd opened the door, then paused and closed it again. 'One more thing. This prayer business. Mortification.' He said the last word in a bitter, mocking tone. 'It has to stop. In its current form. I've spoken to Piers and Ivo, but I'm not sure they're listening, not to me, anyway. Next term, might you try? Before …' He laughed to himself, then said, '…well, if the past few weeks are anything to go by, six weeks of Lent could be catastrophic.' Finally, almost to himself, he said, 'As for that other business, well, the sooner we forget about that, the better.'

He raised a hand in farewell, and without a further word, slipped out of the door, leaving me dizzy and tired in the twilight of my room wondering what on earth he might have meant when he spoke of 'that other business'.

Chapter Seventeen

What is a kingdom without its monarch? A library without its books? A college without its inmates? Piers told me a story about the Oxford don Gilbert Ryle. Apparently, a distinguished, if rather witless visitor to Oxford met Ryle and wanted to be shown the University. Ryle dutifully showed him around various colleges, libraries, introduced him to dons and students; they visited the Radcliffe Camera and the Bridge of Sighs. Ryle showed him ancient manuscripts and dined with him at High Table. At the end of all this, the visitor said, 'Yes, this is all very well, but when are you going to show me the University?'

Littlemore without its motley of students was diminished, yet still recognisable. If an outsider had come I could have shown him 'Littlemore'. Perhaps its essence had been temporarily dissipated, but not lost. In the week before Christmas Day there was still a smattering of staff, mostly support and admin people, and it was possible to find a meal in the refectory. Trudging through the slushy snow from my room to the library and back again it was still possible to bump into the occasional student or academic. Molly and Peter Shanks were staying on campus for Christmas and kindly invited me around for dinner. I lied and told them I'd already been invited to join friends in Oxford.

One afternoon I headed over to Luxford to see if Albertus was on campus. The building, however, was locked up. I hadn't really expected to find him. Charlie had said that he usually visited relatives in Cumbria at Christmas. Yet, in my drained, post-viral state, I felt hungry for some sort of familiarity and connection. In the past couple of weeks, I had become so disconnected from college life, that with my friends gone, it felt natural to go looking for Albertus. I was delighted and surprised, then, that as I walked back to my room, I saw Albertus calling to me from the direction of the main buildings.

'Kitty! Hail! Hail!' With his walrus moustache and academic gown, he looked even more like a throwback to another age, or a theatrical idea of an Oxford don. He wore tweeds under his gown and – comedically – green wellies into which he'd amateurishly rammed his trousers. It was a cheering sight.

'Albertus, how are you?'

'How are you, Kitty, more like?' he said. 'Evie told me you were at death's door.'

'Evie can get a little carried away.'

He laughed. 'True, true.'

'I was just looking for you,' I said. 'Then I remembered Charlie said you go to Cumbria for Christmas.'

'Usually, yes,' he said, 'but my sister isn't up to it this year.' He tried to keep relief out of his voice, and failed. 'That's why I'm pleased I've found you. I wonder … might you consent to come to my house for Christmas lunch?'

I was surprised and my response must have taken a beat too long because he added, 'What was I thinking? What would a youngster like you want with an old, broken dog like me?'

'No,' I said, with genuine enthusiasm. 'No, I'd be delighted, Albertus.'

He studied me for a moment, twirled a strand of his moustache and said, 'Sure?'

'Of course.'

'Good,' he said, with a confident finality. 'Come to mine for, shall we say, 1pm?'

'Should I bring anything?'

'Surprise me.' With that he turned and began to stump back towards the main buildings.

I regretted saying 'yes' almost immediately. Not, of course, because I didn't like Albertus or felt I'd been bounced into it, but because I felt inadequate and insecure. I was not one for Christmas excesses anyway, but I wasn't sure I knew how I'd handle an afternoon alone with Loewe. I felt panicked. The fact I still felt weak after illness didn't help. I was jittery, still troubled by feverish dreams and I considered ringing Albertus up and pulling out, but couldn't quite bring myself to do it. I didn't want to let him down. Yet I had also been immensely touched. I considered again how I'd made him a surrogate father-figure. I wanted to please him and be patted on the head. I didn't want him to think less of me and the invitation flattered me. I felt I would have one over on the others.

'Surprise me,' he'd said. I think part of my anxiety came from my sense that I couldn't. This was a man who had spent his whole life in circles that were alien to my own. My ideas of Christmas were drawn from a cheap and inelegant childhood. Louise and I had grown up with plastic trees and a chicken for Christmas Dinner. We'd ask, I don't know, for a Barbie or Sindy doll and we'd get the cheap version from the local market. Our annual disappointment was something Louise and I had held in common. Loewe's world was not that. Not only had he lived the relatively lush life of an Oxford don, but he'd friends in the highest echelons of society. In his youth, he told us once, he'd spent several weekends at Sandringham with King George VI and his family.

I can laugh at my anxiety now. Now, I guess I might have surprised him by turning up with a bottle of Pomagne and a bag of pork scratchings, saying I was going to show him a seventies working-class Christmas. Back then? I hadn't the confidence. The joke is that I think he'd have warmed to my honesty. He was a snob, but he liked real people. That was why he lived in a modest house in unfashionable Jericho, essentially an old worker's cottage. He was not afraid of Town, even if he instinctively knew which side of the divide was his true habitat. I'd visited his home several times before, and knew his simple habits, but back then I might as well have been about to spend Christmas Day with the Duke of Northumberland. Ultimately, I arrived at his door on Christmas Day clutching that bottle of Krohn Harvest 1960 Port Evie had given me, and – as a kind of joke – a copy of Goldberg's *Queering the Renaissance*. I thought it might give us something to talk – perhaps even to argue – about, if conversation ran dry.

'Come in, come in, dear Kitty!' There was delight and, did I imagine it, a little relief in Albertus's voice as he opened the front door. As I wheeled my bike past him, he added, 'Goodness, you do look wild, Kitty. Cathy Earnshaw in full flight.'

'It's the fag end of this storm,' I said, out of breath. 'It's murder to cycle in. I hear there's devastation up north.'

Albertus helped me take off my coat and hat, led me into his sitting room and said,

'Well, Kitty, devastation is, I've heard, the standard state of affairs in northern climes. Come, let the storm take care of itself, for we are here to feast. Merry Christmas to you!'

'And Merry Christmas to you, Albertus.'

He passed me a glass of chilled *fino* sherry, and proposed a toast to absent friends.

'To absent friends,' I repeated, heartily.

Now I'd regained my breath after my stormy ride across the city – I'd attended Mass at Christ Church – I was in a better position to take stock of my surroundings. Immediately, I registered something odd. It was not so much the room, despite the addition of a carefully decorated Christmas Tree. The room exuded its usual sense of faded, gentlemanly comfort. If Mrs Lodge, Albertus's daily, had tidied

149

away various piles of books and scholarly journals, the extra layer of tidiness could not remove the impression that this was the home of a confirmed bachelor. The red sofas were crumbling into themselves, and their cushions, ratty and frayed from the attentions of Loewe's old cat, Lucius, seemed to be the only things holding the sofas upright. The mirror above the fireplace – which Albertus always called a 'looking-glass' – had a sombre, oak surround, and made the room feel smaller rather than larger. The few pieces of visual art on the walls, including a very fine etching of Florence in the fifteenth century, were in muted tones, determined not to draw attention to themselves.

All of this was familiar. No, the oddness lay, I decided, in Albertus himself. Not so much in his dress – he wore an old blue wool suit, with a pale shirt and a Balliol College tie – but in how he looked. Strained, somehow. Pale. I realised he'd lost a lot of weight and his suit looked loose on him, as if he were playing a fool in a comedy skit, his outsized clothing emphasizing a clownish license. He'd lost none of his instinctive jolliness, but suddenly it looked under pressure. Indeed, he was clearly ill.

Albertus must have noticed my brown study because he said,

'Kitty? Are you well? Would you like another drink?'

'Sorry, Albertus. I'm fine. I shouldn't have cycled. I'm still not one hundred percent. It would have been sensible to drive, but I fancied a drink. Which reminds me!'

I pulled my presents out of my rucksack.

'Ah,' he said. 'Well, I thought we might exchange gifts after dinner.' There was a note of embarrassment in his tone. I wasn't sure if it was because he'd thought I'd committed some sort of social solecism or – as I suspected – he hadn't a present for me.

'Of course, Albertus,' I said, hoping I didn't sound put out.

Then, unexpectedly he said, 'Drink, you say?'

I smiled and pulled a box out of my bag. 'Well, perhaps if I give

150

you this one now and keep the other back for after dinner?'

I passed him the box which he took greedily, sliding the lid off. He sighed like a child given a long dreamed for toy.

'Oh, oh! Kitty! Port wine. Krohn Harvest 1960. Oh, this is magnificent.'

I felt a glow inside, as if I'd drunk half of the bottle in one go. He reached across, pulled me close and kissed me on the cheek, his moustache tickling my face.

As quickly as he'd pulled me towards him, he let me go, and looked back down at the bottle. 'Of course, after its journey through the storm, alas, we shan't be able to drink any. Shame. It'll need at least a week in the cellar to settle down.'

The glow within me faded. Damn. I should have known that. Back then, I was mostly ignorant about port, vintage or otherwise. The nearest I'd got to the stuff, pre-Littlemore, was Cockburn's Special Reserve round at my granny's as a child.

'Yes, I am sorry, Albertus,' I said, trying to conceal my embarrassment. 'What was I thinking? I told you I still haven't recovered from my flu.'

He winked. I was sure he'd seen through my bluster, but was inclined to indulge me.

'Well, never mind, Kitty,' he said. 'It is an extravagant gift, nonetheless.' He laid the box on a small table. 'We shall have to drink it together, soon.' He paused, suddenly struck by something. 'Yes, soon.' He smiled at me, then with his usual bluster said, 'Now! Come into the dining room. Mrs Lodge has laid on a veritable feast.'

It was the best Christmas meal I'd eaten in a long time, though, that may not necessarily count as a commendation. I'd not eaten a proper Christmas dinner for years. The times I'd volunteered to help the homeless and the elderly, I'd eaten the dregs of the meal. When I'd been on my own, I'd not bothered with all the trimmings. Nonetheless, Mrs Lodge had indeed done us proud. She'd left a simple starter of pâté with cornichons, chutney and toasted bread. For main we had goose, roast potatoes and all the trimmings. She'd instructed Albertus carefully on how to heat everything up and he did a fine job. It was the first time I'd had goose and it was a wonder, rich, with crispy, fatty skin. For pudding we had pear tarte-tatin and cream. There were cheeses and port and during dinner, we drank a Pinot Noir that Albertus said had been sent to him by an old friend who owned a vineyard in New Zealand. Afterwards neither of us wanted to move from the table.

Conversation had ranged over a surprising number of topics. I'd long since realised that Albertus loved to dominate and I was happy to play second-fiddle. So, I'd propose a subject, make a simple claim about something and let Albertus respond. He was so used to hearing his own voice, most of the time he would simply discourse on any subject. We spoke of medieval understandings of Christmas, and the limitations of nineteenth-century carols. He became very animated – as ever – about his time spent in the company of the Inklings. After a few glasses of wine, he claimed 'that lot were a bunch of arseholes, really. Half of them spoke like characters in the *Lord of the Rings*, declaiming about honour and glory. Lewis was forever making ridiculous speeches. They saw themselves as modern knights, but most of them were self-publicising shits.' I might have pointed out that this was one of Albertus's faults too, but I was biding my time. On my way to his house, I'd realised our dinner might offer the perfect opportunity to ask about Evie. Had she written to Loewe ahead of his lecture? But I didn't want to blow my chance. I thought, indulge him, get him a bit drunk and he'll be more likely to let loose.

Eventually, we moved back into the sitting room. I was quite drunk and feeling both sleepy and bloated and I needed to find a way to bring the conversation around to Ivo and Evie. Albertus seemed to read my thoughts and said, 'Now I hope you won't be rushing off,

Kitty.'

'I think I should go soon, Albertus. Before it gets dark.'

'Yes, but you have time for a *digestif*, don't you?' I wasn't entirely sure what a *digestif* was. Was it a kind of after-dinner mint? A French biscuit? Nonetheless I said, 'Yes.'

He rubbed his hands together and went to a large cabinet and pulled out a bottle with yellow-coloured liquid in it.

'Limoncello,' he announced, with gusto. 'From an old student of mine who comes from the Sorrentine Peninsula. Have you ever been?'

I said, 'No'. To this day, I have no idea where the Sorrentine Peninsula is.

'Made with the zest of Feminello St Teresa lemons, from his father's farm. They have the most extraordinarily rude nipples, those lemons. You don't mind me saying nipples, Kitty?'

I shook my head, amused.

'As for the connection with St Teresa, that is lost in time, but one suspects it has something to do with her ecstasy, her utter ravishment by God ... With how her nipples must have been as pointy and hard as bullets when our Lord took her for himself.'

He really was very drunk.

'Anyway, this stuff is bloody marvellous.' He poured two small glasses and passed one to me. He was right. It was sensational: Tart, yet sweet; refreshing, yet unctuous.

While I sipped, he went over to a walnut desk, covered with papers, and feebly searched. As he did so, he muttered to himself.

'Where has that bloody woman hidden them? Ah!'

He turned to face me, holding a box and said, 'Cigars! These are ... rare things indeed. Been saving 'em for good company. D'you like cigars?'

'I think so,' I said, noncommittally. I'd never smoked a cigar in my life.

'Then you've never tried a good cigar. Now! Try this.'

He prepared a cigar for me and passed it over. He cut one for himself and then we lit up.

He sat down opposite me and we puffed away for a while. I had this vague memory of my father saying that the thing to do with a cigar is savour the smoke in the mouth. How he knew this, I've no idea. I assume it was something that men, of all classes, knew. Frankly, I thought this treat of Albertus's was a bit grim. I'd have much rather have had one of my gaspers. However, I was keen to impress Albertus so I murmured suitable sounds of appreciation. I also decided this was my chance to ask about Evie. I was drunk, but not paralytic, whereas Albertus was on the verge of tipping over the edge. One more drink and I reckoned he would fall asleep, insensible. He was in the best of moods, displaying none of that melancholy that can affect the seriously drunk.

'Albertus,' I said, as brightly as I could. 'Might I ask you something?'

'Fire away, dear lady.' He was fumbling in his waistcoat pockets for something.

'Um, it's a bit embarrassing really, but … it's about, Evie …'

'Ah, dear Evie.' He found what he was looking for – an ornate key, about three inches long. A mortice key, the kind for locking doors. He laid it on the coffee table between us. I looked at it, wondering what it might open. As I looked back at Albertus I saw the flicker of a smile on his face. 'Yes,' he said, 'she's proven most useful. Wonderful young woman.'

'That lecture you gave at Brasenose. The one on sex and pleasure. Did Evie write to you before it? Saying how much she was looking forward to attending?'

Albertus, who had been in danger of settling back in his chair to sleep, perked up. 'Oh, darling Kitty. Yes, she did. Most gratifying. She'd even read some of my work. I mean, Evie! Of all people!'

I ignored this slight against her.

'I'll be honest with you, Kitty. When you put your hand up to speak, I thought you were her. She'd told me about you, of course, in her note. About how we had this Medievalist in college this year, but I'd assumed she'd brought you along as back-up. I think she thought I'd find you a tempting morsel.'

So, it was true. I breathed carefully, trying to remain calm, trying to tell myself it didn't matter. Of course, it did. I felt like I'd been punched in the guts. Nonetheless, I had to maintain the semblance of cool. After all, I didn't want to spoil this afternoon. It wasn't Albertus's fault, after all. I realised he was studying me, rather blearily, admittedly, but studying me nonetheless. He opened his mouth, as if about to speak, then closed it again. He seemed to be struggling to find the right words. When he spoke, he surprised me.

'You should be kind to yourself, Kitty. You are remarkable, you know. Not like the others. You're a scholar. A pastor. They are amateurs. I should be very sad to see you become bitter about anything.' It was an extraordinarily kind thing to say, so uncharacteristic of Loewe.

I almost cried then. Instead, I said,

'I almost forgot. Your present.'

He raised his eyebrows quizzically. 'Another one?'

I pulled a badly wrapped book-shaped parcel out of my bag and passed it across. He shook it in a pantomime way, and said,

'I wonder what this could be!' He pulled off the paper to reveal the copy of Goldberg's *Queering the Renaissance*. He laughed uproariously.

'I knew you'd get the joke,' I said, with more than a little relief.

'Oh, this is splendid, Kitty. I know Goldberg, of course. Brilliant mind, brilliant. And Richard Rambuss's re-readings of Jesus and Lyric poetry are invigorating.'

'You've read it?' I knew Loewe was widely read, but I was stunned that he might have read something as academically outré as this.

'Well, no, but I knew Rambuss when he was a graduate student. Frankly, my dear, this stuff drives me up the wall, as you well know. But it's the future, I suppose. I can see that. And in thirty years it will be as old-hat as I am. Maybe I'll have a renaissance then.' We both laughed. He stared at the cover and said, with unexpected tenderness, 'Thank you, Kitty. It means a great deal to an old man to spend a day like this with ... well ...' I felt suddenly rather awkward.

'Well, Albertus, I think it's time I was off home.'

'Oh, come now, Kitty. You've time for coffee at least.'

* * *

I don't know if it's only the religious who are inclined to feel their paths are being guided. Perhaps, all of us have a sense of momentum or fate or synchronicity from time-to-time. What I do know, is that at that moment I looked down again at the curious key on Albertus's coffee table and a startling, reckless idea came to me. I looked at it and I thought I knew what it was and where it might lead. Call it instinct, or God, or the Spirit, but – in my drunken state, with my self-control and inhibitions lowered – I felt a path open. For months, I'd been haunted by something Evie had said that day we'd found out she'd be working for Loewe: She'd said, the *quid pro quo* for working for him was access to his private library. His private library. The concept had tantalised me. As I looked at that key I was sure it was the way in.

I looked up at Albertus, smiled, and said, 'How rude of me, Albertus. Of course, I'd love a cup of coffee.'

156

Chapter Eighteen

I have never been an impulsive or reckless person. I've achieved what I have by careful and sometimes ponderous planning and study. That afternoon was as close as I've ever come to throwing every little bit of caution to the wind. It might have cost me my entire Church career. Some risks, however, are worth every scrap of respectability we possess.

From the second I understood where that mortice key would lead, there was no doubt how I would act. You need to understand that this was about more than scholarship or love of knowledge. It was not simply that this key led to a library. In my five decades, I've been in some truly extraordinary libraries. I've studied in the comforting medieval hall of Duke Humfrey's Library in the Bodleian. I've sat in vast reading rooms in the British Library and the US Library of Congress. I once spent a study leave basically living in the UK version of a Presidential Library, Gladstone's in North Wales. I slept with borrowed books. No, this was about the lure of mystery and secrets. From the very first day Albertus had shown us his Chaucer manuscript, we'd been initiated into a secret. Of us all, only Evie – as Loewe's assistant – knew the extent of his secret library, and she had characteristically remained schtum. It gave me satisfaction to think I now had the means – a key – to even-out the advantage she'd had over me for months. More than that, if Loewe had that rare Chaucer, what the hell else did he have hidden away? This was a man who'd spent his whole life among the highest echelons of society. The very thought of what he might have snuck away for himself, made me dizzy. It made me want to throw every bit of caution to the wind and run up the stairs and get into that room. When I finally got there, it did not disappoint. I've studied in so many stunning libraries in my life, yet for all their wonders, their millions of books, none of those experiences come close to what I witnessed in Albertus's house that Christmas Day. What I saw justified every bit of risk I took that afternoon.

Albertus was very pissed and, frankly, unsafe to stumble off to his kitchen to make coffee, but I let him. As he shuffled off to prepare the filter coffee, I shouted,

'Albertus, I'm just going to the loo.'

He mumbled something I couldn't make out, I lifted the key from the table, and slipped out of the sitting room and up the stairs. I had very little time, five minutes tops, but I already knew where I was heading. I'd been in Albertus's house on several occasions and leaving aside the lavatory and bathroom, a guest-room, and the room I reckoned was his bedroom, there was only one other room this key might unlock: the room at the top of the terraced house. I clattered up to the first floor, and, then, as quietly as possible, ascended the narrow staircase up to a floor I'd never been on before. There I found a door with a mortice lock that, even to my inexpert eyes, looked a perfect fit for the stolen key. I slipped it in, turned it, and heard a satisfying click as the lock opened. I opened the door and flicked on the light.

What did I expect to find behind that door? A blazing golden light, as if from heaven? The voice of God telling me to turn around and leave the Holy of Holies alone? I don't know. What I found was both more startling and more ordinary. Inside that small room, no more than ten feet square, were piles and piles of old manuscripts and ancient books. They covered most of the floor, and on the shelves, which covered every bit of wall-space, were hundreds of books, many neatly parcelled up. To my delight, these were arranged medieval style. That is, Albertus had placed the books with their fore-edges rather than their spines facing out. The practice had developed in the days of chained libraries and allowed books to be lifted down and opened without tangling the chains. Albertus's books weren't chained which made his decision to display the fore-edges pure affectation, yet I adored him for it. He was a true Medievalist.

The scent in that room ... There were traces of Albertus – his tobacco-rich and musky scent – as well as a faintest hint of Evie, of 24 Faubourg. In my drunken state, it took me every bit of self-control not to allow the thought of her and her access to this library to flare into envy. I was already more than pissed off with her. Behind their scents, was the warm smell of aged leather and vellum, the echo of centuries of touch and love and study. Just to be there, in the presence of so much work and skill and history, was overwhelming. I reckoned there must have been thousands of years' worth of work and devotion in that room. Indeed, to think that such a trove of history lay within a humble terraced house was beyond overwhelming. It was, frankly, disturbing. When Albertus had shown us that copy of *The Canterbury Tales* months before, surely none of us could have imagined that he possessed – either through theft, or borrowing or acquisition – so many priceless treasures. I didn't know whether to laugh or cry.

Carefully, I stepped inside, conscious that time was against me. How far along would Albertus have got with the coffee? Was he pouring the water on the grounds? Pressing down the plunger? Was he already waiting for me, his fingers drumming on the arm of his chair, waiting to confront me about the fact I'd taken his key? I stepped inside and flinched, expecting an alarm to go off. Of course, nothing of the sort happened. What was I doing here? It had been a symptom of my drunken state, and my nosiness and my envy, that I'd impulsively taken the key. Now I was in the room, I didn't know whether I wanted to leave or start taking books down off the shelves and consume them. It was all too much. Suddenly, I felt foolish. I shouldn't have come.

I was on the verge of forcing myself to leave, when I spotted something on the desk in the centre of the room. The desk was, unsurprisingly, covered in books and manuscripts, but a small section nearest the door had been cleared. On it was a small scrap of paper, and next to it a book I'd recognise anywhere. The paper grabbed my attention because it had one word on it – my name – written in Albertus's aged hand. 'Kitty', followed by a question mark. I stepped over piles of parcelled books, and looked down at it. What could it mean? I picked it up and turned it over. There was nothing on the back. I looked at Albertus's writing again, 'Kitty?', and laid the scrap down. Slowly, my hands shaking, I picked up the book next to it. My mouth was dry and my heart fluttered like a kingfisher's wings. I think I thought, 'At last.' I could barely control my hands' shaking as I opened it and looked down at what Albertus claimed was Geoffrey Chaucer's own hand. It was sloping and neat, the hand of a properly educated man of the Middle Ages. It might have been his. It might have been a scrivener's. Given the famous fact that no-one had ever definitely found a copy of his handwriting, in that moment I'm not sure it mattered. All that mattered was that I held possibly the earliest known copy of part of *The Canterbury Tales*.

How long had it lain on that table next to my name? The juxtaposition was tantalising. Of course, it could be a coincidence. Of course, it could mean any number of things. Of course, it could. But equally I reasoned, it could mean that Albertus intended it for me. In writing, 'Kitty?' was he asking himself whether he should make a gift of it to me? Just the thought of it made my already drunken mind spin again. I breathed deeply and slowly, trying to get a grip. 'Put it down,' I told myself, but I felt frozen. I looked down at the pages before me and read:

A knyght ther was, and that a worthy man,
That fro the tyme that he first bigan
To riden out, he loved chivalrie,
Trouthe and honour, fredom and curteisie.

I smiled. Perhaps these words were a sign. For, in that moment, I was inclined to read Albertus as the worthy knight, courteous and chivalrous. I thought of that picture of Dürer's knight in Ivo's room. Compared to the grim Ritter in that engraving, Albertus hardly seemed plausible – more Don Quixote than Lancelot. Yet, why shouldn't Albertus be the knight's natural heir? Aristocratic, truthful and generous. I thought of that line from the Knight's Tale, where Theseus, the noble narrator, talks of the Universe made to be 'kyndely enclyning'. Why shouldn't Albertus want me to have this book? Why shouldn't he wish to 'enclyne' his love towards me? It would have a natural justice to it.

I was very drunk, not just on fine wine, but on books. I stood there for God knows how long, holding the copy of *The Tales*, trying to decide what to do. I could not lay it down, nor could I take it. Then I heard a sound from the floor below, a clunk. It might have been anything – Albertus stumbling about or the old house creaking in the wind. Anything. I practically jumped out of my skin, though, and time began again. I knew I had to get out of that room and I had to decide what to do with the book in my hands. The rational part of my brain said, 'Put it down and leave.' The drunken, reckless part said, 'He wants you to have it anyway. Just take it.'

Somehow, I found the strength to lay it back down on the table next to the note with my name. I lay the book down and looked at it. The most magnificent copy of the most magnificent book written in the English language, and it could have been mine. I looked at it for a moment longer, congratulating myself on my self-control. And then I snatched it back up, slid it beneath the waistband of my trousers and walked quickly out of the room.

Chapter Nineteen

I know. I am a disgrace and I deserve your opprobrium. Firstly, for the way I'd treated that manuscript. Sliding it into my trouser waistband like that! Any Medievalist knows you never treat an old book that way. I cringe to think of it now. Back then, though, I had bigger issues. I'd failed the test of temptation. My own personal Apple had lain before me and I could not resist biting deep. But before you judge me too harshly, remember I was very drunk and weak, and, more than that, I maintain to this day that Albertus wanted me to have that book.

I ran down the stairs and, in a feeble attempt to cover my tracks, went into the loo and flushed it. Then, I returned downstairs, convinced my face revealed my double guilt – the guilt of effectively breaking into Albertus's private library and the guilt of taking the Chaucer. I need not have worried. I entered the sitting room to find no sign of Albertus. I laid his key back on the coffee table and went into the kitchen. I smiled when I saw he had fallen asleep in a rocking chair near the back door. The coffee remained unbrewed, and Albertus snored with abandon. He looked like a very pleased, sleeping walrus. An idea came to me. I went back into the sitting room, picked up the key and one of the throws off his sofa and returned to him. I lay the throw over Albertus, and slipped the key back into his waistcoat pocket. I reckoned he was so drunk, he was unlikely to remember he'd ever taken it out. I found a piece of scrap paper and a pen, wrote a brief note thanking him for an amazing lunch, and slipped away into the gathering gloom.

Riding back to college, my mind swirled as wildly as the trees which lined my route. I was drunk and quite unfit to ride, but that didn't stop me pedalling as fast as I could. My brain – befuddled on good food, wine and my own stupid daring – was divided between anxiety about my reckless act at Albertus's and a panoply of thoughts about Evie. Her face and the face of Albertus came in and out of focus in my drunken brain. After what Albertus had told me, I wanted to curse her for her conniving. I was also tempted, again and again, to stop and find somewhere to hide the book I'd taken. It was irrational, but I was a mess. By the time, I got back to college, I was thirsty, tired and headachy. I should have drunk a pint of water – my usual trick to avoid a hangover – and crawled into bed, but how could I? The more I thought about what I'd done, the stupider I felt. What had I been thinking? I sat on my bed, scared and angry. For my sins, I blamed Evie for what I'd done. I'd taken the book, I reasoned, because I was angry with her, because of what I'd found out at Albertus's. It had made me act against type. I'd lost control.

I sat on my bed and looked at the extraordinary book I'd taken. It was not, of course, conventionally beautiful. It lacked the gold-leaf and lapis lazuli with which medieval scribes created their visions of the Blessèd Virgin. Nor did it have illuminations of the Saints of such beauty and elegance one wants to weep. It was a simple handwritten document and yet … it was as close to heaven as I was likely to get. I held a miracle in my hand. Despite my anxiety and bewilderment, simply holding it began to calm me. Its beauty and power mastered me. As I held this book written by a long dead literary genius on animal skin it held me in return.

A new thought occurred to me. If I had taken this book without permission, had I really done anything worse than what Albertus must have done himself at some point? Technically, I'd stolen it, but what about him? On the day he'd first shown it to us, hadn't he shadily said he had it 'on loan'? A smirk had come across his face as he said it. Hadn't he sworn us to silence? This copy of Chaucer was priceless. It was so rare, no private individual should have it in his or her possession. I opened the pages and ran a finger over the cool vellum, and thought I might cry. In all my years of studying Chaucer and the Medieval, I'd never really come to terms with the power of its original artefacts. Yes, I'd seen original manuscripts, but I'd always been driven by what I could – forgive me – extract from them. I'd been that worst thing our universities now thrive on: a utilitarian. I'd been blind to what had lain before my very eyes. All that had changed at Littlemore. I'd come here not to further my academic career, but to be formed for service. It had, at a subconscious level, enabled scales to fall from my eyes and meeting Loewe and my new friends had been catalysts for something new. That new thing was summed up in what I held in my hands. I held a lost world. I held the handwritten thoughts of a mind almost immeasurably distant and alien to mine, and yet closer to me than ... well, my own flesh.

A good person, I suppose, would have got back on her bike and cycled back to Albertus's and returned the book. A good person would come up with some sort of half-arsed excuse for her moment of madness and asked Albertus for mercy. But what is a good person? Had Albertus been a good person when he'd taken this book on, as he put it, a 'special loan'? Had he been a good person when he'd taken all those manuscripts that he hid in his secret library? A story came to me, from Marie de France's *Fables*. Marie had been the *nom de plume* of a twelfth-century female poet who collected a series of French Lays and wrote up versions of *Aesop's Fables*. But, embedded within these famous stories, were one or two originals with a subversive feminist twist. The story that came to me was *The Woman and her Paramour*. In it, a cheating wife and her lover are caught in the act by her husband, but the wife is very smart. She persuades

164

him to examine a rain barrel with her before publicly accusing her of adultery. When the husband looks at the water within, the wife asks him if the reflection he sees is real. When he says no, she forces him to conclude that although he *thought* he saw her cheating, his vision is no more real than his reflection in water. Her quick wit (and her husband's slowness) preserve her marriage and her honour. It has always been one of my favourite medieval stories, a sign of what clever women can achieve. The coolest part is how Marie de France praises the wife because of her cunning.

As I sat there that Christmas night, I began to consider how that story might apply to me. The point of the story was not that the wife was praiseworthy because of her virtue (the usual medieval trope), but because of her capacity to handle a tricky situation with cleverness and spirit. I decided I needed to be like the wife: smart and confident rather than apologetic. So what if, arguably, I'd done wrong when I'd taken … stolen … Albertus's book? Was it really any worse than the stuff he'd done? And did I see him wracked with guilt? In a world of mirrors and tricks, what was truly real? All that mattered under such conditions, was what you could believe was true, and what you could get away with. Men like Albertus had ruled the world because of their confidence and boldness, not because of their virtue. Virtue, I reasoned, was just a way men had sought to keep women under control. If Albertus did challenge me over my actions, I guess I'd have to deal with that when it arose, but if he had no more right to it than me? It was his word against mine. That's what I told myself, anyway.

I lay down on my bed and held the book close to my chest. It felt strange and, dare I say it, good. What if Albertus had originally stolen it? It was hard to cast Albertus as a thief, but perhaps he would not have seen it that way. He was a collector and, as he saw it, it had been on special loan. Much as I sought to disengage my conscience, if it were stolen, of course I should not keep it. But to whom would

165

I go? The police? That could only bring heat – is that the term? – on Loewe. What was I supposed to say? 'Well, Inspector, I just found a six-hundred-year-old book lying around on the ground …' A book as rare as this would surely be easily traced and that would lead back to him. From the moment I'd first seen this book, I'd wanted to possess it for myself. I knew that the longer I kept it, the harder it would be to let it go. I lay in the dark and knew that the right thing to do would be to find a way to give the book up – to a library or an academic institution, to send it anonymously to a library. In taking it, however, I also received an unexpected, troubling truth: with a mixture of shock and fear, I realised that I would not be able to do the right thing. I would fight, perhaps even hurt someone, to keep hold of this book.

Chapter Twenty

Term arrived in a flurry of activity. Indeed, having become something of a hermit during the two weeks between Christmas and the start of term, I was a little overwhelmed by the clatter of returning ordinands, their 'Happy New Years', and the bumps of boxes and suitcases as they unloaded their lives and prepared to return to work.

Since that unforgettable Christmas night, I'd sought to get a grip on myself. I'd come to a mind about what to do regarding the book. In short, nothing. I decided that if the matter was raised by Loewe, I would deal with it then, but for now the Chaucer was mine. Yes, I had pangs of guilt and great trembling bouts of fear, but I'd pretty much convinced myself Loewe had wanted me to have the Chaucer all along. I decided to treat my stewardship of it as an extension of Albertus's original loan from God knows whom. I would study it, enjoy it and, in the fullness of time, pass it anonymously on to an institution. About other matters I was less sure. Once the New Year arrived, I began to dread the return of Evie. I now knew for sure that she'd used me as bait to get closer to Albertus. I could go for hours, days even, without thinking about this fact, but as soon as I did, a vile, vengeful mood came over me. I realised I'd always relied on the thought that, for all her faults, Evie – deep-down – was my friend. That she'd valued me for myself. Now, I'd convinced myself she'd never been anything of the sort.

As a Christian, I try to be good and forgiving. I want to be open to grace. I know that holding onto anger and resentment does one no good and eats one up in the end. In the depths of the hurt Evie had inflicted on me, I tried to forgive her. I petitioned God, over and over. I knew it would make life easier if I could forgive Evie for her conniving. After all, we had to survive the best part of three years in this institution together, we had to find some sort of peace. Even if we stopped hanging out, which happens all the time in academic and college settings, we had to find a way to be together in class, most particularly Albertus's class. Yet, I could not forgive her. I could not let my annoyance go.

I was also desperate to see the others, and dreading it too. They were my friends, my best friends and we had a bond that others could not comprehend. Richard's final words – cautioning me against body mortification – had given me pause, but there was no doubt that our shared secret tied us together. And more than that, in their different ways, I bloody loved them. I wanted to see Piers and Ivo bickering good-naturedly again. I wanted to smoke cigarettes and drink with Charlie. I wanted to taste Richard's food and see what outrageous wine he'd turn up with next.

When I heard a knock on my door that first day of Hilary term, I was cast back to my first day at Littlemore: Evie standing there, bright as summer, saying, 'Hallo'. I felt embarrassed to admit how flattered I felt about her friendliness. What if it were her knocking? I sat as quietly as I could, hoping my petitioner would go away. The knock came again and a voice said,

'Kitty? Are you there?' It was not Evie or one of the others, but Jane Sampson. I opened the door and Jane said,

'Oh, Kitty. Thank God!' She looked frantic, though given that Jane had a gift for making a crisis out of the smallest drama, that might not mean much. Yet I sensed that for once, something serious might be taking place.

'What is it?' I had been napping on and off all afternoon and I could hear the sleep in my voice.

'It's Evie,' Jane said. 'Will you come?'

'What's the matter with her?' I asked, as I allowed myself to be led from my room.

'I don't know. She's in the chapel. She's behaving very strangely.'

Jane gave me that look, the one that said, is there something she (and by implication, the whole college) should know about? It implied a question: was Evie having problems with alcohol or drugs? At that moment, I felt sick of Littlemore, the way it drove people mad. Not mad with loneliness or frustration, though it certainly could do that. No. The way it could drive people to a kind of pastoral frenzy, where they wanted to test out their caring skills in front of the whole college. I decided, then and there, that whatever was up with Evie, I'd get her out of sight as soon as possible. I might be furious with her, but she deserved better than a bloodsucker like Jane Sampson circling around her.

As we drew close to the chapel, Jane filled me in on the story as best she could. Apparently, Evie had come back late that morning and, after lunch – which she, like I, had skipped – had appeared in the chapel while Jane's friend Audrey Court had been at prayer. According to Audrey, Evie had been on the lookout for Roddy Peplow. Apparently, having found Roddy in the Sacristy, the next anyone saw of Evie was about an hour later when she was found in – as Jane put it – a 'strange state' in the chapel. She was crying extravagantly, but claimed she was fine. She refused to be comforted and Roddy was nowhere to be found. Jane's story struck me as odd. First, Evie and Roddy got on well, but not so well that she would have made a beeline for him as soon as she'd got back into college. Odder still was the implication that Evie's encounter with Roddy had left her distraught. Had Roddy done something to her? It was absurd. Roddy was a drunk and he was not interested in women. Jane's phrase – 'crying extravagantly' – suggested another image, that of Margery Kempe, Evie's medieval heroine, who engaged in 'ugly crying' as a way to demonstrate her love for her Saviour. Was Evie over-identifying with her heroine? That seemed implausible too. Jane broke in on my reverie and explained that, since I was Evie's best friend, she had come looking for me. I think what she meant was that everyone else was a bit scared to approach Evie. If that was true, I was grateful that no one had yet thought to take the matter up the college food-chain. If Evie was having some sort of an episode, it seemed to me that it was better if we kept the authorities away from it for now.

Whenever I open the door of a church I have a bizarre sense that something, someone, has just escaped through another exit. That I've missed a presence and something tremendous has left me alone. Even though I was fully prepared to find Evie inside, this sensation hit me once again despite the fact I saw Evie lying flat on her face on the chancel steps. Jane was right. It did seem very strange. Perhaps she was merely drunk, though that itself was something I'd never expect of Evie in the middle of the afternoon. I told Jane to stay near the door and walked up towards the chancel.

'Evie?' I said softly. 'Evie, it's Kitty.'

I heard Evie murmur something incomprehensible, but she didn't move. Oh Lord, what if she'd had a stroke? That was possible, wasn't it, even for people in their early twenties? I knelt beside her and gently pulled her hair back from off her face. She looked like she was sleeping. In the month since I'd seen her, I'd forgotten how beautiful she was. Seeing her face in profile somehow amplified that effect. Her chestnut hair was warm and rich in the afternoon light and her pale skin looked soft, almost downy. She might be a saint or a fallen angel. Seeing her like this, I almost forgot I was angry with her. Like so many young people before me, I was inclined to confuse beauty with virtue.

Quite suddenly, her left eye opened and looked intently at me. It opened so quickly and sharply it was almost reptilian and its green hue only amplified that effect. Evie stared and focussed. Then, recognising me, she smiled and said, with a kind of drunken, slurring warmth,

'Kitty! Darling!'

Despite myself, I smiled back. Her tone was sweet and charming. She then tried to push herself upright, and slipped back down onto the chancel stone, face first, with a slap.

'Oops,' she said. Clearly and reassuringly she was drunk and, like many drunken people, whatever she'd drunk spared her any obvious injury. 'A hand?' she added, weakly.

As she pushed again I lent my support, and eventually we found ourselves sat side by side, looking back down towards the main entrance. Jane, I noted, had slipped out of the chapel. Evie slumped against me and rested her head on my shoulder. Given the state she was in, I expected her to stink of alcohol, but she smelt of her usual fragrant perfume. It must, I decided, be drugs then. I said,

'Come on, Evie, old girl. Let's get you to bed.'

'Old girl,' Evie repeated, softly. 'You are sweet, sweet Kitty Kat.' She giggled at this.

'Are you ready?' I said. 'Come on, I'll help you.'

I helped her slide her right arm around my shoulders. 'Okay,' I said, 'up we go.'

Before we could move however, she said, 'Kitty, I'm scared.' It was such a forlorn and lonely voice. Like a sad five-year old's.

'Shhhh,' I said, soothingly. 'It'll be all right, once you're back in your room.'

Still she resisted movement. 'No, listen, Kitty. I have to make it stop.' She looked at me, bleary eyed. 'We have to make it stop, Kit Kit Kitty Kat.' She said this quite seriously, then quite suddenly, she giggled. I began to think perhaps we needed to call an ambulance. Jane was right. Evie was behaving beyond oddly.

That was not the only odd thing. Perhaps I should not admit

this, but at that moment, I found her almost unutterably desirable. Her strange skittishness, which seemed to capture so much of her charm, combined with her beauty, thrilled me. It reminded me of how much – despite the growing rift between us – I still desired her. I wanted to kiss her and I wanted her to kiss me back. And, if Evie had not been in such a vulnerable state, I might not have cared about making a pass at her in a public place.

'You have no idea what I'm talking about, have you?' she said, slowly.

'What have you taken, Evie?'

'Just had a drink with Roddy. Can you take me home, please?'

'Come on then.' I helped her to her feet, feeling very unsure about not bringing medical help to bear. We slowly walked down the nave, Evie leaning heavily on me. Once outside, we passed Jane, who gave a look which said, 'Can I help?' I shook my head and silently mouthed, 'She'll be fine … Drink!' I was sure getting Evie up the stairs would have been easier with Jane's help, but I could not bear the thought of her cooing and soothing over Evie; I wanted to avoid Jane's nosiness. I reckoned that Evie herself would want to be with someone she knew and trusted.

Once we were outside, the fresh air seemed to pick Evie up a bit. She breathed in deeply and smiled again. 'That's better,' she said. 'You're a good person, Kitty.'

'Are you sure you've only been drinking, Eve?'

'Bloody Roddy,' she replied. 'Pink gin in the afternoon!'

As we reached the stairwell that led up to Evie's room I said,

'What did you want to see him for anyway?'

She laughed, darkly. 'Just wanted him to ease my worried mind.' She sang the second half of the sentence.

'Is that Eric Clapton?' She giggled. 'Did he ease it?'

'No. He was far too pissed.' She said this in such a way that it was unclear whether she was speaking of Roddy or Eric Clapton.

We entered her room and, as I manoeuvred Evie onto her bed, she smiled at me.

'You know you really are sweet, Kitty.' She reached up and stroked my face and I felt a surge of electricity. This was the first time anyone had reached out and touched me kindly or gently since Albertus had kissed me on the cheek on Christmas Day. I'd attended a couple of Masses since then, but they'd been 8.00 am BCP services. No touching and no sharing of the Peace. I'd sneak in just before the service and leave without shaking the priest's hand at the end. I felt sudden heat come into my cheek. Jesus's words to Mary Magdalene came into my head, '*Noli me tangere*'.

'Would you like to kiss me?' It was, like many of Evie's comments that day, artless. I felt myself blush a bit. I almost said, yes. She added, as if understanding my reticence, 'You could just lie on the bed with me. Like we used to.'

'I should go and get some help.' I was shocked by the scratchiness, the emotion, in my voice.

'I'll be fine, now I'm in bed,' said Evie. She did seem more at ease, more herself.

'Technically, you're on the bed,' I said, trying to lighten the mood. She giggled again.

I noticed her handbag on the floor next to the bed. A petite Louis Vuitton rainbow shoulder bag. The zipper was undone and inside I saw a tiny purse, a packet of Marlboro Lights, a box of matches, and a packet of prescription medicine. I could see the brand name very clearly. *Remeron*. I'd not heard of it. The end of the box was open and a blister sheet peeked out. Next to the box was a printed piece of paper which looked like the info that accompanies medicines, listing their side-effects. Evie looked very peaceful and had closed her eyes. I saw that behind her, resting on the bedspread was Mr Chatalon. Beneath him, mostly obscured, was a book with a cracked and faded black cover. I couldn't make out what it was for only a small part of the cover protruded. It might, I thought, be a diary, though it looked much too old for that to be likely. I considered picking up Mr Chatalon, partly so that I might slide him under Evie's arm, partly to get a closer look at the book. It would be fascinating if it were a diary or commonplace book. I didn't want to disturb Evie however, and I also fancied a closer look at that leaflet in her bag. I reached into it and scooped the leaflet up. Evie didn't stir.

It was clear that *Remeron* was used for the treatment of depression, suicidal thoughts, and anxiety and panic. It was very powerful and had a list of potential side-effects that covered the best part of the A4 sheet. I studied Evie's face again. It was hard to believe someone like her could be depressed or anxious, yet, now that I looked closer I could see that her make-up was quite artfully applied. There were bags under her eyes that she'd softened with foundation and she was paler than I remembered her. She looked like she'd lost a little weight. I read on, and saw there were contra-indications for alcohol. Apparently, *Remeron* could make the taker 'drowsy', especially in the early stages of use, and alcohol could exacerbate that effect. Was that what had happened? I wondered if she just needed to sleep things off and concluded that that was the most likely case. I reckoned that the likely chain of events was that she'd only recently got this prescription, taken her regular dose, and gone off to see Roddy. Inevitably, he would have had drink and, to be sociable, Evie would have shared a pink gin with him. This had led to an extreme, unanticipated reaction: tears and excitement, then sleepiness and confusion.

As I unfolded the leaflet out fully, a smaller piece of paper fluttered to the floor. I reached down and picked it up. It was a piece of lined paper about three-inches square, with a note written in Ivo's careful hand. It was undated and unsigned. It read,

'Evie, Caution! Now is not the time to get carried away. Remember your Chaucer: Ye been as bolde as is Bayard the blinde,

That blundreth forth, and peril castest noon.' Please! Now is not the time to get carried away. Beware the wages of sin!'

I read the note again, trying to make sense of it. The line from Chaucer was easy enough to figure out. 'As bold as the blind bay horse, that blunders on and does not think of danger.' Ivo was, obviously, issuing Evie with a warning though about what, I could not see. I thought the quote was probably from the *Canon's Yeoman's Tale*, which concerned a pilgrim who arrives late to the party heading towards Canterbury; this pilgrim, a Canon, is – according to his yeoman servant – an alchemist of ill repute. When the Yeoman reveals this, the Canon runs off. The latter part of the tale comprises the yeoman's account of another Canon who gulls a priest into believing that he can make silver from base metal. The yeoman suggests that the pursuit of alchemy has destroyed his life, perhaps even given him lead poisoning. His moral is that we should not seek certain secrets as it's like picking a fight with God.

I looked up at Evie, more than a little confused by this piece of information. Given my meeting with Ivo and Charlie the previous term, perhaps it was some reference to Ivo and Evie's relationship. Perhaps he was simply telling her that they needed to cool their relationship. Then again, given that the story from which the quote was taken had a moral about not dabbling too deeply with certain secrets, perhaps Ivo was telling Evie not to get too deep into … what? Our penitential practices? Perhaps, though of all us, Ivo was by far the most committed to rigorous discipline. And what did he mean by the wages of sin? They were death, weren't they? Was Ivo implying that death lay along the path she was following? That seemed over-the-top. I decided I was reading too much into this note. I thought it wise simply to file the information for now and resist speculation.

Evie seemed to be sleeping quite peacefully, her chest rising and falling rhythmically. I looked across at Mr Chatalon again, considering what I might do. That book looked very interesting. I might have sat there for thirty seconds or twenty minutes. Ultimately, I folded Ivo's note back into the drug leaflet and replaced the leaflet back into the bag. I stood up and looked down at Evie's soft face. I wanted to kiss it. I thought of Ivo's note, 'Now is not the time to get carried away', and thought, 'Very wise.' I looked longingly at her lips, and left. I then went down to the college offices and told the Administrator, Hilary Queensferry about Evie. Queenie, as she was affectionately known by all at Littlemore, had been a fixture in the college since time immemorial. Albertus once joked that the founder of the college, a noted amateur archaeologist, had 'dug her up in Ur of the Chaldees'. She was, however, no hard-baked fossil, but kind and generous, and full of good sense and proportion. When students or staff were throwing toys out of prams, she could be relied upon to say, 'Let me have a look at that,' and within ten minutes most problems were solved. A few years before my time, a college wag – a gifted caricaturist – had made a sketch of Queenie receiving the Nobel Peace Prize. She'd had it framed and put on the wall above her desk.

I told Queenie that Evie had fallen ill in the Chapel, but that I'd tucked her up in bed. Queenie, who always heard about everything, said she'd received a report that Evie had been, quote, 'behaving exuberantly near the altar'. I explained that I thought it was a one-off and said something about how she'd spent time in the company of Roddy. Queenie understood what I'd meant without further comment. I said that I would keep an eye on Evie, but I didn't think it was anything serious. I promised to keep Queenie in the loop and she said she'd appreciate that. Then I went in search of Ivo. When he was nowhere to be found, I looked for the others. They too clearly were not back on campus yet.

I went back to my room and wrote notes to each of my friends inviting them to come to mine for drinks that evening. I checked over these notes carefully. I never trusted the security of the college pigeon-holes. However, I was sure that should anyone read one by mistake or out of nosiness, they could not think I wanted to speak to my friends for any other reason than having new term drinks. I placed the cards in my friends' pigeon-holes, grabbed some cake from the refectory, and returned to my room to wait. While I did so, I thought of Evie. It occurred to me that I should have gone back to check on her. That's what I'd said I'd do. That's what a friend would have done. Instead, I sat on the end of my bed, watching the weak sun disappear behind the trees.

Chapter Twenty-one

I'd invited everyone to come around 7pm. I had no idea if anyone would. I was unsure what I would say if and when they came. I'd been starved of company for weeks, and part of me just wanted to see their faces. I think a bit of me wanted to show off new intelligence the others didn't have. I also wanted to process this new intelligence with people I could trust.

At seven, there was a sharp rap at my door. It was Richard, grinning and holding a bottle of Red Breast Irish Whiskey, ten years old.

'You grew a beard,' I said, somewhat obviously, as he loped in.

'Like an old seadog.' He smiled again, and I couldn't imagine how I'd managed to live without his presence for the past month.

'It suits you,' I said. And it did. It lent his boyish features a distinguished air.

Almost as soon as Richard was over the threshold, Ivo, Piers and Charlie appeared in quick succession. Ivo had a slight tan, the effect I assumed of being in the Austrian Alps. Charlie, as ever, was breath-taking. One never quite got used to her effortless beauty, but a month away from it, made one even less immune. Piers stepped up to me enthusiastically, gave me a kiss on both cheeks, said 'Hello, lovely', and passed me a Harrods bag containing a box of mini shortbread rounds, some Scarpatto panettone, a bottle of crème de cassis, and a few bars of Valrhona chocolate.

'Party food,' he said, by way of explanation.

It was like they'd never gone away. Charlie regaled us with tales of

New York – of snow, and Christmas Day at St John the Divine; of how her father had acquired a new girlfriend, Freya, who was only three years older than herself. We joked about how Charlie would be able to officiate at her father's own wedding if he and Freya waited a couple of years. Ivo was the most subdued of our happy party. I always struggled to read him, but wondered if he and Richard had been arguing again about prayer and mortification. Ivo did perk up, though, when I told them about my Christmas Day adventure with Albertus. Most of the conversation concerned what on earth the confirmed bachelor had served up for us both. The oddest thing about this gathering, however, was how little Evie was missed. No one mentioned her. I thought again of how I'd promised to check in to see that she was all right. If she were gone for good, would this be how it was? A group of friends who had easily forgotten her. We were having such a convivial time that though I wanted to share my news about Evie, I was guiltily aware that mentioning it would put a dampener on the evening.

In a pause between talking about our schedules for the coming term and my carefully edited account of my vacation at Littlemore, someone mentioned Roddy Peplow. This seemed as good a moment as any to say my piece.

'Speaking of Roddy,' I said, 'did you hear about Evie's adventures with him today?' Perhaps I imagined it, but I sensed a beat in the room. Just a moment, as the quality of attention changed. I recalled that comment of Evie's from the first day we'd had tea in Luxford: 'It all seemed a bit staged.' I had that sense again, as if everyone had been waiting for this moment, had been practising their reaction.

Richard said, 'No. Do tell.'

What I told them will not stand as my finest hour. In justification, let me say, that I'd reached a point in my relationship with Evie where I wanted to show off a bit and give her a bit of a mauling in front of my friends. I needed to let off some steam. I wanted to aggrandize myself among them. Did I mean to go as far as I did? No. Once I

179

started, however, I couldn't stop. Despite – perhaps because of – the encounter between us earlier in the day when Evie has been so out of it, once I'd started having a go at Evie I couldn't reel myself back in. I started off by keeping, pretty much, to the facts. They needed little embellishment, after all. When I knew my audience was gripped, I let rip. I told them that, by the time I'd got her out of the chapel, Evie had been raving on about how the church abused women and how she wasn't respected enough by her friends. By the time I began to speak about Evie's use of powerful anti-depressants, I was flowing, though I'd edited out all reference to Ivo's note, of course. My voice – usually so quiet and restrained – rose and rose. I remember calling Evie a 'stupid, selfish bitch' who was going to bring the whole college into disrepute. I called her a second-rate scholar who fucked people to get ahead. I said she wasn't cut out to be a priest.

When I'd finished, I looked from face to face in the low light of my room. Perhaps if the main light had been on I might have spotted something. As it was, I discerned nothing. It was like looking at the shadowed faces in a late Rembrandt. All I remember was Ivo lifting his cigarette to his mouth and taking a drag, the tip of his cigarette glowing in the half-light and giving him an almost demonic aspect. Finally, Charlie said,

'Remeron?'

'Do you know it?' I said.

'Well, yes,' she replied, somewhat coyly. We all looked at her hungrily, rather like vultures around a corpse. Realising we expected some sort of confession, she said, 'Oh, not me.' She laughed, nervously. 'Freya.' When none of us said anything, she went on. 'You all know I've had problems. Well, that does tend to mean one is alert to problems in others and, I don't mind admitting, I have a kind of ex-patient's interest in other people's medications.

'Freya and I got talking late one night. Like all models, she's had to deal with unwanted fans and paps, and she started telling me about how she copes. Apparently, it's the new thing. A wonder drug. All the girls are on it.'

'Is it dangerous?' said Richard. Ivo gave him a rather filthy look, as if to say, 'Of course, it's dangerous,' but Richard either ignored him or didn't see it.

'What do you think?' said Charlie, tartly.

There was a long pause, then, Richard said, 'I guess Evie isn't as robust as she makes out.'

Charlie made a little 'huh' sound, indicating her disbelief.

'Oh, come on, Charlie,' said Richard, sharply. 'Maybe we all need to dial down the medieval discipline.'

'And maybe,' said Ivo, with quiet menace, 'Kitty's right and Evie's just a fucking fruitcake. I always suspected it.'

For a second, I thought Richard was going to hit Ivo. He looked that furious. The tension which had been simmering all night was ready to break through. Then I saw a kind of cold fear spread across Richard's face. As he attempted to stare out Ivo, he shrank, like a dog unable to stand up to the authority of its master. As Ivo glared at him, his grin a leer, Richard cowered. I saw Piers grab Ivo's taut left arm, ready to beat Richard, and hold it tight.

Piers – never really one for swearing – said, 'Richard, for fuck's sake. Not now.' It was impressive. It stopped a chain of events that might have led to Richard and Ivo scuffling in my tiny room. Of all the three boys, Piers was never one for direct assertion. He was the persuader and it was quite shocking to experience him being so forceful.

My room was in the oldest and least well maintained part of the College. In addition to leaky, single-glazed windows and badly fitting doors, its corridors were uneven and given to squeaky floorboards. The squeaks and groans of the house drove us crackers. As Piers told Richard to shut up, I heard a floorboard creak near my door. Later I was amazed at my presence of mind, but my immediate reaction was to hold a finger to my mouth to indicate silence. Everyone stopped. I looked down at the gap beneath the base of my door and the floor. Over Christmas I'd finally succumbed and bought a simple blue draught excluder, but tonight I'd forgotten to lay it across. Light bled through from the corridor into the subdued lighting of my room. I waited, I'm not sure for what. Another creak? A voice? I was sat at the foot of my bed, nearest to the door. In that moment, the gap between door and floor looked enormous, though it can't have been more than a couple of inches. I was so tense I almost gasped when a shadow partially blocked the light.

The shadow just stayed there. Later I would claim that in the heightened atmosphere of the moment, I could hear everything; not simply my own heartbeat, or my own breathing, but the breathing of everyone in the room: Ivo's, slow and steady, Piers and Richard, both fast and ragged, Charlie's, barely perceptible. I'd say I could hear breathing from beyond the door, edgy and troubled. There's one aural fact I am sure of: I heard a quiet sob, like that of a little girl. A little girl in a Victorian novel. I heard sobbing and saw a shadow cast by a pair of feet, just beyond my door. The tension became intolerable. I wanted the figure beyond the door to knock, or say something or just do something. I wanted it to stop simply standing there, sobbing. If something didn't happen soon, I knew I would have to get up and open the door. Just at the point I was about to break, the person creaked away down the corridor.

Everyone in the room looked at each other. None of us spoke. We were like conspirators, almost found out by the police. I looked at Ivo and silently he gestured towards the door with a nod of his head. Slowly I stood up, painfully aware of the creak of springs on the mattress and practically tip-toed over to the door. I turned the lock and peered outside. There was no one there, of course. The only trace they left behind was a faint one – a trace of their scent, 24 Faubourg.

Not that it was necessary for me to smell it for me to know exactly who had been stood outside my door, sobbing. Sobbing, like almost every other activity of the body, is characteristic to the body from which it issues. Just like laughter or speech. The sobbing I'd heard could only have come from one person: Evie. And I was sure she'd heard everything.

Chapter Twenty-two

I dreaded the proper beginning of term. I would have to face Evie, as would the others. It seemed beyond credibility to believe that Evie had not known the rest of us had been in my room that night. The very fact that she would know that and yet we'd done our level best to conceal our presence in the room, was surely conclusive evidence to her not only that we'd been talking about her behind her back, but I'd done a hatchet job on her. Indeed, I was sure she'd heard every word. She must know she'd been called a bitch, a fruitcake and someone who needed to fuck others to get on. I'd cast aspersions on her call to priesthood. Of all of us, I felt this most acutely, not least because, ostensibly, I was closest to her. I'd shown her kindness when she'd been stoned, but had been two-faced. I was the one who had gone into the chapel and persuaded her to calm down and go back to her room. Within twenty-four hours everyone at Littlemore would have known this fact and both Evie and I would be the subject of gossip. If it was seen that she and I were not getting on, that would only feed the gossip machine.

That the chapel incident had immediately generated college gossip was proven the next morning when we had our first Community Meeting of the new term. I tried to time my entrance for the last moment, hoping that would limit opportunities for people to ask intrusive questions. This was a good plan, but one subverted by circumstance. The meeting was due to start at 10am, and I slipped into the room at 9.56. The first thing I noticed was a quietening of the hubbub in the room. I really don't think this was just me being paranoid. I saw Michael Shaw and Chris Eastwood whisper as I walked past them, looking at me out of the corner of their eyes and Jane Sampson and Audrey Court gestured for me to join them, indicating a free chair next to them. It would have entailed pushing my way through a bit of a crowd, so I had a ready-made excuse for not heading in their direction, even if I'd wanted to. The second thing I noticed was the absence of Ivo, Piers, Charlie and Richard. I searched the room for them, but they were nowhere to be seen. Perhaps they'd had the same idea as me and were timing their entrance to the very last moment. Evie was absent too.

I sat down as near to the back as I could. One of the problems of being at an Anglican training institution is that members of the Church of England will always fill a church or room from the back forwards. Most of the decent seats, therefore, were already taken. I squeezed myself onto a decaying sofa next to a second-year ordinand, Luke Cribbins. This struck me as opportune. Luke was a sweet young man in his late twenties, an ordinand from Norfolk who was studying for the first time in his life. Rather gangly, with dusty-yellow hair, he had a constantly bewildered expression on his face, as if the world even in its most mundane forms was beyond comprehension. He was one of the young men who was almost universally popular, not because of any great charisma, but because he was a kindly listener and avoided any distinctive opinions. A dull man, and, therefore, in a risk-averse organisation like the Church, a trusted one.

At 10am, there was still no sign of Evie or the others. Miles Goodhap jumped to his feet with characteristic vigour and to widespread groans announced that that morning's guest speaker, the Dean of Hereford – an old boy – had been delayed, and we should talk amongst ourselves for a few minutes. It was precisely the thing I was dreading. At least I was sat next to Luke.

'How was your Christmas, Luke?' I said.

He looked at me with his big, trusting face.

'Not bad,' he said, in an appealing Norfolk accent. Without bothering to respond conventionally by asking me about my vacation, he said, 'Is it true that Evie had a breakdown?'

My heart sank. If the likes of Luke were asking questions like this, the news must have spread far and wide.

'That's an exaggeration, Luke. She just had a bit of an episode. You shouldn't listen to gossip.'

'She looked terrible when she came in earlier.'

I studied him carefully, trying to process his remark. In profile, the top half of his face was surprisingly handsome and well-proportioned. Below his aquiline nose, however, his bottom lip dropped down, creating the impression of stupidity.

'Evie was here?'

'Oh yeah. About ten minutes before you came in. She looked terrible. She wanted to send her apologies to Miles.' Before I could respond, he added, 'I would have thought you'd have known.'

I don't know why that comment particularly rankled, but without thinking I said, 'Why?'

'Well ...' Luke looked even more awkward than usual. Pale people struggle to blush, I've noticed, but Luke managed the feat. 'Well ... you and Evie. You are ... you are going out with each other.' His speech, which had begun hesitantly concluded with an air of surety.

'What?!?' I was so stunned that I didn't know what else to say.

Quickly, Luke said, 'Not that I mind ...' He gulped, his Adam's Apple bobbing awkwardly in his neck. 'I mean, it's cool by me. It's your business.'

'Luke ... Evie and I are not going out with each other.'

The look he gave me was of complete disbelief. He said,

'Are you sure?'

I laughed. 'Yes, I'm sure.' There was awkward pause. Then I said, 'Luke, where on earth did you get that idea from?'

'I thought everyone in college knew,' he said, blandly.

'Really?' The noise in the Common Room was becoming quite tremendous. I saw Miles get to his feet again and I was sure he was about to clap his scoutmaster hands and attempt to bring us to order. The Common Room door opened and the Principal entered, leading a man I presumed was the Dean of Hereford. The Dean was tall, with a slim, angular face. The most notable thing about his appearance, however, was his greying moustache and goatee beard combination which gave him the aspect of a seventeenth-century aristocrat. One felt he only need put on a wide-brimmed, feathered hat, climb up on a horse and be off to lead the King's Cavalry in defence of Royal Oxford for the image to be complete. I realised I had seconds before Miles brought the room to order. I said,

'Luke. Please. Tell me. Who said Evie and I are an item?'

Miles called the room to order and clapped his hands. Luke scratched his cheek, then said,

'I think it was Charlie. Yeah, it was definitely Charlie.'

Very loudly, I said, 'What?!' at precisely the moment the sound in the room died. My question just hung there, sounding ridiculously shrill. Everyone, including the Principal and the Dean of Hereford, looked at me. There were ripples of nervous laughter. I wished I knew how to dematerialise. I felt colour and heat flow into my cheeks.

'Anything we can help you with, Kitty?' said the Principal, in his plummy, sarcastic voice.

It was a quite horrifying hour. The Dean, who had a reputation as an engaging speaker as well as someone who'd consistently been refused a bishopric because he was in an openly-gay relationship, might – for all I knew – have been brilliant. I didn't take in a word. All I could think about was Charlie. Could she have spread rumours around college about me? Surely Luke must be mistaken. Yet, he was not the gossiping sort. One of the reasons everyone liked him was because he kept his own counsel so carefully. If Jane Sampson

187

had said it was Charlie, I could have dismissed her out-of-hand. Not so Luke. My mind flip-flopped. One moment I'd dismiss Luke's statement as ridiculous, the next I was sure he'd simply repeated hearsay, and, then, I'd accept his claim without question. I was stuck in a loop.

I got out of the Common Room as soon as I could. Once the Dean had finished, I told Miles I had a splitting headache and left. As I walked away, I heard one or two murmurs. By leaving early I would only add to the rumour mill, but I simply had to get out of that airless room. I imagined the gossips, 'Kitty didn't look very happy did she?' 'Do you think she and Evie have split up?' 'I bet Kitty's the reason Evie got stoned yesterday', and so on. I pictured Jane whispering and laughing behind my back. I realised why Jane had come looking for me the previous day: she'd thought I was Evie's partner.

Outside, the wind whipped freezing rain against the stone and brick of the buildings. I didn't even bother to go back to my room to collect a coat. I simply left my seat in the Common Room and took the shortest route towards Charlie's. I just had to have this out with her. I was soaked and furious by the time I arrived at Charlie's building. Macavity, the Shanks's old tom, was sat in a small dry patch outside the entrance to the flats. I was so angry I almost kicked him. He must have sensed my antipathy because he hissed malevolently as I passed. I dripped great globules of water on the stone stairs as I clattered up to Charlie's apartment, but I was beyond caring. When I reached her door I thwacked it so hard my hand throbbed. Charlie was usually prompt in answering, a sign of neediness I'd always thought. When there was no response, I rapped again, almost swearing at the pain in my knuckles. In frustration I shouted, 'Charlie? Open the door.' I was about to leave and head towards Ivo or Piers' rooms, when the door opened a crack.

When Charlie saw it was me, she opened the door wider. She was dressed in a red silk dressing gown with a dragon print on it. I was about to launch into my speech, such as it was, when her appearance gave me pause. Sure, she looked like she'd just got out of bed, but I saw something else on her face other than half-removed mascara and eyeliner. It was pain. She tugged her right dressing-gown arm down over her wrist, as if there was a cut or bruise on her right arm. I guessed she was basically naked beneath the wrap. Through her sleepy, pained eyes, she assessed me coldly. I must have looked a frightful sight. She wrapped her right arm around her waist, as if about to stroke her belly. I wondered if she'd just come on.

She scratched her scalp with her left hand and said, without a hint of warmth, 'What do you want?'

I was surprised. We were friends and in the very least I'd expected her to ask me inside. Her coolness triggered my anger.

'What have you been telling people about Evie and me?'

This question was clearly so unanticipated, she laughed. It wasn't a sarcastic laugh. Indeed, it was quite indulgent. It defrosted her, at least momentarily.

'Me? What am I supposed to have said?'

'That Evie and me,' I said, awkwardly. 'Well, that we're an item.'

She visibly relaxed, leant again the doorframe and said, 'Oh, bloody hell, Kit.' She shook her head. 'Do you really think I'd do that? After everything I've said about Evie?'

'Luke Cribbins said you'd told him.' The words sounded brittle, petulant and childish. Teenaged.

'Luke Cribbins? God's teeth, Kitty, why would I even speak to Luke Cribbins? He's so nervous around me he practically vomits every time he sees me.'

'So what are you saying?'

'Well, don't take this the wrong way, Kit, but I think you could do with a break from this place. It's all got a bit … intense.'

'So where did he get that rumour from?'

'Who knows? People make up all sorts of bull. He got it from Evie herself for all I know. It's the kind of crappy thing she'd do.'

* * *

As I walked back to main college, I was gripped by two thoughts. Firstly, I had to speak to Evie. My hunch was that Charlie was right: spreading rumours was precisely the sort of thing Evie could do. Did I believe that she had spread the rumour about us? I was unsure. Charlie's words, that it had all got a bit intense for me at Littlemore, hit home. By staying in college over Christmas I'd not found a way to refresh or recharge my energies. I'd failed to get any perspective. The bizarre end to the previous term, marred by fever and illness, overhung into the new year. Yet, given Charlie's words, I felt compelled to find Evie and clear the air about this rumour. I had to get a sense of whether, among her other sins, she'd spread a frankly silly, but irritating, rumour about us around college.

The other thing on my mind was of a different order. As I walked away from her flat, I was absolutely convinced Charlie was not alone. How did I know? How do we ever know these things? I suppose one piece of evidence lay in the fact that Charlie didn't invite me over the threshold, though that might have been for a dozen reasons. We'd had a pretty boozy time the night before and it was entirely possible she had carried on back at her flat. Her flat might have looked as bombed-out as my room. Yet as I walked in the direction of Evie's, I was certain that someone else was with Charlie. It's tempting to say, though it would be overdramatic to say it out loud, that behind the stench of stale cigarettes and old alcohol was the smell of sex. A faint tang of sea and salt. Whatever was the case, I was convinced that as I left Charlie's I was leaving a site of private triumph. Or failure. Either way, Charlie didn't want to share it.

If I was certain there was someone else with Charlie, I was equally certain, when I knocked on her door, that Evie's room was empty. It gave off a hollow chime. I weighed up my options. I could wait. Given how soaked I was, that was hardly attractive. Alternatively, I thought Evie might be in one of three places: the library, the chapel or Luxford House. Fifteen minutes later, having checked the library and the chapel to no avail, and properly dressed for the weather, I headed towards Luxford House. It was where I had always thought she would be. She had a key to Albertus's rooms, after all. Yet, when I arrived at Luxford, there were no signs of life. The front door was locked and all the lights were off. I suppose Evie might have been inside, but it seemed improbable. It looked like Evie was not on campus. Maybe she had the right idea. I thought about getting in my car and driving off somewhere to clear my head. I tramped off in the direction of the car park, then realised I didn't have my keys. I considered going to the bicycle sheds and jumping on the old bike I'd bought in a flush of enthusiasm the previous September. It was not a day for cycling, however. The rain had eased, but it was still cold and grim and the wind was penetrating. Yet, now I was here, there was something satisfying about being outside and alone.

Almost without thinking I began tramping off down High Street in the direction of the old Asylum – now re-branded Easter Villas – and the panopticon. The panopticon looked especially dismal in the rain, its blacked-out windows looked like they were weeping. I paused besides a commemorative plaque, which read, *'Littlemore Asylum Memorial. Erected in 1857, the panopticon was considered the height of Victorian rationalism. Inspired by the work of Utilitarian philosopher, Jeremy Bentham, it enabled the supervision of many inmates by few guards. It is left here in tribute to those who were interned in this place, often against their will. It challenges us to care for the most vulnerable with kindness and understanding.'* Beneath was a list of sponsors and donors. Someone had sprayed an ejaculating penis in red paint over them. Unbidden, that scene in *Mrs Dalloway* where Clarissa retreats into her room and pictures it as a tower, came into my mind. Lonely, brittle Clarissa adrift in lost opportunities, pondering her failed love for Sally Seton and what might have been if she hadn't married Richard Dalloway. Christ, I hadn't read it since I was a teenager. It felt like decades ago.

'Hello.'

The word, pronounced in soft and careful tones from behind me, made me jump violently. I turned and saw Evie, in wellies, jodhpurs and her ancient Barbour, all muffled up against the cold. Her red bobble hat gave her a faintly gnomish appearance.

'Evie,' I said.

She looked up at the panopticon.

'There's a petition, you know,' she said. When I said nothing, she added, 'Against the tower. Has been ever since they turned the old asylum into apartments. They say it's morbid. Everyone wants to forget.' She shuddered. 'Can't say I blame them.'

She said this with such force, that it made me pause. I said, 'What's wrong, Evie?'

Evie licked her lips. It was one of her characteristic gestures, the kind of thing she did when she was trying to come to a mind on something. Finally, she said,

'Nothing.'

Until that point, I had felt wrong-footed. I had so little expected to meet Evie out here, I'd been instantly on the defensive. This one word, this blocking of access, reignited my anger.

'For God's sake, Evie. Why can't you just be honest with me?'

'*Wovon man nicht sprechen kann, darüber muss man schweigen,*' she said quietly, almost to herself. 'Don't you think that's beautiful?'

'Please, Evie, stop showing off.'

'Whereof we cannot speak, thereof we must keep silent. Wittgenstein', she continued, as if I hadn't spoken.

Something snapped within me. I stepped up to her, took hold

of her arms, and shook her. She was so limp she might have been Mr Chatalon. I shouted, 'For the love of God, Evie, what's wrong with you? I know about the pills. I know about your lies. I know how you used me. I know, I know, I know …'

Tears of frustration fell down my face. Evie just looked at me. She had the serenity of the Virgin, even as I shook her. I rambled on. I can't remember what else I said. Something about how much she'd hurt me, something about how I didn't want to see her anymore.

When my rage and frustration had burnt out, we just stood there, next to the panopticon. The silence was dreadful. I wanted to escape, be anywhere but here. Evie quietly took my hands in hers. Neither of us wore gloves and our hands were red raw. Evie's hands were smaller than mine and more elegant. My hands were, in my estimation, agricultural, square and heavy and I'd always hated them. My nails were chipped. Evie had what I called 'artist's hands' – thin, long fingered – an effect enhanced by the talon-like nails painted in a rich dark red. Her hands were as chilly as mine.

She looked at me and, again said, 'Whereof we cannot speak, thereof we must keep silent.'

This time she spoke kindly and carefully, her eyes alive with intelligence. I saw she was on the edge of tears.

'One day, Kitty, one day. I'll explain. But not now. It's …' She broke off. She looked utterly miserable. The marks under her eyes were black and purple. Just then I think I drew as close as I ever did to Evie's utter despair. I saw how trapped she had become. It was shattering. My sister, when very moved or freaked out, always said, 'I can feel it in the back of my eyes'. We'd laugh about how strange that idea was. Right then, in front of Evie, I understood Lou's words properly for the first time. I felt Evie's despair in the back of my eyes.

Then, quite suddenly, I saw a spark of something in Evie's face. Hope? She let go of my hands and reached into one of her deep jacket pockets. It was the kind of pocket from which one might expect twelve bore cartridges to be pulled or treats for the hunting dogs. Instead she pulled the tatty, black book I'd seen on her bed the day before. She looked down at it, rubbed her thumb across the cracked leather, as if it contained a code, instructions for use. I could not read her face. She said, 'I'd like you to have this, Kit.'

She passed it across to me and I reached out to take it. She didn't let it go immediately. Not before she said,

'Just remember, there is no one good, but one, that is God.'

She smiled weakly, kissed me on the cheek, and walked off towards Littlemore, leaving me alone, holding a strange black book in the lee of a tower on a desperate day.

Chapter Twenty-three

'The question is,' said Albertus, 'just how Catholic was the 1549 Prayer Book?'

It was the first Loewe seminar of the term. As he spoke, he leaned forward and poured himself a cup of tea. He added milk, then sat back and surveyed us owlishly. 'Us' was all of my friends, except for Evie. After her incident in chapel on the first day of term, she had acquired a sick note for 'flu'. According to Albertus, she'd been given a week's exeat and had gone down to London to be with family.

The Reformation was hardly my area of interest or expertise. In one sense, it was none of our strengths. Ivo had once called it, 'The Second Peasant's Revolt', because – as far as Ivo was concerned – Luther was a peasant with an excrement obsession. It was not so much that Ivo disagreed completely with the Reformation; rather he insisted on two points. First, that the C of E represented the best of all possible Churches for it was 'both catholic and reformed' and secondly that the Reformation in England was – quote – 'honest, at least'. When challenged he'd explain that in England it was clearly about power, whereas our European neighbours sought to conceal this fact with holy posturing.

'It was a transitional text,' I suggested. The claim sounded dry and academic, even to me. When no one responded, I added, 'I mean, it carried the echo of the Medieval into the Reformation era.'

Loewe twirled his moustache, a faint note of amusement on his lips, and said, 'Explain.' While I considered my answer, I glanced at him, testing my conjecture that he was ill. At first sight, it was not hard to refute. There remained a kind of ruddiness in his cheeks and his eyes and mannerisms were as alive as ever. The moustache was still magnificent. But these were superficial factors and behind the surface, was a thinness and a hint of strain. Albertus was working very hard to stay still. I read somewhere that, sometimes, the very sick have a season when they look almost preternaturally alive. Albertus had lost weight and it created the illusion of a second youth. It was as if his white hair and moustache had been stuck on with gum-araby and he were a youthful actor playing an old don in an end-of-term show.

I was, if I'm entirely honest, also waiting for Albertus's axe to fall on my neck. This was the second time I'd seen him since the Christmas Lunch and my break-in to his private library. The first time we'd met we'd been alone, he tramping across campus towards Luxford, I on my way to the library. I had been awkward and stilted in my conversation. I drew close, again and again, to confessing my theft. How could he not know that I'd taken it? Yet, he had been breezy and friendly and kind. He remained profoundly grateful for my company on Christmas Day and only wanted to know if I'd had a good time. It made my sense of guilt worse, as if Albertus wanted to shame me with kindness, but I was determined to stick with my agreement with myself. I would only speak of the book if Albertus challenged me, and so far he'd been discreet. Now, on this second occasion, I wondered if he was enjoying my squirming. Was he deriving a vengeful pleasure in delaying the inevitable exposure of my sneakiness and thievery? I could already see how my shame, over time, might become exquisite, excruciating even.

Finally, I composed myself and said, 'Well, consider the differences between the funeral services of 1549 and 1552. The former was intended to take place in church. It included a commendation of the deceased, an echo of the language of the Requiem Mass; the 1552 version drove a coach and horses through that, leading to a service that was supposed to take place at the graveside. That's even before we talk about damage to the Mass struck by 1552, or the Black Rubric.' The Black Rubric was the nineteenth-century name for Cranmer's 1552 explanation as to why communicants should kneel rather than sit; he wanted the communicant to understand that kneeling did not indicate undue reverence for the Body and Blood.

If all this sounds dull and uninspiring, it reflected the lack of enthusiasm in the room. Ivo seemed lost in private thoughts. Richard was sat as far away from him as politeness would allow, periodically yawning. Charlie chain-smoked and Piers kept lifting a cup of tea to his mouth, as if to drink or blow on the liquid, before placing it back down on his saucer. Usually all four of them were neat and trim, fastidious indeed, and though their clothes were smart and fresh, they all – except for Richard – looked tired and worn-out, as if they'd had a night on the tiles. Perhaps they had. As for me, I had more things on my mind than my guilt about taking the Chaucer, not least my unease about the book Evie had given me.

Before opening it, I'd snuck back to my room, closed the curtains and locked the door. I laid my draught excluder across and turned on the bedside lamp. If it were a treasure or even if it were – as I suspected – Evie's commonplace book or diary, I didn't want to be seen reading it. I wanted to keep my reaction to myself. Evie's book, however, was something else entirely. Firstly, it was very, very old indeed. No later than the twelfth century, I thought. The cover was soft calf-skin, possibly original, and in a real mess. Its black leather was peeled and dented. The spine was badly bumped. However, it was inside that the book came alive. The parchment retained a milky translucent quality, an indication that this work had been produced to the highest standards for a very discerning audience. The language was Latin and it had illuminations which shone. Its gold leaf and use of lapis lazuli were first-class. At first glance, it might have been a psalter or book of hours, but it was something far rarer. It was a copy of *The Penitential of Cummean*.

Perhaps that means nothing to you, but – for me, if it was nowhere near the class of the Chaucer – it was heart-pounding stuff. *Cummean's Penitential* was the classic of its kind, the precursor of all the penitentials of the medieval era. When the medieval Church had begun to code its penances for sexual, corporate and personal sin, this was the book it reached for. In need of a steer on what punishment should be doled out for having sex with a donkey? Want to find an appropriate penance for defecating on a neighbour's sheep? Consult *Cummean*. Attributed to a seventh century Irish monk, its prescriptions of punishment for sin were drawn from the fourth century. It was a text that, along with Chaucer, had formed the basis of my PhD. It was, also, a flagellant's delight, containing hundreds of prescriptions for self-discipline.

Cummean's Penitential was hardly a rare book. There were dozens of extant copies and, in edited form, hundreds of further medieval copies. Yet, a copy of this quality was exceptionally rare, possibly unique. For the person who'd created it, it had been a work of profound love. That didn't explain either why Evie had it or why she'd passed it to me. One thing was obvious, however: she'd acquired it from Albertus. He might have given it to her, I suppose, but instinct told me not. I reckoned that she, like me, had lifted this book from his private library. As to the why, there was an obvious and straightforward answer: Evie had acquired it to enhance her disciplinary prayer. I chewed this over and over in my mind. It had a core of truth to it, but I was sure there was more to it than that. It wasn't like she couldn't acquire this text in any other format. So, I reasoned, her interest had to lie in this specific copy, and, if its beauty was enough to fascinate anyone, I wondered if there were more to it than that. As to why she'd passed it to me, I was flummoxed. Was it that she – like Richard – had felt she'd got too deep into self-flagellation and passing this book to me was a symbol of rejecting that way of prayer? Perhaps. Was it a peace offering, even? She knew I'd studied the *Cummean* extensively. Did she simply want me to possess a copy of transporting beauty? Over the following days, I came back to the book again and again, flicking through its elegant pages. I don't know what I was searching for. I simply felt led on to study it for something that might unlock the disquiet in my bones. There was something about it – a hint in its pages – that would not let me go.

* * *

'Kitty? Kitty?' I looked in the direction of the voice. It was Albertus, staring at me expectantly.

'I'm sorry, Albertus. What did you say?'

'I said, your analysis was sound, but felt rather too textbook. I was hoping for something a little more radical. What with your fascination' – unexpectedly, he comedically raised his eyebrows in the manner of a vaudeville villain – 'with the outer limits of acceptable scholarship.' Ivo laughed quietly. Loewe said all this in a good-natured way, but there was a note of steel behind it, as if he'd been disappointed I hadn't been giving him his full attention.

He added, 'You're not playing it safe are you, Kitty? For the sake of a tired old man?' There was something unexpectedly sad in the way he said this. It stirred everyone's attention and I wondered if any of the others suspected or knew about Loewe's illness. He stood up, slowly and heavily, as if he were in pain and walked over to an oak table.

He looked so pained that Charlie stood up and said, 'Albertus, I can get whatever you're after, if you like.'

'No, Charlie. It's fine. Just a little stiff today. Always happens in January. Need to keep my bones moving.'

He opened a drawer, took something out and shuffled back across. It was rather distressing to see him looking this shaky. He sat back down and laid two small black books on the coffee table in front of us.

'Two books,' he said, 'both alike in dignity. In fair England where we set our scene.' He grinned at his little joke. 'Well, not quite. Before you, ladies and gentlemen, are two examples of the Book of Common Prayer. One 1549, the other 1552.'

'Originals?' said Piers.

'Of course. What do you take me for?' Albertus smiled, showing a line of uneven, yellowed teeth.

If these copies of Cranmer's first English prayer books were not exactly rare, they were hardly commonplace. Many of the 1549 copies were destroyed with the arrival of the 1552 edition; with the accession of the Catholic Mary as queen in 1553, many of the 1552 copies were collected up and burned. As I considered this, that line of Heine, written centuries later, came to mind: 'Where they first burn books, they will soon burn people.' It was apposite for Cranmer's fiery fate.

Ivo had picked up one of the books and was studying it, with rapt attention. He must have been holding the 1549 edition, for he said, 'To think, this little thing caused riots across the West Country.' He was referring to the violent 'commotions' its introduction at Whitsun 1549 generated, especially in Cornwall and Devon. 'Cranmer was a fool to ban the people's processions and festivals. It was sacrilege.' He shook his head. 'What have we now, four hundred years on? Empty Methodist chapels across Cornwall.'

'You really think Cranmer was a villain, Ivo?' said Albertus, gently. Charlie had picked up the 1552 edition and opened its pages.

'Don't you?' said Ivo, a trace of real bitterness in his voice. It was extraordinary how deeply Ivo seemed to feel the slight to medieval England.

'I think Kitty has a point,' said Albertus, nodding respectfully at me. Before Ivo could speak, Albertus went on, 'Stephen Gardiner said that the 1549 text was "patient of a catholic interpretation".' Albertus's point was well made. Gardiner had been secretary to Cardinal Wolsey. He was no fan of Cranmer, had lost his bishopric in 1547, and was imprisoned in the Tower. He was released and restored by Queen Mary. He died soon after Cranmer was burnt at the stake.

'Before it went through the protestant theology-grinder, I think Cranmer's original text revealed a deeper generosity than many give him credit for. Indulge me, Ivo, but were the 1549 edition a handwritten manuscript, I'd bet you could scrape off the text and find the words of the Mass hidden underneath.'

Ivo softened at this, laughed warmly, and said,

'A palimpsest? You're incorrigible, Albertus.'

A palimpsest. While Ivo and Albertus wittered on, and Charlie, Richard and Piers began talking about the 1552 edition, I zoned out again. A palimpsest. Was that it? Could it be that my disquiet about Evie's book came down that? A palimpsest. For the rest of the seminar, I was hardly present. Albertus might have been unfolding the very secrets of the universe and Ivo might have found the key to heal the broken relationship between Eastern and Western Christianity. I didn't care. All I wanted to do was escape and get back to my room. All I wanted was to re-examine Evie's book. A palimpsest. Was that the solution to the secret of her book?

Chapter Twenty-four

As I hurried back to my room, my hands shook with excitement. For days, I'd been bugged by a hunch that there was something more to Evie's book than met the eye. Now I was sure that if that hunch added up to anything, it was because it was a palimpsest. A palimpsest, you may be wondering? A manuscript from which the text has been scraped or washed off so that it can be used again. In its original Greek it simply means 'again, scraped'. In the early Middle Ages, when parchment was rare and valuable, it was not unusual for writing to be 'erased' using milk and oat bran. Later on, pumice was used.

Why was I so sure that Evie's book was a palimpsest? Was it any more than just clutching at straws or desperate instinct, a need for the book to have some sort of extra significance? Perhaps. Except for one thing. On a couple of occasions, as I'd studied the *Cummean's* exquisite pages, I was sure I'd seen something, just a hint of something on a page. I hadn't processed it at the time. It wasn't until Albertus mentioned the concept of a palimpsest that a lever had shifted. Yes, as I'd desperately flicked through its pages I'd spotted something. A ghost. A trace of a lost past bleeding through.

Back in my room, I locked my door and found the loose floorboard under my bed. I'd discovered it in my first couple of weeks at Littlemore. Now, I lifted it up. I reached inside and took out my special box, containing my most personal items. I sat up, dusted off my arm, leant back against the door and opened the tin. It was an old Cadbury's biscuit tin with a print of a soldier of the Royal Horse Guards sat on a horse, sword raised, outside a palace. It was scratched and sorry, but it had travelled around with me ever since I'd left home. It had been my granny's, at least I remember seeing it at her house when I was a little girl. A few years after she died, I found it in a cupboard at my parents' house. I took it and used it as my secret keepsakes store. It was one of my private treasures.

I felt physically sick as I took the book out of the tin. I felt like I was on the verge of discovering something extraordinary. I told myself this was ridiculous – if the book were a palimpsest, it was as likely to contain a list of medieval shopping as anything else – and, yet, I was sure Evie hadn't sold me short. She'd given me this book for a reason. It represented a clue to something, perhaps even a guide to the shadowy mysteries that had dogged my time at Littlemore. I just had to find the right page again, a page where the characteristic brownish marks of old, erased writing had bled through the milkiness of the vellum. The first time I'd seen them I'd put it down to old age, a little bit of spotting that can affect any old manuscript.

I flicked the *Cummean's* pages again, concentrating this time, and then I saw them, about half-way through. Just the ghost of some words, a faint brownish stain. I went over to my window to see if the extra light might make them clearer. The words were unbelievably faint. It was only when the page was angled away from my eye-line that they began to stand out, white on cream. Greek. Αυτό είναι το δέντρο της ζωής. Greek is not my strong point, but I thought it might be, 'Here is the Tree of Life.' The Tree of Life. It was a phrase redolent with meaning. It was mentioned both at the very start of the Bible in the Book of Genesis – as being planted with the Tree of the Knowledge of Good and Evil – as well as at the very end of the Bible in the Book of Revelation, where its fruits will be offered for the healing of creation. Some theologians had even argued that the Tree of Life represents Jesus Christ himself. But if it was a biblical idea, it was also a concept that was found in almost all cultures, especially those which influenced Christianity. The idea that all life could be traced back to an immortal Tree predated Christ by at least three thousand years.

The thing that gripped me in that moment of discovery, however, was that this book Evie had given me held within it much more than the words of Cummean. If this copy of his penitential was at least seven-hundred years old, behind it was another text, even more ancient. Was that Evie's point? Was that why she'd gifted it to me? And now that I'd noticed the writing, I began to see it everywhere, as if I'd brought a lens into focus. The page was covered in a spidery hand and just trying to decipher a few letters behind the *Cummean's* Latin text made my eyes hurt. Yet, it was clear at last that this was very far from a conventional book and page after page had markings upon them.

There was a sharp knock on the door. I almost jumped out of my skin. The rap came again.

'One moment,' I said, trying to keep my tone light. I placed the book back in the tin with my other treasures, replaced the floorboard and straightened my hair. I then unlocked my door and opened it. It was Richard.

'Kitty. Fancy a drink?'

'Sure,' I replied. 'Where?'

'The Trout?'

* * *

'Shouldn't you be off on that placement of yours?' I said, half an hour later, as we nursed our pints.

'Probably,' replied Richard. The river was high and fast-moving that afternoon, almost threatening to overflow the banks. It was not unlike that day Louise died, although the Thames at this point is much narrower than the Severn back home. I wondered how quickly it would wash a body away. I shuddered. I was glad we were indoors looking out through French windows while the fire blazed. The dangers of the river were placed at a safe distance.

Shouldn't you be starting your first one about now?' said Richard.

'Not till March, and then only a brief attachment with a parish. I'm still waiting to hear with whom.'

We fell into an amicable silence. I never failed to enjoy Richard's company. He was peaceful to be with and he had none of the spikiness of the others. Eventually, he said, 'Actually, that's what I wanted to talk about.'

'What? My placement?'

He laughed and said, 'No. Mine.' I waited for him to continue. 'I won't be continuing it.'

'Really? I thought you were having such fun.' Richard had spent the past few months alongside a rather eccentric country parson who'd given up a successful career as a hard-rock musician. Richard said he had a wicked sense of humour, a store of extraordinary anecdotes, and a profound sense of freedom in his ministry, no doubt conferred in virtue of being independently wealthy. Apparently, his downstairs loo contained a mix of religious tat and gold records from a dozen countries. Richard had promised to introduce me to him.

'I was,' he said. 'But there are deeper issues.' He offered me a cigarette and I took it. We lit up and he said, 'The fact is, I've decided to leave Littlemore.'

'What?!?' I almost choked on the lungful of smoke I'd just inhaled. He calmly smoked his cigarette and looked out at the river.

'I'm not like you, Kitty,' he said. I shook my head, reeling from this news. 'Really, I'm not. Your vocation, golly, it's incredible. I saw that the moment we met. You have an amazing generosity. But me? I have the history and the connections, but this life ...' He sighed heavily. 'I'm not made for it.'

'Has this got something to do with Ivo?'

He rubbed the bottom row of his teeth across his top lip. It was one of his most charming habits. It made him look like he was pretending to be a monster. It was a gesture that Louise and I used to call 'teeth-out'; we'd do it when we wanted to make a silent protest. Then he said,

'That's exactly why you should be a priest. You get to the heart of the matter, every time.' He took a drag on his cigarette, then said, 'I can't stand it anymore, Kit.'

'Come on,' I replied. 'If Ivo, Piers, or any of us are pissing you off, it's not like you have to live cheek-by-jowl. What with placements and the different courses we do, how much time do you actually need to spend alongside Ivo?'

He looked at me with kind of hopelessness. 'You think this is about disliking people?'

'What then?'

Something extraordinary happened then. He began to speak, and – usually so fluent – he stumbled and stuttered his words, as if we were in a fairy tale and a witch had sealed his tongue with a curse. He took a series of deep breaths, as if composing himself. When he spoke, it was in fragments.

'I, I, look, Kitty, I want ... I can't ... Not now.' He closed his eyes and pinched the bridge of his nose as if he were suffering from nosebleed. He then ran those fingers down over his neat beard. I decided to try my hunch, to see if it would tempt Richard out of his shell.

'Is this to do with our experiments getting out of hand?' When he said nothing, a flash of inspiration hit me. I said, 'Just nod,

Richard.' I thought it best to keep my words as coded as possible. You never knew who might be listening. I'd not forgotten what Richard had shown me that day in my room – his infected wound. It had shocked me, made me wonder if we had gone much too far, though I still kept my cilice. I thought of it a lot, although I hadn't worn it since the end of Advent. I missed wearing it. I enjoyed its sharp reminders of God's passion for us, but I didn't want the whole world to know about it.

Richard – his eyes still closed, as if he needed to keep away a world that frightened him – nodded once. Remembering his enigmatic words as he'd left me before Christmas – 'As for that other business, well, the sooner we forget about that, the better' – I tried a hunch.

'Is this about that other business?'

He looked pale and pasty, ghastly. He nodded again, then, quite suddenly, he stood up, opened his eyes, and ran towards the loo. I considered going after him, but was sure that a woman barging her way into the gents wouldn't help. As I waited for him to return, I tried to make sense of what had just happened. First, I couldn't imagine Littlemore without Richard. I realised I'd come to rely on his kind presence, indeed, in a profound sense I rather loved him. Perhaps this sounds wrong, even calculating, but he was precisely the sort of person I could imagine marrying. If I am not really the marrying kind – I'm not sure I either have the passion, consistency or focus to carry it off – I could imagine being 'companionate' with Richard. I could see a world in which we were together, living out a marriage as public friendship, while happily pursuing our private lives separately. I suppose, I'm just trying to say that, of all my friends, he was the one I trusted the most.

As for his reaction to my questioning, well, of course I knew something was terribly wrong and, at the same time, I didn't. I mean, back then I don't know if I – if any of us – had quite the language for trauma and abuse that we possess now. When a man cannot speak of what has happened to him, when he can only nod and rushes off to the lavatory to be sick, then only a monster would fail to appreciate that something horrific was at stake. And yet … I am trying to be honest. On that January day, I cannot claim the twenty-twenty vision that hindsight gives us. Yes, we'd all got a little deeper into ancient religious practices than any of us had quite bargained for, but I didn't know how bleak those practices had become for someone like Richard. I didn't know what one human could do to another in the name of God's love.

Richard returned five minutes later. The front of his hair looked damp, as did his beard. I guess he'd splashed water on his face, but apart from that he looked quite refreshed. Indeed, he looked like his usual, unconcerned self. He sat down and grinned rather sheepishly, then said,

'Sorry about that, Kit. Don't know what came over me.' He held himself in a curiously formal way, as if he were on parade. 'Must have been the beer.'

'Richard,' I said, a note of pleading in my voice. This re-formed Richard – the stolid, controlled, public schoolboy – was even more disconcerting than the one who'd run off a few minutes before. I didn't want to let him bring down the old shutters again so quickly. I considered offering what I knew about the book Evie had given me as a gambit, as a way of trying to keep Richard open. I sensed that 'that other business' had something to do with the *Cummean* and the text that was hidden behind it. I considered it, and dismissed it. I wasn't ready to gamble my new knowledge so soon.

He smiled confidently and said, 'Fresh air?'

* * *

We'd cycled to The Trout and, as we headed back towards college, we pushed our bicycles besides us towards Binsey. I enjoyed the feel of cold air, almost burning, in my lungs. Soon, I thought, as we walked in silence, soon, he'll speak. Soon, he'll tell me what the hell has been going on, but, of course, he didn't. Well, not directly, anyway.

'Can I ask you something, Kitty?' he said, eventually. I nodded. 'About your sister?'

I stopped, surprised by this turn in conversation. He stood beside me and breathed a long white plume of breath into the Oxfordshire air. Then he said, 'I don't want to pry, but how did you cope? With losing … Louise.' He said the name carefully, as if it were holy. I felt my breath catch in my throat. It was the first time I'd heard her name in public for years and it felt almost sacrilegious to hear someone else speak openly of her. Her face came into my head, fixed as she'd been at thirteen on her school photo: long chestnut hair tied back, almond-shaped eyes, an open smile, her teeth a little uneven on the left side. The open-hearted face of a bright and responsible girl.

I thought of my parents and how they'd loved her so dearly, not least – I thought – because she died before she'd really gone through adolescence and had screwed up like all kids do. They never understood how hard I found it when she pushed me around, and how it annoyed me that I had to have her hand-me-downs. I loved her all the same, of course. When we were little, she was never afraid, and she helped me take risks I'd never dream of. 'Come ON, Kitty!' she'd shout, when I was too scared to go into the sea on holiday or was afraid to go back to school after the summer, and she'd laugh, that giddy little laugh, and I'd laugh too, and follow her. Then she died.

Mother, father and I, we got through it – the aftermath, the funeral, the looks on our neighbours' and friends' faces. The pity.

It might have made us closer as a family, but – forgive the watery metaphor – we all became submerged beneath a sea of grief. I know that each time my parents looked at me they wanted to see Louise, and they didn't. And when I looked at them, I saw Louise, well, parts of her at least, and I wanted to get away.

'Kitty?'

'Yes?'

'How did you cope?'

'Oh, like everyone. I pushed it down.'

'Did it work?'

'I'm at Littlemore, aren't I?'

'What do you mean?'

I began to walk again and Richard followed. I said, 'Never repeat this … promise?' He nodded, then I said, 'I had a breakdown at University. A crisis of faith or hope or whatever. Nothing like Charlie's, but real nonetheless. I needed to know there was something more than …' I gestured to the road and hedges, '… this.'

'So, you're saying one has to face stuff?'

'Some day,' I replied.

We walked on in silence for a few minutes, then Richard said, 'How's Evie?'

'I don't know,' I said, honestly. 'She's been away.' Then, on a hunch I added, 'Does all this concern Evie?'

He looked across at me. 'Kitty, you're smart. I think you can work it out.' He rubbed his face with his left hand before continuing. His ungloved hand was very white, corpse-like. 'I'm not ready to speak. I'm not sure I ever will be. But perhaps Evie and I are different versions of the same problem …' Then, almost to himself he said, '… the problem of loving the wrong thing … I hope she'll have the sense to leave, too.' He paused again, then said, 'Do you know that god-awful tower in the village?'

'The panopticon?' He grunted to himself, almost in disgust. 'The panopticon. Yes. Visit it, Kitty. One Thursday night, say. Arrive no later than nine and wait.' Then, almost as an afterthought, 'Don't be seen.'

With that he resumed his usual cheery demeanour, slung a leg over his bike, and said, 'Come on. We'll be late for evening prayer.'

Chapter Twenty-five

I've never had a gift for prayer. I mean, I know how to use liturgy, but I'm not one for contemplative prayer. I cannot sit and rejoice in silence. For me the Church of England's great gift is its prayer book. It requires not that priests look into men's souls or that we sit around moping or meditating; rather it gives us a liturgy around which to unite. The Prayer Book and its successors are the things that hold me in prayer. I've known people who can achieve profound levels of concentration and devotion, indeed, who can spend hours and days in silence, contemplating the Lord and all his works. Not me. I need words or, failing that, visual stimuli – an icon, a stained-glass window – to hold me to my task.

Never, then, have I been more grateful for the Prayer Book's ministrations than that evening. We arrived back just before Evensong began, stowed our bikes and snuck into chapel as Roddy said, 'Almighty and most merciful God, we have erred and strayed from thy ways like lost sheep. We have followed too much the devices and desires of our own hearts ...' We collected books and headed towards our usual seats. None of the others was there. For once, I was glad.

The gift of liturgy lies in how it holds us. That night it enabled me to control my mind to a degree. Even so, I felt torn and confused. The events of the afternoon only added further questions and concerns into the maelstrom. Richard's remarks had destabilised me further. I felt like I faced a tipping-point, a precipice, and it was taking all my energy not to fall in. What the hell might lie in the panopticon? I tried to pray for grace not to rush to judgment. Most of all, I prayed for Richard that he might find it possible to change his mind and stay. Perhaps he was making an idle threat, although he was not the sort for drama. I suspected he'd already spoken to the Principal.

As soon as Roddy had led us in the final Grace, I fled. I didn't even say goodbye to Richard. It would be overdramatic to say I wanted to be alone. Rather, I simply wanted to be where others were not. I rushed to my room, foregoing the usual sherry and college supper, filled with an urge to do something I hadn't done since I was a child: to simply go to bed and hide under the covers, pretending that the world outside might thereby go away. I wanted to lie down, sleep and discover my world had become magically reordered in the morning. I wanted to wake and find that fairy-tale land was back.

I opened my door, switched on the light, and was about to step inside when something made me pause. I stood on the threshold and looked at the space I'd come to think of as my home. It looked as it always looked: neat, ordered and perhaps a little sterile. None of the chaos that so often characterises students' rooms. My little haven. And yet, I was sure something was wrong. I blinked and considered, then stepped inside and locked the door. I looked from bed, to desk, to shelves; from looking-glass to wardrobe to dresser. I looked at my small collection of shoes near the door and the cheap rug on the floor. It was faultless and just as I'd left it, and yet ... Perhaps because of my conversation with Richard I was alert to something beyond the ordinary. A violation. At first sight, everything looked like it was in order, and yet I was sure this room had been broken into. I knew it at a gut level.

I have always had an acute sense of smell. During my PhD I shared an office with another student, Mindy Auerbacher, an American from North Dakota whose mother owned a perfume-making business. Over the two years I shared that office with her,

Mindy would turn up wearing a whole panoply of scents given to her by her mum. Mindy became so impressed with my capacity to distinguish between the nuances of the perfumes, that she offered to set-up a meeting with her mother. Indeed, Mindy said that if I could only give up the cigarettes I could set my price as a scent-tester. Over the years since, I've often amused myself with the thought that if the priest thing ever went belly-up I could ring Mindy and take up that invitation.

It was that sense of smell that guided me now. I sensed just the vaguest note of something different in the room. Yes, there was the usual background hint of tobacco, and my own perfume – the last of a bottle from Mindy called *Stolen Winter* – as well as hand moisturiser, coffee, and traces of my deodorant. However, there was something else, something more masculine in the air. I couldn't quite pin it down, though if pushed I'd say it was an after-shave. However, even though I couldn't pin the details down, I knew the scent was extraneous. I rarely allowed people into my room, and it had been weeks since one of the boys had been around. Unless I was losing the plot, I was sure someone had recently violated my room.

I double-checked my door was locked, then got down on my knees and lifted-up the loose floorboard I'd laid down only a few hours before. I reached inside and breathed a sigh of relief. My special box was still there. Whether it had been opened was yet to be seen. I sat on my bed and checked inside. Everything was intact, most particularly my newest treasures, the *Cummean* and my copy of the Chaucer. I took it out and stroked its cover, then kissed it. I laid both books on my lap and looked at them. Two ancient books. Both once part of Albertus's collection, one given to me by Evie, the other taken by my own hand. My treasures, and they were safe, but I was still sure someone had been in my room.

More to the point, I was sure it had been searched, unless, of course, I was just becoming paranoid and my sense of smell had somehow got messed-up. After what I'd been through in the past few weeks that wasn't beyond the bounds of possibility. Even at this stage of the term, I was conscious that I hadn't fully recovered from the flu. It still left me with patches of time when I felt woozy and lightheaded. Could a virus affect one's judgment? Or sense of smell? Probably, and yet, I knew that I'd been broken into. I laid the books and the tin on the floor and stood up and looked at my study again. I slowly revolved on the spot, trying to take in minute details. Anything that might be unusual: a mug slightly out of place on a coaster or a book faintly out of synch with its neighbour. Nothing.

It was on my second slow revolution that I spotted it. The top drawer on my desk was closed shut. In and of itself that was hardly remarkable. I was the kind of person who instinctively closed drawers and shut doors. However, that drawer had never been inclined to stay shut for very long. It was a quirk I'd become used to. For my first few weeks at Littlemore, I'd persistently shut it, only to find it popping back open an hour or two later. Eventually, I'd taken to pushing it to the point where it was almost closed and leaving it. Whoever had been in my room had – I reckoned – a very clear understanding of my habits. They knew I was not the sort of person to leave drawers and cupboards open and in their haste, perhaps, they'd failed to realise that that drawer wasn't completely shut. After searching through it, they'd shoved it shut. It was the one I kept bits of stationery and old pens in and it was obvious from the merest glance that my intruder had not bothered to disturb its contents.

I sat down on my desk chair. Having found the drawer, I felt vindicated in my initial assessment. Clearly, while Richard and I had been away in Wolvercote, someone had broken into my room and made a search. It was more than alarming. Could it simply have been someone on the off-chance? A sneak thief, say. There had, after all, been incidents when townies had broken into college. I was sure I locked the door when Richard and I had left, though that meant very little. It was a standing college joke that half the room keys acted as masters to the rest. No, the sneak thief thesis didn't strike me as very likely. The previous college incidents bore all the hallmarks of small-time burglars: messy, short of time and desperate for easily handled and fenced goods. Cash was always stolen. I kept my small stash of cash in the bottom drawer of my desk. I checked it and it was intact.

No. Whoever had broken into my room had wanted to leave no trace. This perhaps offered a partial answer as to 'Why?' Whoever broke in wanted to look for something, perhaps find it, but not take it away. For if someone had wanted to steal something specific, surely the best cover would be to make it look like an ordinary burglary. That was my first thought. However, the more I considered this, the less it appealed. Concealing the theft of something specific beneath what appeared to be a conventional robbery was all very well, but I'd report the break-in not only to the Bursar, but to the police. If the police were brought in, they would take fingerprint samples and so on. If the intruder was a college member I can't imagine they would enjoy the police taking fingerprints.

Another thought occurred to me. The intruder might simply have wanted to photograph something. My mind rushed to images drawn from spy novels: Of charming old mountebanks using *Minox* cameras to snap away at private documents. Enjoyable as it was to toy with such images, it was beyond ridiculous. Spy stuff? At Littlemore? Even if I'd often thought that the world of espionage and the Church of England shared common traits – a love of secrecy and back-room deals, of nosiness bordering on prurience – this was a connection too far. Even though I possessed a couple of books of dubious provenance, I couldn't see why anyone would want to resort to the techniques of espionage.

Finally, I arrived at a point that felt closest to solid ground. It concerned the books. I possessed two medieval manuscripts that, at best, were borrowed and, at worst, filched from some collection

216

or individual. This, I reckoned, left me in a rare situation. I could see how an intruder might break in for reconnaissance purposes, reasoning that if they had a look around without raising suspicion, they could come back again. However, given the illicit nature of my manuscripts, should they come across them they might take them, arguing that I would not report the theft. This latter point struck me as exactly right. If, for example, my money and ID had been taken I would, of course, report it; on the other hand, if my Chaucer had been taken, I would not. For, furious and distressed as I would be, it was not something I would want the police or the college authorities to know about. There would simply be too many questions that might lead to criminal prosecution and me being sent down from college. Equally, others – most especially Albertus – would be drawn into the debacle.

If I felt I had a pretty solid 'Why?' that still left me with 'Who?' The potential answer to the latter was more than troubling, for the field was obvious and tiny. Having arrived at the conclusion that my intruder had been targeting one or other or both of my manuscripts, it was impossible to consider anyone other than my small circle of friends. Essentially, the field came down to Ivo, Piers or Charlie. Evie was away. Richard had been with me. With discomfort, I had to acknowledge a troubling thought: It was not beyond the bounds of possibility that Richard's invite was a set-up, just to get me out of the way. Could that be true? Just to acknowledge the possibility was disturbing. Was my grip on reality so poor that I'd misjudged my relationship with Richard? My heart said it was impossible, but my head said otherwise.

I got up from my chair and sat down on my bed. I picked up the two medieval books. On the surface, they looked so innocuous, nondescript, even, and yet they held a kind of magic, capable of exercising a power of possession. If I felt it, so must the others, indeed, I knew they did. How could I forget that first conversation

217

with Richard and Ivo about the power of manuscripts? How I'd almost mocked Ivo when I'd suggested that one didn't need to have held an original Plato to write confidently about his philosophy. It seemed a lifetime ago. Now I knew the power of ink on vellum, of illumination at a learned hand; of the magic of hand-created texts.

However, I was equally sure that – leaving aside the crazy idea that Albertus had told the others about me taking the Chaucer from his library – none of the others knew about the secret copy of the *Canterbury Tales*. No. As I held both books in my hands, I knew it was the *Penitential of Cummean* they wanted, either for itself or because of the palimpsest concealed behind it. I set the Chaucer down on my bed, and looked more closely at the oddity Evie had passed me. I ran a finger across one of the pages, felt the slight roughness of the hairy side, felt an animal body at least eight-hundred years old. Why had someone – possibly quite soon after Evie's book had been made – erased the text and covered it with the *Cummean*? I made two decisions. First, to keep this strange book close to me from now on. I really could trust no one. If someone wanted it they would have to exact a price from my own flesh, take it from me by force. And, secondly, to figure out exactly what it was that someone had carefully erased away from its vellum pages. I would expose its secrets again.

Chapter Twenty-six

The age of wonders was over and Camelot was in flames. At least, that is how I felt as January drew close to February. It is a hellish month at the best of times, interminable and grey, and that January, as I remember it now, was as dreary, damp and dismal as any I've known. Some days it was only light for four to five hours. We tramped from artificial light to light, cold room to cold room. If the lights had only been candles we might have been mistaken for nuns or monks.

I was in a pretty bad way and it must have been noticeable. Over the next few days, half the college asked me, 'Are you all right?' From Miles Goodhap to Molly Shanks, I couldn't seem to go ten paces without some sort of kindly solicitude. I deflected it as best I could. If seminary is supposed to be a kind of dismantling or deconstruction of our personality and faith, so far I'd learned two things: First, be careful who you trust, and secondly, know how to hide your emotions. Regarding the first, I wasn't sure I trusted anyone. Regarding the second, I felt I'd learned a lot, primarily from my friends. As I saw it, it was – for the most part – their key skill, perhaps the effect of private education. Until that week, I thought I was doing well in imitation of them, but given the attention I was drawing from the pastoral vampires, I was clearly failing.

I did my very best to present my usual cool, unconcerned self, to be polite to all who I met, but I was preoccupied. Even for the best actor – and I was and remain at most a modest one – I suspect it's difficult to conceal preoccupation. I was simply overwhelmed with thought. Like most introverted people, I've always been inclined to live mostly inside my head. My own thoughts tend to consume me, ravish me, delight me or torment me. There is a lot to be said in favour of this approach to life. It is insulating. That is all very well if one can keep one's thoughts in order and I usually can, but that January I was simply overwhelmed. I was caught up between trying to figure out which one of my friends had broken into my room and not becoming completely paranoid. I was torn between my deep affection for Richard and the sneaking suspicion that he'd conspired with the others. Equally, I could not dismiss what Richard had said, or not quite said in the pub that day, specifically his instruction to go into the panopticon. I knew I would have to go there. It was calling to me, it had been for months. Like someone walking along a cliff, I was both terrified of what lay over the edge and yet had the urge to jump off.

Then, there was Evie. Evie returned from her break at the weekend, the very model of her old self. She appeared at Community Meeting on Monday looking relaxed and refreshed. It was interesting, even moving, to witness how warmly she was greeted by the wider college body, even by the likes of Matt Smith and Bob Hawkins. Would you believe me if I said it was quite lovely to behold? I hope so. We are all messed-up creatures, after all. If I could not get over my sense of being used by Evie, and if I could not quite acknowledge the depth of my feelings for her, I was secretly pleased to see her back, and back to her old self. Even now, decades on, I can close my eyes and see her smile as she was greeted by the college – open and undefended, full of delight – and be cheered by it. Few of us, even the most manipulative, are wholly bad and in those last few days before the curtain drew down on Evie's life there were still opportunities to see Evie at her best.

There was that Biblical Studies class that showed Evie's fearlessness and her willingness to stand up for women in a still male-dominated world. The class was on the opening chapters of the Book of Genesis. Our lecturer, Dr Walter Finch, a thick-set man with a significant under-bite, was taking us through the different accounts of the Creation, noting how there were at least two different versions: first, the creation of the earth in six days, and the second, the creation of Adam and Eve in the Garden. In the hands of a supple and generous lecturer, the subject would have galvanised the whole class. Finch, however, was a chauvinistic pedant with no poetry in him, and the class began to sink beneath the weight of his heavy words. As Finch ponderously insisted that the account of the creation of Adam and Eve was evidence that God placed men over women, Evie took her chance to strike.

'Dr Finch?'

'Yes, Evie,' said Finch. His voice – as ever when speaking to women – was supercilious and patronising, as if he was sure he'd already thought all the thoughts Evie could ever have.

'I wonder what your thoughts are on feminist criticisms of traditional readings of the Adam and Eve story?'

Finch looked at Evie carefully, weighing up his response. Bob Hawkins, who always enjoyed a bit of sport, opened his sleepy eyes and came to attention. One-by-one, members of the class came back to life.

'Well,' said Finch, extending the word into two separate syllables. 'There's some interest in that. But I think for your purposes, Evie … for the purposes of ministry, I think we can treat feminist ideas …' – Finch said 'feminist' as if it tasted of vomit in his mouth – '… as a little marginal. Traditional readings are more than sufficient in parish settings.'

Evie raised her eyebrows in mock incredulity and said, 'Aren't clergy supposed to be scholars? Teachers of the faith?'

'Well, yes,' said Finch, smiling indulgently. 'But …'

'So, shouldn't we be asked to read people like Phyllis Trible or Elisabeth Schüssler Fiorenza? I don't see their names on the reading list …'

It was marvellous. Evie was her old, bold self: calm, composed and powerful. The kind of woman I wanted to be. Even if no one had heard of the likes of Phyllis Trible – and even I could only claim a passing knowledge back then, her work on the equality of Adam and Eve revolutionary – everyone was attentive now. My heart soared. It was a testimony to Evie's passion for eccentric versions of Christianity that she'd displayed the previous term, of her eclectic reading and self-possession that she could take Finch on, on his own turf.

'Ah, well, they are rather new, Evie,' Finch blustered. 'Very specialist.'

'But both of them have been writing since the seventies. Our own Principal told me before Christmas that he was considering inviting Professor Trible to guest lecture next year.'

If Finch had been a more likeable man, Evie's handling of him might have struck an awkward chord. As it was, even those who were unsympathetic to 'shouty' and 'strident' women, wanted to cheer Evie on. Finch crumbled. He leant on his desk and his shoulders slumped. Within a week, Trible and Schüssler Fiorenza were on the reading list.

Between classes and chapel, I retreated to my room claiming I had a journal paper to work on. It was a good and plausible excuse, one that most of my peers, including my friends, were inclined to believe. Of course, my retreat from communal life was driven by other preoccupations. I wanted to get my mind in order, and I wanted to dissuade further attempts to break into my room. If I'd taken to keeping my rare manuscripts close to my skin, such was my anxiety that I half-expected to be mugged for them, even on campus. Some mornings I'd wake from dreams in which I'd been drugged whilst Ivo or Charlie stole them off my person.

When I wasn't in my room, I was quietly and discreetly trying to figure out the text in Evie's book. I toyed, again and again, with approaching Evie about it. I felt sure she could supply the clues to speed my analysis up, but it was as if there was a blockage in my head that I couldn't overcome. Despite moments in class like that between Evie and Finch, I could not overcome the definite tear in our relationship. Looking back, I can see what a fool I was, but back then I'd become a locked room. I would not let Evie in again. I tried to press on on my own, but I was not making much progress. After weeks of study, the most promising – if curious – discovery was a few quite striking phrases about Jesus' wounds being God's κόλπος. It's a weird word that can mean any hollow space, or a fold, even – in geographic terms – a bay. However, in the context I found it, 'kolpos' would most obviously translate as 'vagina'.

This association of Jesus with a vagina is not as strange as you might think. In the Middle Ages, there was a whole devotional tradition which considered Jesus's wounds on the Cross as feminine. It was what enabled some of the great saints like Bernard of Clairvaux or Julian of Norwich to speak of Christ in feminine terms. Yet, there was something troubling about the fragments I'd managed to translate. They were, in historical terms, far too early to be associated with Late Medieval devotional practices. Julian and Bernard had been writing in the High Middle Ages, after theology had broken ground unforeseen by early Christianity. This text, however, pre-dated them by centuries and was in Greek rather than Latin or early Italian. Given its subject matter one might have expected it to be frivolous or deliberately blasphemous as some of the stories in the *Decameron* were. This text, however, was nothing of the sort. In the section I translated, Jesus' 'vagina' was being presented as the hope of the world. It was revolutionary. The only thing that kept me going was a nagging sense that I'd read or heard some of this text before somewhere, perhaps in a conversation or argument I'd overheard. Every now and then I'd come across a line and a distant chord would strike. But I was so exhausted after my slow and painful deciphering I could not make the connection.

Outside class, I quietly kept my distance from Evie. It was on the Wednesday before her death, that we finally met face to face. Wednesday afternoon was always games time and the communal areas were usually quiet. I was in the common room, sat in the seat I'd occupied that famous night when Evie and Bob Hawkins had gone toe-to-toe and Hawkins had stormed out. I was sick of my room and the library, and was examining some 'Dead Vicars' books in a desultory manner when I heard Evie's voice behind me.

'Hi, Kit. Mind if I sit down?'

I turned. 'Of course not.' The only other person in the common room was Luke Cribbins. I reckoned his presence would stop Evie from making a scene, if that was her plan. It was too public. Evie sat opposite me and said, conventionally,

'How are you?' I took a moment before answering. It would be easy to answer in equally conventional terms, but I thought she deserved something better. Our relationship might have become broken, but – in college terms at least – we were old friends.

'Oh, you know,' I said, wearily. 'This place. These people. All driving me insane.'

'You should do what I did. Get away.'

'It's clearly done you some good. You look great.'

I wondered how long we could keep up this chat. Evie did look refreshed and renewed after her break. The gossip round college was that she'd spent a week with some monks in Northumberland or else she'd been shopping in Rome. Charlie had another story: Evie had spent a week in the Priory getting clear of alcohol and sleeping pills. I wanted to ask Evie what the truth was, but Luke Cribbins showed no signs of leaving the common room. Indeed, I was convinced he was deliberately ear-wigging. I remembered how he'd said we were lovers. Then, Evie did something I didn't expect.

'Kitty, I want to say sorry.' She spoke quietly and clearly. Luke, who was sat ten yards away, pretending to read a copy of Ken Leech's *Soul Friend*, sat a little straighter.

'You already have, remember?'

'No, Kitty, that was different. When I was unwell, I was a prat. I promise ...' She paused and smiled to herself. 'I promise, on Our Lady, the martyrs, and all the saints, that I won't bother you again.' She stood up, and was about to walk off, when she stopped and added, in a whisper,

'Oh, and Kit. For the love of all that's holy, look after it.' She walked away.

I often think about that brief encounter. It wasn't quite the last time I saw Evie alive, but it was the last time we spoke alone. Should I have figured out what was going to happen to Evie based on that short exchange? 'I promise, on our Lady, the martyrs, and all the saints, that I won't bother you again.' It's a line that affords multiple meanings. When I was interviewed by the coroner after Evie's death, she asked if I'd had any hint of Evie's state of mind. We were all asked that. I said that I had nothing definite, indeed, that the last time I'd spoken to her alone she'd seemed very bright. I mentioned that line about her not bothering me, but said that I'd read it as Evie saying she wouldn't be clingy or over-bearing. But, of course, her words could have been read in a different way. The coroner said as much, though she accepted my account as valid.

225

Of course, I said nothing about her final line. 'For the love of all that's holy, look after it.' That, I decided, was not for public consumption. It was for me. It was whispered so quietly that not even Luke could hear it. At the time, I'd assumed I'd find time to speak to Evie properly about the book. We had all the time in the world. Looking back, I can see I was deluding myself; Evie's actions proved that. I draw close now to the defining and definitive act, Evie's death. There is one more thing I must talk about first: what I saw in the panopticon on that Thursday night.

Chapter Twenty-seven

I haven't spoken properly of Ivo, Piers, Charlie and Richard for ages. I suppose I've been doing my best to avoid them. It was only by setting them to the side that I've managed to convince myself to get to this point: the climax of my little story. But, if I am to confess properly, I can avoid them no longer.

In the run-up to Evie's death, I'd hardly seen them. This was partly to do with the simple fact that Albertus had scheduled few seminars that term. Loewe could be puckish and capricious at the best of times, but that term he was around even less than usual. The reason, I thought, was simple: he was seriously ill, though at that point I don't think any of us guessed just how bad things had become. For all of us, in our different ways, Albertus was immortal. We thought he would just go on and on. We weren't ready to acknowledge his frailty.

There were other reasons I'd seen less of the others. Quite apart from my creeping paranoia about how they saw me, the others were fully committed again with placements and preparations for dissertations and theses. Since our chat at The Trout, Richard had practically vanished. It was clear he was going through with his plan to leave. I still saw him occasionally, but it always seemed to be at a distance. We had our usual Friday nights, of course, but there was no joy in them anymore. All I remember of those last weeks before Evie's death is how – sometimes with Evie and Richard present, sometimes without them – we'd sit playing piquet and what Piers

227

called 'German Games' and chat in a desultory manner. Evenings ended early and, more often than not, I would try to get away for 9pm, pleading work as my alibi. No one ever questioned me or asked me to stay.

That Thursday, then. There were flurries of snow in the air and I remember a fat old crow sitting on Old Quercus, the oak in the Quad beneath my study-window. The crow would come back day after day and skip up and down the branches. It made me want to curse Quercus, as Christ had cursed the fig tree, and make it wither and die. On that day, however, I just hoped the snow would stop or turn to rain. I'd resolved to go to the panopticon that evening and I had no desire to leave traces of my tracks. After morning chapel, I worked alone all morning and shared a dismal hunger lunch of mushroom soup and a roll with Piers in the Refectory. He asked if I fancied going out for a decent bit of grub early evening. I told him I wasn't feeling myself, though I just wanted to be alone to prepare for my visit to the old tower. Piers vigorously tried to change my mind. He seemed utterly sincere, only interested in his grumbling stomach. The human face I decided was a treacherous and beautiful thing. I had convinced myself that his offer was just another ruse to get me away from my room for a while.

I had something else on my mind. No one had mentioned anything about prayer and mortification since Christmas. I wondered if Piers – who had always been my way into that world – wanted to sound me out, to see if I was up for something during Lent, which was just a few weeks away. To draw me in again, like a drug dealer and provide me with what I secretly wanted and secretly feared. I often took my cilice out and looked at it. I kept it under my pillow. I don't know why. Perhaps it was a kind of bizarre analogue to Evie's comforter, her stuffed cat toy, perhaps. At my most secretly pious, I sometimes longed for dreams of my Saviour, like a second-rate Teresa of Avila or an Anglican Catherine of Siena. I felt closer to

Him when I was near the mode of pain and discipline. Yes, I would wear it too, from time-to-time, on high days and holy days, though Richard's words had sobered me, as well as his infected wound. Could this practice really be right if it could lead to damage like that?

Day turned into night, and I felt paralysed. It all seemed ridiculous. A piece of Gothic theatre. And once I was at the tower, what was I supposed to do? Just sit there, lurking in the shadows? Waiting for some of my friends to turn up? I even began to suspect that Richard wanted to lure me there. Oh God. I was a mess. Once I'd allowed the thought that he had been in cahoots with the others, anything was possible. Yet I'd seen how awful Richard looked that day. It was no fakery. Whatever else might be going on, when he'd said I should visit the panopticon he'd been utterly sincere. And, in the end, that was what frightened me. This evening would be the end of something.

It was a starry night and even by seven o'clock the ground was beginning to freeze. At least it meant I wouldn't leave tracks in the rock-hard ground. Quite how I was going to keep warm while I waited for the others was another thing. I had visions of giving myself away with chattering teeth. As I approached the tower, I checked, as best as I could, that I wasn't being watched. I saw no twitching curtains from the apartments. I saw no one lurking in the dark. The door, however, was intimidating. It had a heavy rusted bolt and a security lock on it. It looked, frankly, impregnable. Still, I thought I might try the bolt and, to my surprise, it slipped free quite easily. Someone had put in a lot of work to get it free. There was no handle so I pulled at the protruding lock and the door swung open. I slipped inside and did my best to close it again. I decided that the safest, darkest place to wait was in a recess in the first downstairs room. I pushed myself as far back into the shadows as I could, shuddering at the damp chill of unheated brick and metal, and set myself to wait.

Everyone knows that time is subjective. That night, I swear

I learnt that fact in my very DNA. It was bone-achingly cold and pitch black. I'm not easily spooked, but sitting, at night, inside a dark, creaking asylum building as the wind whistles around the door would be a challenge for anyone. I tried to soothe myself by reciting the Rosary in my head. When I lost my way, I tried the Jesus Prayer: *Lord Jesus Christ, Son of God, have mercy on me a sinner ...* over and over. It would work for a few minutes, then the creaks of the building and the scratching and crawling of God-knows-what – the Devil I thought at one point – would overwhelm me. The stench in the place was obscene, the stink of cat piss and decay and stale air coming over me in waves, making me want to retch. At one point I thought someone had died in there, the smell of rot and filth got so bad, then I realised I'd sat on some old clothes that a tramp or someone had discarded in there. It was like sitting on the remains of the dead. The worst moment, the moment when I nearly screamed, when I nearly lost it completely, came when I felt something damp and hairy crawl over my left hand. It rested there just for a moment. I felt its slimy tummy move, its tiny paws tap on my skin. To this day I don't know exactly what it was, a rat or a mouse, I guess. Sometimes still I wake up in the night, my body shaking and damp from visions of being trapped in a creaking cell filled with slimy rodents crawling all over me.

After two hours, cold and weary and desperate for the loo, I'd just about had enough. As I grew agitated, a thought struck me: the door. It had been barred when I arrived and there had been no way for me to slide it back across once inside. It was an amateur's mistake. If anyone was looking, they'd notice that straight away. In my anxiety, I began to move my stiff limbs, thinking I had to get away. Then, I heard muffled voices outside. Whoever was there, they were discussing something. I was sure it was the state of the door. I felt every muscle in my body tense, then the door creaked and squealed and I heard multiple pairs of feet tramp in. From the sound, I reckoned that at least three people must have entered. I heard the door pulled shut again and I waited for someone to switch on a torch. Nothing. Then I saw a couple of red points flare bright in the dark. Cigarettes. I watched them move across the dark space and ascend the stairs. These were people so familiar with this place they could negotiate it in the dark. My need for the loo vanished. My mind became focussed and alert and I'd stopped noticing the cold. I told myself, 'Don't hurry.' I had to give them time. This was the hardest thing. My body was desperate for action. I was stiff and sore, but the adrenaline shot prepared me for anything. And still I had to wait.

I wanted to leave it half-an-hour before I acted. Ultimately, it was more like twenty. I crawled up slowly on my hands and knees, stopping at the slightest sound. I paused as I reached the first level, peeping over the step into the open space. Nobody was there. My heart was beating so hard I swear it could have given me away. Not that I should have worried. Other sounds were now beginning to fall from the floor above. Muffled, at this distance, but real nonetheless. The sound of human voices and something else I could not quite make out. A repetition. A faint thwacking sound perhaps. In the dark, I almost lost my nerve. I thought, a person could go mad here. I wanted to get up and run away or scream and shout. I forced myself to carry on.

I knew I was at the point of no turning back. I felt like a medieval supplicant, a sinner at the end of a pilgrimage of grace, crawling to her goal. I must have been covered in dust. This thought only added to my sense that I was a sinner forced to do penance, crawling the last part of her journey back to the holy community on her hands and knees. I began my final ascent towards the room at the top of the tower and I looked up and saw a dim light bleeding out onto the top step. I heard the sound of voices and the sound of something else cracking and snapping. When I reached the final chamber, what I saw was shocking. I could – especially when seen through my tired, already scared eyes – easily embellish the scene with *grand guignol* features. I shall attempt to resist.

First, what I saw, as I peeped over the top step, were four people illuminated by candle light. They were Ivo, Piers, Charlie and, to my surprise, Evie. I suppose the next thing to acknowledge was that they were all naked. Their clothes were piled against a wall. I am not especially shocked by nakedness, per se. It's fair to say I've seen a few naked bodies over the years. The oddness of my friends' bodies lay in how their nakedness seemed part of a form of worship. It was a well-known medieval heresy, especially among the poorer Lollards, that worship should take place naked. The belief arose from the idea that – through Christ's saving work – we have all returned to a state of innocence, like Adam and Eve before eating the Apple. In such a state of grace, we have no need of robes or priests; we can simply be as nature intended us.

You might suppose, then, that what I witnessed was an orgy, all writhing bodies, with everyone fucking, grimly and relentlessly. Well, it was a scene of excess, but it was no orgy. In the moments before I turned tail and slid away, only one specifically sexual image impressed itself on my mind, though it was stripped of eros. It was Piers' priapic penis. He simply stood there riveted by the scene unfolding before him, his penis erect. He looked like one of those fertility statues one sometimes sees in museums, a totem of a middle-eastern cult devoted to virility. He was so still. It was as if he were unaware of his erection.

No, this was no orgy or a hippy ritual from Midsummer's Night. It was ... well, it is so difficult to find the right phrase. It was torture, if that is not too over-the-top. Despite the half-light, it was clear that all four of their bodies – excepting head, neck, lower arms and legs – were covered in bruises and old, healed or partially-healed wounds. Charlie's body was the most shocking. As I've said before, she was tall and slim – a model of the conventional feminine ideal. Somehow it was more disturbing to see marks on her flesh. Across her chest, straddling her breasts, were three dark lines which looked like scourge marks. Around her waist were a series of dark marks where a metal cilice belt had bitten deep. One area looked like it had scabbed. All of them, including Evie, bore the marks of serious and repeated flagellation across their shoulders and chests.

If their bodies presented distressing sights, it was what they were doing which will remain with me for as long as I have a mind. Piers, as I said, simply stood there, statue-like, transfixed. To his left was Ivo. Cradled in his hand was an open book. He read out loud with the slow, didactic tones that I'd heard him use before, monkish, as if he were a priest reading from some edifying book during an otherwise silent meal. The Latin was delivered with the clean, prissy tones of a Cambridge scholar. Insofar as I could understand – my Latin has never been great – Ivo was reading a list of penances: 'those who befoul their lips' shall do penance for four years and so on. There were lots of references to fornication and pollution of the body and soul. He was reading from the *Penitential of Cummean*.

While Ivo read, Charlie slowly and rhythmically whipped Evie's back with a scourge. The sound of it was terrible, a gurgling, tearing sound. Even today, I can still hear that snap and crack as Charlie brought the leather down against Evie's body. That was not the worst of it. The worst of it was Evie herself. She knelt on the floor in front of Ivo and Charlie and Piers and she submitted to their violence. There was a line of sweat on Evie's brow and she stared straight ahead, only wincing when the leather clattered against her back. There was a kind of severe dignity about her, mixed with something inhuman, in the way she just knelt there while Charlie hit her and Ivo read and Piers looked on. It was monstrous. Why did she just take it? Why did she not scream when the scourge ripped her back?

I could not breathe. I had to get away. I was terrified of being seen by them. I thought I would never be able to make my muscles move again. I felt like my face and head had been turned to stone, making me unable to take my eyes from the scene. I don't know what enabled me to move, except perhaps an instinct that if I didn't move then and there, my cover would be blown. As I began to slide backwards down the staircase, Evie did something remarkable. Without moving any other part of her traumatised body, her eyes flicked in my direction. They were pleading and desperate, or that is how I read them now. Given the dim light, I think there was no way she could have seen me. Yet, was it beyond the bounds of possibility that, in that sordid scene, she sensed me lurking in the dark? If she did, it makes my retreat even worse. In that moment, I had the means to end the torture, but I ran away. No, worse. I betrayed her. Though, as subsequent events proved, that was not my ultimate betrayal.

Part Three

1. He who long harbours bitterness in his heart shall be healed by a joyful countenance and a glad heart.
2. But if he does not quickly lay this aside, he shall correct himself by fasting according to the decision of a priest.
3. But if he returns to it, he shall be cut off until, on bread and water, he willingly and gladly acknowledges his fault.

'V. Of Dejection. The Penitential of Cummean'

Chapter Twenty-eight

I'm close now to that morning in Chapel when I found Evie suspended from the rood screen. However, I am not quite there, yet. There is one final element to be set in place before you can judge for yourself what kind of monster I am, or, how closely I approximate to a human being.

Unsurprisingly, I did not sleep that night. The selfish, paranoid part of me lay awake expecting the sound of hands hammering on my door, Ivo or Piers or Charlie, or all three of them, telling me that they knew I'd been there with them and now it was my turn to be punished. Another part of me expected the knock to presage Evie's arrival, bloody and bruised and feverish, asking why I did nothing to help. The greater part of me was just overwhelmed and traumatised. Every time I closed my eyes, I saw Evie or Charlie or one of the boys. I saw their fevered, focussed faces, grimly set on their task. Ministers at a vile ritual.

As I lay alone in the dark, I tried to figure out what I should do. Would a good person report it to someone in authority? Probably. We were not simply private citizens. We were, through Littlemore and its Principal, under the Church's discipline. People had been thrown out of Littlemore for far less than what I'd witnessed. Yet, there were also people high up in the institution who'd committed far, far worse and they'd flourished. So, yes, a good or pious person would have decided to go to the college authorities and make an accusation, but that strategy itself was also not without its risks. This was the Nineties. I was just an ordinand. Would the Church reward me for rocking the boat? I considered doing my duty, for the briefest moment, and dismissed it. I was not going to play Judas. I would approach matters a different way.

I want to confess something. Ultimately, it was the hurt generated from being left out that prompted me to action. Isn't that pathetic? I still wanted to be an insider. I still wanted to know. I still wanted to be part of their gang. Thus, when morning came, I got up, showered, prayed and breakfasted, and went around to Ivo's. He was always in on Friday morning. Indeed, we used to joke that this was the day he 'held court'. I felt clear-headed and ready to deliver my news and verdict. I rapped on his door and heard his characteristic, 'Come.' After the events of the previous evening, entering that room was a disconcerting experience, for, there was Ivo, dressed in his usual tweedy manner, the very picture of landed respectability. He sat in his office chair with that rather sloppy, loose-limbed aspect that was so characteristic. As I walked inside, he looked up from a letter at me, squinted slightly and then grinned boyishly. It was incredibly disarming and almost convinced me the previous night had been a complete mirage. He swung his chair around and said, with real warmth,

'Kitty! How lovely to see you. Put the catch across would you?' He gestured for me to sit. 'What brings you to me on this fine morning?'

I knew that if I allowed myself to be deflected for a second, I would not be able to say my piece, so I just said it.

'Ivo, I was there last night. When Charlie beat Evie, and you and Piers watched.' There was a long pause, during which Ivo considered his response. Finally, he said,

'Ah. I see.'

He sat quite still, his fingers steepled, part-don, part-holy man, as if his brief speech had settled some dispute. It was infuriating. I wanted to dive in, start arguing, but I knew it would do no good.

It would only weaken my hand by giving him something to react against. It was his tactic for dealing with any situation – let your opponent reveal their weakness – so I returned his gaze. Then he did something I hadn't expected. He breathed in carefully, and said,

'I know.'

'Know what?' I could have kicked myself for speaking.

'I know you were there.'

'What?'

He rubbed his nose meditatively and said, 'Well, that's not strictly true. I didn't see you, but I knew you would be there at some point. On one Thursday, I mean.'

I'd arrived feeling I held all the decent cards. Now I felt like I was playing catch-up with a player of superior skill.

'How?'

'Oh simple,' said Ivo. 'Richard told me.'

While I processed that piece of information, he went on. His tone became ever drier, more academic.

'What one needs to understand about Richard is that he's a deeply divided and torn man. Troubled. Aren't we all, you might say. Well, to a point. Richard's mind flip-flops so easily he's always torn between commitment and inaction, between rebellion and conformity. In that respect, Kitty, I think he's quite different to us. You and I are much more like Dürer's resolute knight. However, that is by-the-by … He'd wanted to speak to you for a while. He felt it would bring him relief. I'm sure he dropped hints. Perhaps even showed you things.'

Something must have shown up on my face, perhaps a memory of Richard's infected wound, for Ivo then said, 'Ah, I see he did. But! He is also loyal to older friends and other perhaps less definable things like class and honour, ridiculous though those ideas are.'

He paused in his disquisition, took a sip of his coffee, then said, 'After your trip to The Trout, Richard came to see me.' I tried

239

to interrupt, but Ivo raised his hands and said, 'Not to tip me off. Not because he was conspiring, but because that's what he does. He thinks himself into a corner and gets confused. There's no malice in him and, Kitty, that is a marvellous thing.'

'And now he's withdrawn from training,' I said, weakly.

'And that's a shame. He would have made a fine priest. Though I think he would have been walked over by his parishioners.'

'Like he was walked over by you and Piers?' It came out more angrily than I intended.

Ivo was about to retort, then breathed carefully, nodded his head. 'Yes, I'm sure it appears that way to you.'

'So, tell me how it was, then, Ivo?'

'I'm just saying it's not as simple as you think.'

'Please,' I said softly. 'Tell me.'

He picked up a packet of Marlboro Red, took one out and lit it. He did not offer me one. After a couple of drags, he said,

'If you gave me back my book that would be a start.' So, we were coming to it, I thought. It had been him who'd broken into my room in search of the *Penitential of Cummean.*

'I'm not sure it was ever yours, Ivo.'

Quite suddenly, he slammed his left hand down on his desk. It was nasty and loud and made me think of the crack of that whip on Evie's back. Then, with cat-like speed, he jumped up from his chair and grabbed my right arm. I reeled in shock and pain. He held his lit cigarette half-an-inch over my bare skin with his free arm. I felt my skin begin to scorch. I thought I was going to scream. When he spoke – in a soft whisper – it only underlined the violence.

'There are things you don't understand, Kitty.'

I was terrified, but with all the cool and defiance I could muster, I stared into his furious eyes and said, 'Then tell me.'

He let me go. He breathed slowly and deeply, wrestling I thought with his fury.

He returned to his chair, then said, 'Are you sitting comfortably? Well, whether you are or not, I'm going to tell you a story. And like all good stories it began a long time ago, in a fantasy land ... Once upon a time, there was a young man called Albertus. He was very bright, very well connected and, well, a little greedy and selfish. He had access to all sorts of unusual places: To private libraries in draughty country houses ... To college depositories ... He was a personal friend of curators in grand establishments ... the British Library, the Bodleian, you get the picture ... And dear old Albertus, because he was greedy and charming and admired, would persuade his friends to let him take books away on loan. And, sometimes ... sometimes he would forget to take these precious items back.'

Ivo paused in his narrative to give me time to process his words. As I tried to regain my composure, as I tried to overcome the pain where he'd grabbed my arm, I understood he might be lying. However, even if Ivo was overstating things, he offered a plausible case. I thought about the books I'd secreted about my person. Both absurdly rare. Both of dubious provenance. Both connected to Albertus. Ivo's account reminded me of a story one of my PhD supervisors told me about how lax many of the great libraries had once been. How they'd been little more than gentlemen's clubs in which even the rarest books were passed around from hand-to-hand. Scholars would walk out of places as august as the British Library with manuscripts so rare that these days one might wait for months to touch them. Is that what happened with Albertus?

'Then,' Ivo said, 'many years later, along came a modestly talented cohort of students with a passion for the Medieval and a willingness to plumb the depths of prayer.' He smiled to himself. 'Albertus indulged these ordinands. He was, after all, getting very old. Indeed, he wanted to get his affairs in order, so, he took on an assistant, one Evie .... What he didn't appreciate was, well, that, despite appearing kindly and perhaps a little gullible, Evie was as

241

ruthless as he'd been. And, it has to be said, a little more needy.

'Evie was given access to Albertus's fabled treasure trove. Piles of manuscripts and incunabula locked away. Albertus had become sentimental in his dotage and wanted them to be catalogued in preparation for their return to proper libraries after his death. He had so many he didn't know what he had. You think that copy of the *Canterbury Tales* was something? Not according to Evie. Evie, for all her charm, has always been secretly insecure. And she wanted to impress us, us being Piers, Charlie, Richard and me. She wanted to tell us all about the cornucopia of rare books she'd come across.'

'So, when she came across my ...' he smiled, then said, 'that copy of the *Cummean* she was practically wetting herself to tell us. She'd overheard us talking about our penitential plans and she thought it a way to go deeper. "Ivo, you won't believe what I've found ..."' His impression of Evie, if mocking, was surprisingly good. '"More complete than any surviving text ..." "Full of unique penances ..." You know what she can be like ... So ...' He paused again and pushed his specs up off his nose towards his forehead. He was embarrassed, I realised. 'So ... that was the deal. Get me the book ... and she could join the magic circle.'

'You made her steal for you?'

'I wanted a closer look.' He grinned, without a hint of humour, then added, 'Well, that's what I told myself. But it's never that simple, is it?'

'What do you mean?'

'Oh, come on, Kitty, grow up. Do you think this is just about ancient books? This is about the truth. This is about protecting the faith.' He looked avid, almost mad. His face was alive with the passion I'd glimpsed in the half-light of the tower the night before.

'What?!?'

'Yes, Kitty, it's about the fucking truth.'

'And the *Cummean* is what exactly?' I spat it out, angry

now. I thought of Evie kneeling there while they doled out their punishments.

'It's an instrument,' said Ivo, with finality. 'It corrects the sinner.'

I stood up and shouted, 'And what ...' I stopped and breathed deeply, then said, in a whisper. 'And what does that make Evie?'

The silence was appalling. Monstrous, even. I looked at that copy of Dürer's knight on the wall. The cold hard face of the knight, and the Devil by his side. I'd always seen Ivo as the knight. Now I wondered if he was the Devil. Ivo glared at me, then smiled. He said,

'Kitty, please. Sit down.'

I hesitated, then obeyed.

'Cigarette?' I shook my head. He took one out of the pack and lit up.

'Where is this leading, Ivo?'

He took a drag and said, 'There was this beak at school, a clergyman, who said that God sends us the people and the books and the art we need, if we are only wise enough to spot them. Do you believe that?'

'I don't know,' I said, testily. 'I'd need to think about it. Why?'

'I suppose I'm saying I find it hard to believe that we haven't all come together for a reason. The books, the people, the shared passion.'

I lost my temper, and said, loudly,

'Christ, Ivo, I saw Charlie leathering holy fucking hell out of Evie while you read out penance, and Piers stood there with a hard-on. I saw the wound on Richard's ...' As soon as I'd said this, I regretted it. The last thing I wanted was for us to be overheard. I whispered, 'This is not blessèd of God. It's fairground medievalism.' My pomposity sounded hollow in my mouth.

'So why are you here, Kitty, and not in the Principal's office?'

'I'm here ...' I broke off. 'I'm here because I ... I just want to understand.'

243

'Are you sure? Are you sure you're not jealous?'

'Don't play games, Ivo.'

'I wouldn't dare. You forget, I broke into your room. I found your cilice under your pillow. Have you been sleeping with it?'

'Fuck you.'

'It's all right,' he said, putting up his hand. 'I understand. Oh God, I, of all people, understand. I've understood since I was a kid. Piers too. We've understood since we were together at Christian summer camp. The things the leaders and counsellors did to us. They'd make your soul weep.'

'And Charlie?' I left the question hanging there. 'Evie?'

'Would you believe that Charlie thinks she's ugly? I suppose you do. You're a woman. You know how it works, though it bewilders me. Anyway, she's been searching for years for a way to purge herself of shame. Piers and I provided it.

'As for Evie,' he said, in a drawl. 'There's things you don't understand. Yes, she fancied a taste of God's discipline, just like you. Just like all of us. But she crossed a line. Got above herself. Found out stuff she shouldn't. I've had to bring her back to the fold.'

Without thinking I said, 'Ye been as bolde as is Bayard the blinde, That blundreth forth, and peril castest noon.'

Ivo pursed his lips, then said,

'I see you are better informed than I thought,' then almost to himself, 'though not as well as you think.' Almost absently he picked up the delicate biscuit by his coffee cup and pushed it into his mouth.

Did I think he was mad? I wish I could say, 'Yes'. As Ivo chewed that biscuit – wafer-like and elegant – my mind was cast back to that night when Evie had turned up at Charlie's with oysters, and told us how Matthew Hopkins liked to eat a dozen before he set a witch ablaze. I wondered if Ivo was what officers of the Spanish Inquisition had been like: by turns, cool, detached, then furious and zealous. I remembered an account of how Crassus

– the general who'd crushed Spartacus's Slave Revolt – had slept soundly while, on his orders, thousands of slaves were nailed to crosses along the Appian Way. Yes, there was something fanatical and righteous about Ivo, but mad? I'd spent hours and days and weeks in his company. The world had got out of all kilter, but there was still a part of me that said he and the others were my friends. My best friends. And what you must remember is that even if I'd never been admitted into their closest circle, I appreciated the power of mortifying prayer. I'd shared in that strange mix of pain and joy and mystery. I thought then (as I still think now, in weak moments), that I was more like him than any of the general run of people in College.

I understood, after all, the fever of ancient books. When he described the copy of the *Cummean* as 'his book', I understood in my very bones. That's exactly how I felt about my – yes, my – copy of the *Canterbury Tales*. I knew the obsession with old things, of course I did. Yet, what struck me, however, was that there was something more at stake for Ivo. Why did he need *that* book so badly? Yes, our obsessions are often mysterious to others, but Ivo's hunger for this copy was palpable. I remembered Evie's words, 'For the love of all that's holy, look after it.' Evie, I realised, had stolen this book back from Ivo. She wanted to keep it away from him, at all costs. I considered Ivo's words of a few minutes before: 'She found out stuff she shouldn't.' Finally, I understood the significance of the palimpsest. Whatever she'd found behind the words of the *Cummean*, she didn't want Ivo anywhere near it. He could not be trusted with it.

'Why did Evie steal the book back off you?'

'Oh, well done. Figured that out have you.'

I said nothing, determined to make him fill the silence for once.

'I wish I could trust you, Kitty. I really do, but on this, I can't. I like you enormously, but you'll never understand …' He paused, assessing me again. 'Yes, I was quite wrong about you. You're not like the knight at all. You're like his dog. Loyal and trusting. And I see that, for all her treatment of you, you'll be loyal to Evie and all your sex.'

I should have been insulted, I suppose, but I was not. If I was yet to fully un-fog the mysteries around Evie's book, and what lay beneath its surface text, I was curiously grateful to Ivo. He'd helped me see myself a little clearer. We are all divided selves, and so easily confused, but he had shown me to what I must be faithful. If I was a dog, I was not his dog.

'What now?' I said. Ivo stood up and stretched.

'Forgive me,' he said. 'A little cramp.' He rubbed his left leg. I shuddered. I didn't want to picture the kind of wound that lay beneath the tweed of his trouser, itching angrily away against the wool. A thought occurred to me: was that why he always wore tweed? Because wool on wounds only aggravates. He walked over to the window and looked out. I watched his broad back, sealed inside a country check shirt, his trousers held up with braces. I thought of the marks and bruises that lay beneath that shirt. It all seemed so surreal. Bizarre.

Suddenly he turned and said, 'A deal, I think.'

'What do you propose?'

'I'm grateful, Kitty, that you came to me first, rather than speak to Evie or, heaven forfend, the Principal or the Chaplain. I think it best for all concerned if we keep this quiet. I appreciate that you're a woman of principle and, perhaps, you feel you should bring this affair into the light. However, if you do that, I think I have enough on you to get you thrown out with the rest of us.'

'Are you threatening me?'

Quite coolly, he said, 'Of course I'm threatening you. Just, as I think, you're threatening me. However, if we can put this all behind us for now, I think I can offer you something you want.'

'Yes?' I said, with a little puzzlement.

'Well, I thought it would be obvious. Give me the book and I promise to leave Evie alone.'

I sat considering this. Ivo spoke softly, almost kindly, as he proposed his bargain. He might have been offering me a choice between a pre-dinner sherry or Madeira, rather than a choice between a secret book and the well-being of Evie. I wondered how far Ivo might go in hurting Evie. I remembered Richard's terror that day he'd sought to speak of Ivo. I thought again of what I'd witnessed in the panopticon. Ivo would do anything to promote what he saw as his righteous ends. I remembered what he'd written in his note to Evie: 'Beware the wages of sin.' The wages of sin was Death. Did that mean he would kill? I shuddered again and saw Ivo smile. When I thought of it in those terms, it was obvious: give Ivo the book and save Evie. And yet she had said I must not give it to him under any circumstances, which meant not even when her life was threatened. I had to stall, play for time. Perhaps if I could only speak to Evie, make her see sense. Finally, I stood up, and said,

'Sorry, Ivo. You need to give me some time.'

He nodded, a sad little nod.

'I see … That's a shame.' He looked at the hot tip of his cigarette and then back at me. I rubbed my arm where he had held hot coals over the skin. Then he said,

'Okay, Kitty. But do not be like Boccaccio's valiant men and fair ladies, eh?'

It was such an innocuous sentence, but it was pregnant with so much threat. His reference to Boccaccio concerned the indiscriminate death meted out by the Plague. Boccaccio says that, in the Plague of 1348, many breakfasted with the living and dined with their ancestors. Not only was Ivo telling me to make a quick decision, but beware of the consequences of delay. A thought occurred to me: I could destroy the book, put it beyond use, but it was a hopeless thought. I could no more destroy an ancient manuscript than strangle a cat. Perhaps, I could run away. But where? Even then, I needed to see Evie, first. Let her guide me in my final decision. Even if our relationship had been poisoned for a long time, I still owed her that. Didn't I?

I walked to the door, then Ivo said, quite affably, as if we hadn't spent the last half an hour talking about violence and lies,

'See you at Charlie's tonight?'

'Probably.'

'Super.'

I spun the internal lock around to open it. With my back to him, I had this sudden image of Ivo smashing me over the head with a cosh. It made me turn back, but Ivo, of course, was at the other end of the room, by the window still. Just as I was about to leave, I said, on impulse,

'Ivo, come back, please. Come back from the dark.'

He turned and said,

'Kitty, it's not me who needs redemption.'

Chapter Twenty-nine

I searched and searched for Evie that afternoon. No one had seen her and she wasn't to be found in any of her usual places. Her car was still in the car park, and her bike in the shed. She might have been at the panopticon, but I thought not. If I couldn't bring myself to go back there, how could she? No. It was as if she'd been wiped off the face of the earth. In my anxiety, I almost wanted to report her missing, though even in my febrile state I could see how ridiculous that was. I just needed to wait, hold my nerve and she'd turn up. Unfortunately, as the day wore on, my tiredness and anxiety turned in on itself.

My encounter with Ivo had chilled me. No, terrified me. My aching arm bore testimony to what he was capable of. As the day rolled on, I wanted to retreat to the only place I felt some semblance of safety, the place that had become my home: my room. So, as soon as I dared, I retreated there and barricaded the door. I shuffled my bedside table across and piled it up with books. I checked and double-checked the lock, aware that Ivo could easily break in, should he choose, but determined to take as many precautions as possible. I lay on my bed and tried to stay awake. I lay there, looking at Evie's book in the half-light, running my fingers across the vellum as if it were braille. As if touch might supply the clues to the book's nature.

As so often when one tries to stay awake, I fell asleep. I dreamed that Evie was her biblical name-sake, up to her neck in a pool of stinking water and excrement, desperately trying to remain dignified.

I dreamed that Ivo was Adam berating her for her faithlessness and hitting her with a scourge. Piers was the snake, offering the Apple of temptation. Charlie, her face swollen and marked with pox, shouted obscenities at them all. Then the scene shifted to a library. I saw Albertus as a young man, his hair and moustache transformed into a deep chestnut colour. He skulked around among the books, occasionally sliding a volume into his trousers, adding to the size of his vast belly. I dreamed of a silent Louise, her clothes sodden with water, pointing the finger of judgment at us all.

It was still dark when I woke, cold and shivery. I lay on top of my bed and Evie's book was gone. In my panic, I reached for my bedside light, realised there was no table by the bed, and slowly came back to sense and remembered that the table and the lamp were pushed against the door. I got up, turned on the light and saw that Evie's book, my book, was on the floor. I picked it up, and walked over to my window and looked out on a wild morning. I checked my watch and saw that it was 7.00 am. It would soon be dawn and I was gripped by an urge to go and pray.

Later on, the police asked me why I chose to go to the chapel at that time. They were intrigued. Did I do it regularly? Was it common among the students? The lovely Police Liaison Officer, a thirty-year old female sergeant who told me to call her Lizzy, was bewildered by the idea that people might pray at any other time than during profound distress. I told her I went there to think and pray. What I was discreet about was what I went to think over. For, as I crept down into the chapel, I was going to think over a theory that had come to me about Evie's book. Given that I didn't want anyone outside of my immediate circle, let alone the police, to know about my manuscripts, I told Lizzy I went down to pray about my upcoming placement and what God wanted of me.

I've never felt the same about the dawn since that morning I found Evie hanging from the Rood in Chapel. Freud said that the uncanny is an effect of the ordinary – fear is generated by the familiar placed in strange relief. Until that morning, I'd never dreaded the dawn. I'd never sensed in it the odour and bleakness of death, it always gave me hope. Things changed that morning when I found Evie suspended between worlds, hanging from a low beam, her body infused with an odd glow by the breaking dawn. To put it another way: It was just grim. There was, as I've long since discovered in priestly ministry, very little dignity in death. It's just banal and cheap, and there is no way of protecting the dead from the intrusions of the living. I was simply the first to intrude, and over the coming days, Evie's broken, pathetic body got used to it. As I've said before, my first thought was, 'How could that beam take Evie's weight?' I still marvel at that fact sometimes, when Evie comes back to me, as she does with increasing frequency now. If I intruded on her death, she now repays the compliment and intrudes on my half-life. Sometimes, I wake from sleep and I can still feel the coldness of her skin where I checked for a pulse. It makes me think of winter rivers, of dead fish.

The rest of that morning was a mess. I banged on the front door of the Principal's house till it was opened by his wife, bleary-eyed, sulky. I saw two young girls, the Principal's children, lurking in the shadows. I guess we all like to imagine that in a crisis we'd be clear-headed and precise. As I tried to explain the situation to Mrs Palmerston, I discovered I was not. I felt a curious wave of panic in my chest. The Principal earned his keep that morning. He – like an old-fashioned Colonel – rallied the troops magnificently. Hilary 'Queenie' Queensferry, the College Administrator, was characteristically immense, protecting the student body from the press, who were on the scene more quickly than anyone might reasonably imagine. After speaking briefly to the police on their arrival, I was permitted to go back to my room, on the strict proviso I wasn't to be left alone. Several of the pastoral vampires lined up to be my comforter and chaperone. I told them – to my abiding shame – to bugger off and leave me alone.

It was in my room, later that morning, that the pact of silence began to form. Charlie had come to find me, and somewhere along the way Ivo and Piers had attached themselves. When they arrived, I was attempting to reach for my bottle of Dalwhinnie on the top shelf inside my wardrobe. I was shaking almost uncontrollably. I remember Charlie stepping in and taking control. I was, in that moment, inordinately grateful. I needed to sit and breathe and be calm and I sat on my bed, while Charlie poured. Piers and Ivo, dressed in dark suits I think, looked down on me in pity, like funeral directors. We drank quietly and I felt the bitter bite of the alcohol steady my nerves. Finally, Ivo said,

'I think we should agree on some things.'

'What?' said Charlie, softly.

'About Evie.'

'Is this the time?' The question was out of my mouth before I could engage my brain.

'It's the only time,' said Ivo, coldly.

It was Piers who continued. 'We have to accept that questions – difficult questions – are going to be asked in the next few days. I'm sorry to say this, but Evie's body will be subject to a post-mortem. Her body will be examined minutely. All of us know that her body is covered in bruises and lacerations.'

If the alcohol was going to my head, it also gestured towards the truth: I realised that the three of them had already discussed this before they'd met me. In those brief minutes before arriving at mine, they'd begun to formulate a plan.

'Ivo and I,' said Piers, 'have already disposed of the evidence from Thursday. I think we simply play things cool from here on. There is one thing, though.' He coughed, embarrassed.

'What is it?' I said.

'Well,' said Ivo. 'Your cilice.'

I closed my eyes and nodded. I gestured towards the pillow.

It was done quickly and kindly, Ivo reaching across and sliding the item inside his jacket.

After another long silence, I said, 'We can never speak of this, can we?'

'No,' said Charlie. There was a bleak finality to it. Later on that night, as I churned over the day's events, I thought about this conversation again. Second-time around, I was sure her comment was a threat.

'What do we say? About the wounds? If they ask?' I said.

'Oh, they'll ask,' said Charlie.

'That we thought that Evie had been troubled for a while, but we didn't know how bad it was,' said Piers.

'And, anyway, they'll find items, scourges and such like, in Evie's room,' added Ivo. He poured another slug of whisky for each of us and passed them around. He said, 'Kitty, where's your Bible?'

I pointed to one of my shelves. Ivo took it down and said, 'We never speak of this. We swear to it – on the Blessed Virgin, the Apostles and the Martyrs. Now.' He held the black leather volume out in front of us. We all placed our hands on the cover and made our oath of silence. And that was that.

It was later that Ivo's line, 'And, anyway, they'll find items, scourges and such like, in Evie's room', came back to me in a troubling echo. In the days to come, I was in a permanent state of unease and near breakdown. Why shouldn't Evie – who had gone so much deeper into a world of pain and discipline than me – have a whole selection of mortification devices? Among them might be any number of things that could cause wounds across her flesh. Yet there was something disconcerting about the way Ivo delivered that sentence. 'They'll find items, scourges and such like, in Evie's room …' In the days that followed, my traumatised mind began to brood

253

on this line. I began to connect it with the conversation I'd had with Ivo the day before Evie's death. About how I should not delay too long in speaking to Evie. I began to suspect that Ivo had got to Evie before I had. That he was even more ruthless than I'd imagined. That he knew how to push Evie over the line. It raised the age-old question that surrounds deaths like Evie's: did she, metaphorically speaking, 'jump' or was she 'pushed'? Or to put it bluntly: in those vile days after her death, I asked, if Evie jumped into oblivion how much was Ivo responsible for pulling on her feet?

Chapter Thirty

One of the things I discovered in the aftermath of Evie's death is how much power the very wealthy can still wield in England. After twenty odd years of being ordained, it's bloody obvious, but back then I was still naïve. In the past twenty years, I've witnessed again and again how money – sometimes in the hands of old clerical families – can be deployed to lessen the effects of sexual impropriety and even sexual criminality. On more than one occasion I've witnessed bishops and deans with old money spray it around on smart lawyers to get friends and family better deals when they've crossed a sexual or financial line. Back then, I'd never seen anything like what Evie's parents did. It was a lesson in a very English form of corruption and, I'm embarrassed to say, I was grateful for what they did.

Sir Angus and Lady Miranda Kirkland appeared at Littlemore on Saturday afternoon. Sir Angus – who insisted I call him 'Gus' when we were introduced – was much shorter than I expected. For some reason, to this day, I tend to expect those who've worked in the higher echelons of civil or public service to be tall. Gus was a stocky man, no more than five foot seven, with a thick head of black hair and a steely glint in his eye. There was an energy to him that verged on anger. He'd been an ambassador to various parts of Europe and the Middle East and there was something of the perma-tanned jetsetter about him. Piers told me he was known as a fixer who'd ruthlessly work his old school and university contacts to get results. Whatever else he was, his suits, hand-made in virgin wool, were magnificent.

As for Lady Miranda, she was stick-thin and taller than her husband. I noticed that she always wore flat shoes, presumably so as not to embarrass him. Like her husband, her clothes – Chanel and Versace – were immaculate. Physically, I'd expected her to be an older version of Evie, yet she was not. Evie's features were a hotchpotch of her parents. She had her father's lips and her mother's nose and chin. I was glad that she hadn't inherited her mother's tendency to look at every person she met as if they'd created a terrible stink in her nostrils.

Gus and Miranda were magnificent in the face of Evie's death. It seems wrong to say it, but it was precisely the kind of situation for which they were trained and in which they excelled. Their whole upbringing had prepared them for crisis. Not so much the death of their only child – which I later discovered broke both of their lives – but a preparedness for tragedy. They handled the hurriedly prepared press conference on Sunday morning with a dignified, patrician calm. Gus's voice – refined and precise – was shaped for delivering dramatic and sad news. When he asked for the family's privacy to be respected at this tragic time, he might have been asking the nation for calm on the eve of war.

On Monday, the Principal gathered the whole student body to tell us not to speak to the press. It was one of those occasions when a great number of people embarrassed themselves. There was much weeping and hugging. I have vague recollections of Michael Shaw and Chris Eastwood weeping over me, among others. The College President attempted to look dignified in his hiking gear, and there was already talk of a Charity or Trust in the name of Evie. The Bishop of Oxford turned up towards the end of the meeting, offering prayer and anointing. I will never forget the way he looked at the Principal: with a kind of cold grimness that said, 'This is all your fault.' It did not presage well. Indeed, within weeks there was a major internal investigation into pressures being placed on young ordinands.

Through it all, Gus and Miranda offered a kind of quiet and discreet presence. They took up residence with the Master of Balliol, an old Foreign Office friend of Gus's. They kept court there during that frenetic week and it was during a visit to the lodgings, with Ivo and my friends, that I discovered just how much the old Establishment could conceal and smooth over. We were invited over for drinks on the Tuesday evening, though we were not, it should be noted, invited to dinner. None of us. Not even Ivo who, as a scion of the old gentry, I thought might have been. Not even Charlie, who'd known Evie at school.

It was an exceptionally awkward three-quarters of an hour. Miranda and Charlie kept trying and failing to find links via the school connection. Gambits were offered and declined. Gus attempted to show some interest in my research area; he said that Evie had spoken very fondly of me when he'd last seen her. I tried to hide my surprise and said I was very fond of her. He said how sorry he was that I'd found her 'like that' in the Chapel and he thought me very level-headed for taking things as I had. He said, 'If there's anything Miranda and I can do, please let me know.'

As I processed this offer, he tapped his glass with a fork to gather our attention. 'Friends. I'm so sorry to gather us together on this sad occasion. I don't need to tell you what Evie meant to each of us. She spoke with great affection about you all, especially you Kitty. None of us can imagine what her state of mind might have been on Friday night. Indeed, Miranda and I shall always be ... tormented by the thought that we could not prevent what happened.

'I suspect we all feel guilty. We shall all ask ourselves, could we have done more? I know I shall. But I don't want any of you to blame yourselves. I've spoken to the police and the coroner today, and I want to assure you that everyone ...' He paused and took a deep breath, before continuing, 'Everyone wants this tragedy cleared away

257

as soon as possible. And as discreetly. I want us to remember Evie at her best, not as she …' He paused again. 'Not as she left this world, but as she lived. She was young, vibrant, talented. In many ways, easily led, but in others bold and courageous. In token of that, I ask you to raise your glass. To Evie.'

'To Evie,' we all mumbled. Charlie was chalk-white. I thought she might faint.

It was, on reflection, extraordinarily well-done, a testimony to the diplomat's art. At no point did Gus look at his watch, and yet he timed it precisely so he could deliver it to full effect, whilst ensuring that – to allow time for Miranda and him to get to High Table in a seemly manner – we had to leave as he ended his speech. As we walked back to the car, Ivo said, 'I think the Kirklands have spared us a very hard time.'

'What do you mean?' said Charlie. Something of her colour had returned.

'Well, based on that speech, my hunch is that they want nothing unseemly to come out about what their daughter might have been up to … with us …'

'He knows?' I said.

'No, of course not. But he suspects something. That line, "In many ways, she was easily led." Dear God … It's code. It means he's seen the state of Evie's body and seen the items in her room. So yes, he suspects something. He, err, well, he suspects something about you, actually, Kitty.'

I stopped and watched the others walk on for a few paces.

'About me?' I said.

The others stopped and turned. Ivo said, 'Calm down, Kitty.'

'I am calm, Ivo.'

'It's going to be fine,' he replied.

'What do you mean he suspects something about me?'

'Piers,' said Ivo, softly.

Piers said,

'I got talking to Sir Angus yesterday afternoon. He wanted to know about you. About your relationship with Evie.'

'What?'

'He had this idea that you and Evie were together.'

'And what did you say?'

'What do you think?' he said, defensively. 'Come on, Kitty. It's nothing. We just need to stick together on this.'

I sat silently in the back of Ivo's car on the way to Littlemore. I had barely slept since I found Evie three days before. That's hardly surprising. I was in shock. I can handle stress and strangeness, but finding a dead body – let alone the body of someone you once adored – is dreadful. Suddenly Evie was everywhere: in my thoughts, in everyone's fevered prayers, in the newspapers and in conversation. It may almost be blasphemy, but this omnipresence of Evie was almost Christ-like. Indeed, ever since, whenever Easter comes around I think of her; of how violent death can leave a space in which everyone suddenly starts seeing the dead person everywhere. That applied as much to Evie as it ever did to Jesus. As we drove back to college, I had another anxiety. Was I now going to become the focus of police attention or the coroner's? I had no idea how that stuff worked. If Gus and Miranda suspected I was, what? Evie's girlfriend? Her partner? Then what might the authorities think? I thought back over our relationship of the previous term – the times we'd slept together, our mutual attraction. Was there any evidence left that might connect Evie and me as lovers? Might I be suspected of inflicting horrific wounds on her body or of driving her to suicide? I had visions of interrogations in smoky, airless rooms. I thought I might vomit or scream.

I clung on to Ivo's words: 'I think the Kirklands have spared us a very hard time.' Ivo could be infuriating and, as my recent encounter with him revealed, quite frightening, but he was speaking into his world: the world of privilege and position, where the Establishment looks out for their own. Surely he could not be so very wrong. I played back Gus's words, 'Everyone wants this tragedy to be cleared away as soon as possible. And as discreetly.' Discreetly. It was the key word. I was someone who'd learnt to be self-sufficient; I needed to be in control and now I was in the hands of figures who might offer me up to keep their hands clean. I thought of Gus's fingernails. They were so neat. I'm not sure I'd seen a man with such manicured hands before. He would never want to have a thread out of place on his hand-made suits, even less Lady Miranda. Scandal was the very worst thing they could imagine and they would do anything to avoid it. I, indeed all of us were relying on that fact. As we travelled out into the countryside on that chilly night, I prayed it would be enough.

Chapter Thirty-one

Who said that a symptom of trauma is an inability to order time and events properly? They were right. Trauma breaks the lines of connection on which our routine lives rely and in the following weeks I was in an iconic state of trauma. I cannot guarantee that what I say happened exactly in the order I describe. My memory of that period is shot and damaged.

I do know I was properly interviewed by the police and gave my statement. It did not happen in an airless cell, but in my own room. It was gentle and kind and respectful. All the officer was interested in was my account of what I'd found, what I saw and what I did. I was offered counselling and support. I could not have been handled with kinder gloves. The same was true of the College. They offered me a professional counsellor and time off and a restructuring of my course of study, if I wanted it. I even had a meeting with the Principal and the Bishop who were most anxious to impress upon me how much the College cared for its ordinands. They were clearly crapping themselves and desperate to avoid scandal. An incident like Evie's could lead to the closure of a small college like Littlemore.

Despite my shock and stress, I began to think Ivo was right. Everyone – from the ecclesiastical authorities through to Evie's family – wanted to smooth things over. The Coroner's Court confirmed this. As an Agatha Christie fan, I expected the coroner to be a beaky late middle-aged man who had to repeat questions to stumbling country bumpkins; the reality was, of course, quite different. The coroner was a woman in her late thirties, brisk, calm and kind. She guided us through proceedings with courtesy and warmth. The surprise for me came regarding Evie's name. When the case was called, Evie was described as 'Evelyn Clarissa Kirkland'. In my naivety, I'd always assumed that Evie's name was just that, 'Evie'. This minor revelation seemed to me to sum up how elusive Evie remained for me. We'd spent half a year hanging out with each other, but I'd never even known her full, her real (as I now thought of it) name.

When I gave my evidence, I felt held and understood. It was nowhere near as terrifying as I imagined it would be. The other key witnesses were, in their differing ways, impressive. Gus Kirkland, speaking on behalf of his family, remained dignified and controlled. He spoke of long-term concerns that he and Miranda had held about the state of Evie's mental health; he spoke of Evie's time in the Priory to deal with alcohol and prescription drug issues; he noted how her involvement with the Church and her selection for training had offered a real boost. He outlined how supportive Littlemore had been and how he felt the institution bore no blame. The real issue was Evie's long history of self-harm and depression.

Ivo, Piers and Charlie were models of quiet respectability. They were humble and discreet. They spoke of friendship and of Evie's sense of fun and joy, and of her troubles. When asked about tendencies towards self-harm, they each said they'd had an instinct this might be the case, but had no idea how serious it might be. Piers said he thought Evie's final act was inexplicable. Ivo was cool and urbane, with no hint of the monster I'd glimpsed that morning after Evie's torture in the panopticon. I tried to see them as the coroner and jury might see them. Could they even begin to see behind the act? I thought not. If I were not aware of the details I couldn't even begin to imagine that these three were any other than the quiet, prayerful people they presented themselves as. Quietly, all of us betrayed Evie.

Richard appeared on one of the two days of the hearing, not

as a witness, but in the gallery. He was there when Ivo began his statement and had gone by the time he had finished. He was waiting for me outside the courtroom at lunchtime and we went to a little café he knew and chatted politely over sandwiches and soup. He looked dreadful, even more angular than usual. This effect was made even more pronounced by his decision to shave off his beard. His cheekbones protruded and his clothes seemed ill-fitting. He seemed all planes and angles. Behind his specs his eyes were hooded. I didn't think he'd slept much recently. I asked what he was planning to do now. As soon as I'd asked it, I realised he might think I meant, 'Are you going to tell everyone about what we did to Evie?' Instead, he said,

'I'm off to Greece tomorrow. I'm going on retreat to a monastery. Just to clear my head. Who knows from there. What about you?'

'I don't know,' I replied, honestly.

I attempted a couple of conversational gambits, discreetly attempting to sound out whether he might speak out about Evie or felt the need to correct the impression the rest of us had given in the courtroom. He would not bite. The only thing he said before he left was, 'One day, Kitty. There are bigger issues at stake than the death of a troubled woman in a college chapel.'

That was the last time I ever saw him.

The Coroner came to her inevitable verdict: Evie's death had been caused by suicide. She ruled the case closed and Evie's body was released to the family. I remember there being some sort of line-up later that day, it might have been at the court or it might have been at the College. Ivo, Piers, Charlie and me, all the other students and staff walked in front of Gus and Miranda and shook their hands. It was like being at a funeral without a body. As I passed Evie's grieving parents, I said how sorry I was. All I remember was how neither of them could look at me. And yet, I received a message a few days later that the Kirklands wanted me to read the Lesson at the funeral.

When I found out, I wanted to run. I just wanted to get in my car and drive north. I wanted to see the hills of Cumbria or the wide-open expanses of the Yorkshire moors, somewhere I knew, far away from the claustrophobia of Littlemore. But, of course, I did not. I accepted and when the day came I drove alone down to the little village church in Wiltshire where Evie's earthly remains were to be interred. The weather was bitter, but I could not think of a more beautiful place to bury her. The church was twelfth century and tiny. It has an original strong box on display in which the old parish treasures would have been locked away in medieval times. The Kirklands had connections in the village going back hundreds of years and Evie was to be interred in the family plot.

I have taken the funeral services of many young people. They are usually powerful and incredibly charged events. They are massively attended and the level of tears and sadness is, understandably, extravagant. There is usually popular music and countless tributes. I don't judge this. The death of the young will always generate potent reactions. What was striking about Evie's funeral was how subversive it was. It was not a memorial or a celebration of life, as has now become standard. It was an old-fashioned funeral using the *Book of Common Prayer*. There were a couple of hymns – 'Lead, Kindly Light' and 'Pleasant are Thy Courts Above' – and the vicar delivered a very simple tribute. The church was about half-full and I realised that apart from family and a few representatives from Evie's school and university life, this was a deliberately quiet occasion. I was asked to read from 1 Corinthians 15. The funeral was so old-fashioned that, clothes aside, it might have taken place any time between 1662 and about 1980. I thought it more impressive for its restraint.

None of the others turned up. After the service, I spoke briefly to the Principal about it. He said that Ivo had come to see him that morning with a card and a small wreath of orchids. He'd said that – due to an undisclosed family issue – he'd been called away. He said he would write privately to Sir Angus and his wife later. As for Piers and Charlie, he had no news to deliver. He'd expected them to be here. Then, again, he added, it was clear that this funeral was less for friends and more for close relatives. Where that left me, I don't know. He finished his speech, probably the most extended he ever had with me, by saying he was sure everyone would be at a College Memorial service in a few months.

* * *

I was so lost. I was so lost I didn't realise for days what had gone missing, or, as I discovered, had been stolen. In those days after Evie's death my usually neat life had, perhaps unsurprisingly, become chaotic. Clothes and possessions became disarrayed. I lost the motivation to tidy in the obsessive way I usually did. That chaos – of mind as much as of physical space – meant it was days before I realised that the *Cummean* was gone. Before Evie's death I'd begun keeping the books close to my body, but in the aftermath, I put them down in my room. In my traumatised state, I paid them less mind than I'd used to. I spotted them, from time to time, poking out of a pile of clothes, or so I thought. It was about a week after the suicide I discovered the truth.

The Chaucer was safe. That was the good news. The *Cummean*, however, was gone. The book that, in my tiredness and confusion, I'd thought was Evie's, turned out to be an old leather Bible. Once I looked with even half my proper attention, it was obvious. I turned my room upside down. I made so much noise that my next-door neighbour Audrey Court turned up. I suspected she was already on high alert, waiting for me to break down, and came a little too quickly.

She stood there in the doorway saying, 'It'll be all right, Kitty. I understand. It feels impossible right now, but one day you'll heal.'

It was all I could do not to punch her or tell her to eff off. Instead, I stood dumbly, surrounded by books and mess and clothes, until she left.

The book had to be in my room. All I needed to do was be more systematic. It would then simply appear as these things often do when one stops looking. So, I began tidying, quietly and carefully, trying to concentrate on my breathing, anything to keep me calm. It meant I slowly managed to reassemble and tidy my room, but there was no sign of Evie's book. I sat on my bed, exhausted and desperate. For the first time since Evie's death I cried. I wept and wept, like a little girl. When my tears had burnt out I tried to reconstruct events. When had I last been sure I'd had the book? I was sure it was on the morning of Evie's death. Before going to chapel, I'd put on an overcoat and slid it into one of the pockets. Insofar as I was sure of anything I was sure it was still with me when I'd come back to my room before Ivo and the others had turned up.

I considered this. I'd thrown my coat on the bed and then sat with my back to it. What had happened after that? It was all a blur of drinking and chat, but someone had picked it up and hung it on the door. They'd moved it so that they could sit down. It had been Ivo. Ivo had gone behind me, picked up my coat and – with characteristic tidiness – had hung it up on the door peg. That was when he'd taken his chance. Perhaps he felt the extra weight in the coat or seen it sitting inside the pocket. Either way, he'd taken his chance and claimed his prize. He'd stolen my book.

I felt too burnt out to weep any more. I was too hollow for fury or outrage. I just felt cold and empty and sick. I'd been played. At my most vulnerable – reeling in shock and in need of friendship and kindness – Ivo had been ruthless. When presented with 'his book' as he called it, he'd not hesitated. Evie was dead and he had what he wanted all along.

In the end, I'd let Evie down. I could not keep her book safe from his clutches and the worst of it was I knew why she wanted to keep it away from him. On that morning I'd gone down to chapel and found Evie hanging there, I'd puzzled it out. And if I was correct, not only could I see why Ivo coveted it, but also why he thought he had to punish Evie. The text that Evie had found concealed behind the words of his penitential were quite extraordinary. They held within them the power to disrupt and rework pretty much all of the assumptions of the Church. It offered justification for much of what Evie had claimed about the radical and feminist foundations of Christianity, which I – to my shame – had too often treated as a joke. In short, the book that Evie had found was pure dynamite.

Chapter Thirty-two

I was short of people I could trust. There was, in fact, only one person left: Albertus. Yet, he'd become as much of a ghost as Evie. Since her death I'd seen him once, the day after the Principal had called the whole student body together. I'd been walking back from Chapel when I'd seen him in the distance talking to Charlie. He looked a shadow of his former self. I was about to walk over, when something made me stop. Even at forty yards I could see the tension between them. It looked like they were arguing about something. Albertus seemed to be trying to make light of it and Charlie was pressing her point. Then Albertus said something which made Charlie stop. She let her head fall, as if in defeat. Albertus could do that to people. He then did something I never imagined he ever would: he hugged Charlie. It was so uncharacteristic, it was almost difficult to witness, obscene, somehow. He was just not that sort of man.

Given how ill he looked, I was unsurprised when Albertus did not make the funeral. I was disappointed, of course. Evie had been his research assistant. She had been his chosen one, after all, and there was a part of me – quite a significant part – that thought he should have made the effort. Instead he sent a most extraordinary floral tribute with a brief note attached. The tribute comprised a single lily, violets, a sprig of columbine and some purple monkshood or 'Our Lady's Slipper'. It looked so bizarre when placed on the grave that the Principal said, 'Oh dear, I think Loewe is going completely gaga.' I didn't have the heart to tell him that those flowers were medieval symbols of the Virgin Mary. The note read simply, *'Sicut lilium inter spinas, sic amica mea inter fileas Adae'*, a quote from the Song of Songs, which translates, 'As the lily among thorns, so is my love among the daughters of Adam.' It was beautiful, tender and surprising. I had not thought he held her in such esteem. To this day, I can never hear Palestrina's setting of that text without thinking of Albertus's tribute to her.

No matter how ill Albertus might be, I needed to speak to someone, and he was the only person I could trust. It was pointless going to look for him in Luxford House. At the best of times, Albertus was disinclined to be on campus without good reason, and right now, surely he had none. There were no seminars scheduled. It was not even as if Ivo, Piers and Charlie were around to entertain him. They had vanished. No. He would not be on campus. So, on the first properly spring-like day of the new year, I cycled off towards Albertus's house in Jericho.

I rapped and rapped on his door. No answer. I called his name through the letterbox. Still nothing. Yet I was sure there was someone in there. Eventually, I saw a figure approach through the glass of the front door. The door opened and I was greeted by a woman in a dark blue nurse's dress. She was in her mid-forties, perhaps mid-fifties, with straggly red hair, flecked with grey. She looked at me severely and said, in an Irish accent, 'Well?'

'Um, I'm here to see Albertus.'

'Professor Loewe isn't seeing any students.'

'I'm not a student.' It was a lie, but an instinctive one. In one sense, it was true: I was no undergrad, here for a tutorial. I was, I thought, more like a friend. We'd shared Christmas Day together, hadn't we?

I heard a voice, weak and faint, issue from the sitting room.

'Who is it, Eilidh?'

269

'Just a student, Professor.' Eilidh looked severely at me. I decided this was my chance.

'Albertus,' I shouted, 'it's me, Kitty!'

I heard Albertus say something indistinct. Eilidh continued to study me, then said,

'Come back another day. He's not well.'

I thought she was going to slam the door in my face, when Albertus said, more strongly than before,

'Kitty!' There was real delight in his voice. 'Eilidh, bring her to me.'

I didn't wait for Eilidh to object. I pushed my way past and entered the sitting room.

It was a dreadful, shocking scene. Where six weeks before, this room had been the very acme of a bachelor don's inner sanctum – dog-eared chairs, piles of books and magazines, and the scent of pipe tobacco – now it was little more than a hospital room. Someone – perhaps Nurse Eilidh, for I couldn't imagine Mrs Lodge doing it – had removed the books and magazines from sight. In place of the comforts of home was a hospital bed. It was surrounded by medical equipment, including a drip, a blood pressure monitor and some sort of pump device.

At the centre of this web of wires and tubes, lay Albertus. He looked beyond dreadful. The oddly youthful look of a few weeks before had departed. He was skin and bone and his eyes were sunken. His skin almost had a translucent quality. He grinned warmly at me – his smile, at least, had not changed – and said,

'Come now, Kitty. I don't look that bad do I?' His voice was scratchy and weak. I smiled back at him and said,

'You look a fright, Albertus, but I won't hold it against you.'

He laughed, as heartily as his shrunken frame would allow. His laughter turned into a cough and while it burned itself out, he gestured towards the door through which I'd just come. I shut it, and sat down next to him.

'Won't the nurse be annoyed?'

Between the last few hacks of his coughing fit, he said, 'Oh, I do hope so.'

'You haven't lost your mischief, Albertus.'

'Oh, Eilidh brings it out in me.'

'Where did you dig her up? She's worse than Nurse Gamp.'

At that moment, the sitting room door opened and Eilidh poked her head around the door.

'I'll be off now, Professor. I'll be back at seven. If there are any problems, just press the button around your neck. And, young lady, don't go tiring out the professor.'

Albertus rallied at this and said,

'Be off with you, woman. Before I sling you out.'

Eilidh smiled indulgently and left. I waited till the front door clicked shut, then said,

'What's this all about, Albertus?'

'I'm dying, Kitty.'

'That much is reasonably obvious. I mean, why didn't you say anything?'

'What good would it do?'

'We ... I ... might have helped. Rather than you having to rely on Nursie here.'

'I'd have liked that. You'd have allowed me my pipe. Though I don't think you're the nursing kind, Kitty.' He paused, then more firmly, much more like his old self, 'I thought you and the others had enough on your plate. Evie and all that.'

'Was that what you and Charlie were arguing about? This?' I gestured at the equipment in the room. He nodded. I realised it had been Charlie comforting Albertus, not the other way around. She had been hugging a dead man walking. A sudden, renewed love for them both flowed through me.

'How long?'

271

He raised his gnarled hands and shrugged. 'Who knows? A week? A month? My doctor says I might go on for months. The tumour is inoperable. Has been for ages. It's the pain, Kitty, that's what I can't stand. And the bloody drugs.' He gestured feebly at the pump-device.

'But, there must be something,' I said.

He grinned warmly, once again. 'Sometimes the only "something" is to accept the facts. I think I've accepted the facts.'

I realised tears were sliding down my face.

A friend once told me that in Germany, one's PhD supervisor is known as one's 'Doktor-Vater', or, in these egalitarian times, 'Doktor-Mutter'. When I wrote my PhD my director of studies had been like a mother to me, helping me bring the thesis to birth, offering wisdom and advice and the occasional chiding. In the end – like all good parents – she let me go. I realised as I sat by Albertus's bed, that in the short time I'd known him he'd become the closest I'd ever had to a real father. Twenty years on, I wonder if that signals just how messed up my relationship with men must have been. Albertus was hardly an unambiguous man. He was, I knew by now, a man of dubious moral character and to latch on to him and see him as my true father was not exactly healthy. Back then, however, he was what I had, and I had to learn to let him go. Everyone gets orphaned in the end.

In that moment, it was as if he were the last priest in England and I were the last sinner. I felt like we were nearly out of time and I needed to find some peace. It was time for the truth, free of any pretence.

'Why did you steal those books, Albertus?'

Owlishly, he tipped his head slightly to the side. 'You're not going moral on me, are you, Kitty?'

I shook my head. 'Steal might be a little strong,' I admitted.

He licked his cracked lips and said,

'I'm a borrower and a reader. And words are ravishing. I think you know this yourself.' He sighed, then added, 'But I think I've borrowed them for long enough.' He looked at me with his extraordinary, intelligent eyes, as if daring me to challenge him.

'Why …' I stopped and tried again. 'Did you mean …'

'Did I want you to take the Chaucer?' said Albertus, kindly.

I laughed and said, 'Yes.'

'It's not that simple. I wanted to see who you were, Kitty. Of all my students, you're the one who's puzzled me. So, consider it a test.'

'Did I pass or fail?'

'Let's just say, I was reassured. There is no one good …'

'… except for God.' I finished the line for him, remembering it was a phrase Evie had used the afternoon she'd given me the *Cummean*.

'Yes,' said Albertus. 'Call it an old man's vanity, but I've always needed to know what makes my students tick. I've always needed to show them as much of their true selves as I can. I think I'm ready to let you and the Chaucer go now.'

'Is that why …'

'Is that why I encouraged Ivo and Piers?' He closed his eyes and said, 'Don't remind me. I'm not sure I can stand the shame.'

'Perhaps it's time for confessions.'

He seemed suddenly agitated and tried to push himself up. He gestured towards a couple of spare pillows on the settee and said,

'Get those would you? Slide them behind me.'

I did as he asked and he settled back more comfortably. He closed his eyes and said, 'I am not a good man, just a clever one …' He sighed again. '… Not clever enough.' He opened his eyes and glared defiantly at me. 'How could I know what Ivo would become?'

'Because you know what makes your students tick.'

Albertus looked furious and seemed ready to fight back, then said, in a defeated tone, 'You're right, of course. I should have seen

… there is a monster in all of us, Kitty. But, I am old and I no longer want to look so closely at others or myself.'

'But…'

'But nothing,' he said harshly. 'I thought it would be good for you all to pray your way back to another world … a world where God still mattered. I thought I was being so clever. I didn't see that I was sowing your fields with salt. Forgive me …'

'And Evie's book?' The room had become hushed. Even the machines around Albertus had fallen silent. Neither of us spoke in more than a whisper. On a hunch I said,

'Did you just happen to pass it her way?'

He smiled. 'It was very carefully done, though I say it myself … she was convinced she'd found it herself … it brought me such joy to see her so excited.'

'Why did you do it?'

'Do I need a reason?' he said harshly. Then, like a chided child he added, 'Because I am old, and stupid and bored and thought it would be fun to give Evie something to play with …'

I wanted to leave, then, to get away from this absurd, capricious old man whose lack of judgment had helped to bring Evie's world crashing down, but I could not. I still loved and needed him, and I still needed to understand. I arrived at the only question I really wanted an answer to.

'Did you know what was concealed behind Cummean's words?'

'No,' he said sharply.

He closed his eyes again. I realised he was on the edge of exhaustion. I thought he was going to cry.

'*Father, forgive them, for they know not what they do.* How, I've come to rely on those words.' He looked at me again, an exhausted old man and said, 'I may be mischievous, Kitty, but I'm quite old-fashioned. You may have helped me be less of a fuddy-duddy, but if I'd have known what … unorthodoxies … what radical claims …

lay beneath the Penitential, I would never have passed it to someone as impressionable as Evie. I would most certainly have not let Ivo anywhere near it.'

'He has it, you know.'

'Ah. I'm sorry to hear that.'

'Will he destroy it?'

'He will want to … and he won't … it is not his instinct to destroy ancient things, even those he despises.'

I wanted to cry again. I felt overwhelmed and exhausted. I felt ancient. Though I am not much of a one for poetry, as I sat by Albertus and observed his brokenness, two lines came to me. That line of Yeats's: 'An aged man is but a paltry thing'. Albertus had become 'a tattered coat upon a stick'. That, and that line of Penthea in John Ford's *The Broken Heart*: 'Alas, poor gentleman! He look'd not like the ruins of his youth, but like the ruins of those ruins.' And despite it all, I loved him. Despite his selfishness and vanity. Despite his self-deception and the way he'd blithely led us to our doom. I should have left him then to rest and sleep. Instead, I knew it was time to talk about what was hidden in the book Evie had given me. I knew it was time to speak truth. I said,

'Father, would you hear my confession?'

Chapter Thirty-three

Now I am the best part of fifty, I've learnt to accept I'm not the myth I have of myself. I wish I were. I wish I were the confident, competent priest everyone believes me to be. I am not like the colleague who told me about a cell group she belongs to. In it, she and the other members take off their masks and try to reveal themselves to each other. They are, in her words, 'dangerously intimate'. The very thought of it makes me queasy. I now see, I've never achieved intimacy. I've slept with people, of course; I've created illusions of intimacy, but I've never let anyone in.

Except on that afternoon with Albertus. As he lay there dying I just let go. Perhaps, I simply felt safe because he was so close to the end. He was asleep for most of what I had to say and he was not, when I finished, sufficiently conscious to offer me absolution or penance. I don't think that matters. The rest of my life has been penance. In *Cummean's Penitential*, penances are precise and detailed. Thus, a monk who commits the sin of gluttony is required to live for forty days on bread and water; one who commits femoral intercourse does two years and so on and so forth. If I am happy about one thing, it is that my life has become a penance. Sometimes, in my more febrile moments, I almost think I'm cursed. Do you know that some medieval books were so priceless that librarians would curse them? Some borrowers had to take oaths: return the book or die. Images showed thieves being taken down to hell by Satan's ministers. Perhaps, all of us, in the end – Albertus, Evie, the lot of us – were cursed by the books we obsessed over.

What did I tell Albertus, that afternoon? My spiritual director had taught me to keep confessions simple and orderly. As someone with too many words, that's always been a struggle. That day, I finally understood my spiritual director's point. My confession came down to one thing, fractured into a dozen differing things: betrayal, most especially my betrayal of Evie. I've no regrets about what was done at the inquest. It would not have helped matters if we'd gone into details about manuscripts and cilices and hair shirts; or about how Evie and Ivo and I had crossed lines that surely had less to do with the Medieval than our damaged upbringings. I still think about what Piers said, about how he and Ivo blithely killed that cormorant to make a potion. At the time, it didn't bother me. It amused me. But, frankly, what kind of a person does that sort of thing? Or Ivo, who said he learned early about the power of discipline at Christian summer camp. God knows what that entailed. Perhaps one day we shall know. We were all screw-ups and, as I spoke to Albertus, I said so.

I spoke about Evie. I attempted to tell the truth: That I hated her; that I loved her. I wept like a child while I confessed how much I wanted her and had loved the taste of her lips, the scent of her body. I wept when I said I wanted to be her, to have had her life. I wept when I spoke of how young and sad she'd seemed that day I discovered she still clutched her worn-out little teddy, Mr Chatalon, to herself when she couldn't sleep. I spoke about how I could never see her straight because I was jealous. Years on, I see more clearly how enemies can supply us with value and passion. That afternoon, for the first time, I admitted the aridity of my life. I admitted how I used Evie to help me feel something, anything. If our time at Littlemore had been a Mystery Play, I would have been well cast as Judas, and Evie my Jesus. Nowadays, I am inclined to read myself through the lens of the Fisher King: my life is a wound that can only be healed by a fool, pure-in-heart. But the world has grown thin and all the fools are corrupt. Indeed, they have no heart at all.

Most of all I spoke about books, specifically the words that lay concealed in the copy of Evie's *Cummean*. While Albertus slept, I talked about what Evie and I had found: the world's only known copy of *The Gospel of Eve*. To even say that out-loud made my pulse thrum. It was one of the great lost books of western literature, a book that had been thought lost for sixteen-hundred years. It was a text that was explosive and would lead to a rethink of the foundations of Christianity. It had been suppressed because of its feminist understanding of Christ, of women and sexual relations, and I had not understood what I'd had until I'd deciphered a passage containing one word on the night before Evie had died: Borboros. *Βόρβορος*. It simply means 'mud' or 'filth'. It led me back to that argument Ivo and Piers had had in Chapel months before. They'd mentioned the Christian sect the Borborites – the filthy ones – who were supposed to have used *The Gospel of Eve* and other questionable books as the basis for their 'grubby' rites. When I'd woken from my night of dreams, my mind had connected the dots. Yet, what I understood that morning was a revelation: that Christian tradition had got *The Gospel of Eve* all wrong. The Borborites hadn't been the wicked ones, at all; they had – as Evie had argued all along – been those who had been stereotyped as vile by prudish, judgmental 'Christians'. The Gospel they protected had been about radical equality between men and women; *The Gospel of Eve* spoke of Jesus' closest disciples being women as well as men. If Evie had got so many things wrong – there had never been libertine Lollards in Oxfordshire – at a deeper level she had been right. There were ancient, egalitarian traditions that went back to the very foundations of the New Testament.

Finally, I understood Evie's obsessions of the Michaelmas term, all those excited conversations and trips out to find out more about a suppressed version of Christianity lost since the fall of the Roman

Empire. Finally, I saw that all her talk of Lollards and feminism, of sexual delight as a kind of 'freedom in Christ', could be traced back to what she'd deciphered in the palimpsest behind *The Penitential of Cummean*. Her discovery had set her on a path that could only lead to conflict with Ivo, a man who – through violence and self-mortification – had appointed himself the defender of orthodoxy. He truly saw himself as Dürer's knight defending Christendom from all comers. If I still didn't yet know the full details, I was smart enough to have figured that much out. Ivo had appointed himself Inquisitor to Evie's heretic and he'd drawn Piers and Charlie into his scheme. Only Richard had enough sense to resist, but insufficient strength to speak out.

As I confessed to Albertus, I began to appreciate how much I'd been played by my friends. Charlie, Ivo, Piers, even to an extent, Richard. I'd been mesmerised by them. Even more than Evie, they were people I wanted to be like and to be liked by. I appreciated how much I'd read Evie through the lens they'd supplied for me. I'd been so ready to accept Charlie's assessment of Evie's manipulative nature. I'd let myself be so blithely charmed by Ivo and Piers. Of course, it wasn't so much that Charlie was wrong about Evie. Evie was no saint or angel, but, as events transpired, I think Evie cared for me more completely than I knew. Evie loved me, whereas Ivo was both cruel and ruthless, as demonstrated in the way he stole the *Gospel of Eve* from me. Perhaps my greatest betrayal during those months, then, was of my own judgment. The fact is, all of us deserved to be counted among the *Borboros*. Not the *Borboros* Evie had found – the ones who had been misunderstood and painted as filthy by the narrow-minded and pious – but those who make themselves filthy with their hate.

Do I have regrets, then? Yes, and yes, and no. Looking back, my time at Littlemore would have been simpler if I'd never known my friends. In the months after Evie's death, as the rest of them withdrew from Littlemore, I began to find a quieter, more sustained way of living college life, though it was touch-and-go for me too. I almost left, but where was I to go? I didn't have trust funds and family estates. After Evie's death, in the quiet rhythms supplied by Littlemore, I found a way to live within the confines and the spaces of the Church. But for all my bruises, how can I write off that time completely? I never felt more alive. Those months, when I mortified my flesh, when I was part of a select and separate group were – if I'm honest – the best days of my life. Of course, I wish Evie had lived, but her death doesn't wipe away the glories. If that makes me a monster, then we were all monsters. We found each other and gave each other strange animation.

* * *

Perhaps, I should tell you what happened to my friends. I never saw Richard again after that lunch in Oxford. He, however, has found his own peace, I think, in Greece. About five years after our last meeting, he sent me a card from a monastery on Mount Athos. God knows how he found my address. *Crockford's,* I guess. He revealed that he had become an Eastern Orthodox monk and was about to take life vows. He had taken the name 'Dionysios' and wished me every blessing in my life. I couldn't quite picture this transformation from ultra-English ordinand with a love for food and drink to bearded monk, but God has a sense of humour. Perhaps, in taking the name Dionysios, a reference to the old puckish god of the Greeks, Richard found a way to acknowledge the joke. I comfort myself that this quiet, troubled young man has at last found peace and community. He always suffered from a deficit of love and found in feeding others with his amazing food a way to escape from loneliness and abandonment. I trust he is now fed by his community and his God in ways which truly satisfy.

Charlie reappeared in college a week after Evie's funeral. She was not well. When I went round to see her in her flat, she was drinking heavily and chain smoking. She said that she wanted to stay at Littlemore, but didn't think she could. She'd spent the previous week in a Carmelite nunnery in Norfolk, trying to find some peace, but it had only made things worse. That afternoon, she told me things that made the scene in the panopticon seem tame. It's not my story to tell so I shall be discreet. However, I found out it had not been Piers she'd been with that day I'd found her half-naked in her flat. It had been Ivo, and Ivo had turned his gift for chastisement onto her. My encounter with Ivo's love of holding cigarettes close to human skin was, shall we say, as nothing compared to what he did with them on Charlie's flesh. Evie's death had proven a wake-up call about the depth of his power over her. We talked into the night and I suggested she speak to the police. She said she couldn't, not least because it would bring the world down around us all. She felt ashamed of the way she'd used Evie as her punch-bag. If I could have heard her confession and given her absolution, I would. Like me, I think she knew how close love is to hate and vice versa.

Charlie packed her bags the next day and I heard nothing of her for over a decade. There were rumours, of course; comments and insinuations made when, over the years after ordination, I'd bump into old Moreans (as alumni are known). Charlie had been seen in Thailand running a bar; Charlie was working in Eastern Europe in an orphanage, and so on. The truth was only confirmed when I was appointed to my Cathedral role. A letter came, along with a photograph, from Rwanda. It congratulated me on my promotion and said how much she missed me. The photo showed her and a man she said was her husband, along with a girl, her daughter. Charlie looked happy and relaxed in the photo. She was older, more mumsy somehow, there was even a streak of grey in her hair. She wore khaki 'jungle' gear and, to my amusement, I noted how fabulous she looked even in these nondescript clothes. She explained that she'd found her way, and a modicum of peace, working for the rebuilding of that shattered country.

As for Piers and Ivo, they didn't even bother to return to

Littlemore. When I asked the Principal about this, he explained that independently they'd resigned as ordinands. Apparently, in the light of Evie's death, they needed a time of profound reflection and reconsideration. The Principal said that, at one level, he wasn't surprised. When he'd been at seminary, there'd been a violent death and it had shaken the faith of many. I almost said I didn't think Evie's death would shake either of them one jot, but I stayed my tongue. The older I get, the more certain I am that their faith was not so much shaped by the Living God, but by a fascination with death. Perhaps that's always a risk with religion: like sex, it always runs close to the deathly, to an emptying of self that is final and definitive. Piers and Ivo were like men longing to be soldiers in a war – not so much for glory, but because it offers the promise, indeed the near certainty, of death. They were attracted to the Eros that lies in Thanatos. Their approach to faith was an offer of destruction.

Perhaps, they got what they wanted in the end. Piers and Ivo disappeared from my life and, over time, even my fury at Ivo's theft of *The Gospel of Eve* began to lose its force and fire. It was a couple of years later, just as I was about to be ordained, that I came across Piers again, or a photograph of him, at least. It was above a headline on page ten of *The Times*. The story ran, 'Piers Halliwell, youngest son of Mr Leonard Halliwell, the noted financier and close friend of the Royal Family, was found dead at the family home in Chelsea yesterday. Halliwell, who had recently become engaged to Lady Harriet Coutts, was known for his hedonistic lifestyle. More to follow.' I read and re-read the scant information. Over the following days, more news came out. It became quite the scandal at Littlemore among the few remaining students who remembered him. Cocaine and heroin had been involved. It turned out that what killed him, however, was auto-asphyxiation. It was a cheap and shameful way to die, and I couldn't quite match it up with the young man I'd so adored and admired. He had, it seemed, become a worshipper at the altar of Bacchus, and his offering had been accepted. I quietly attended the funeral at a swanky church in West London, full of society types. I arrived late and left early. I'd only gone to see if Ivo turned up. Of course, he didn't.

As for Ivo. Ah, Ivo. He was, I guess, the trigger for this confession. A few months ago, idly googling his name on the internet, I came across a brief notice of death on the BBC World website. It said, 'It has been reported that the Hon. Ivo David Matchings Termagent, brother of the 12th Viscount Crantock, has been killed in Ukraine by a breakaway faction of the Russian Orthodox Army.' I read on, but details focussed more on the current Viscount, a noted landowner, than on him. I searched ever more dubious sites, searching for clues, but most accounts were just as sketchy as the BBC's. Over the following weeks, however, certain disturbing facts came to light. Ivo had fallen very far indeed, it seems, and had become associated with increasingly fanatical Christian extremist groups. He'd smuggled guns and child soldiers for the Lord's Resistance Army in Uganda and had links to Chinese group Eastern Lightning as well as the Russian Orthodox Army. There were rumours of support for White Nationalist Christian groups. His family had long since disavowed him. It was the reports of how he died, however, which I found shattering. His charred remains indicated that he'd been systematically tortured before his death. Apparently, the torture included the use of the 'Gerard's Shoe' technique. Named after a man who'd attempted to kill William of Orange, it involves forcing someone to wear oiled, soft shoes made too small for him. His feet are then held in front of a fire until the shoes contract and crush the wearer's feet. There was evidence that broken glass and lit cigarettes had been forced into his anus, and his genitals had been removed, apparently, while he had still been alive. Some reports speculated that this was a sign he had been punished for homosexual acts.

Last week, I received a small parcel through the post. There was a letter in it from a grand sounding firm of City Solicitors, 'Renfrew, Locksley and Black', indicating that the enclosed comprised a legacy to me from the late Ivo Termagent, Esq. In addition to a neatly sealed box was a hand-written note. I recognised the crabbed, prissy handwriting immediately. Ivo's note was crisp and simple, and it constituted a confession of sorts. It began with general salutations, asking after my health and saying how fondly he remembered me from Littlemore. He said that if I was receiving this note he must have, as he put it, 'come to a sticky end'. Then he spoke of Evie. He began with a quote: 'The kiss burns his heart, but the old man remains firm in his own ideas and unbelief.' It was from that story of the Grand Inquisitor from the *Brothers Karamazov*, the one where Jesus comes back in the time of Torquemada and, despite being embraced as the Christ by the people, is arrested by the Inquisition. In the story, the old Inquisitor explains to Jesus that most people cannot handle the freedom he offers; only the rules of the Church are sufficient. Before Christ is released, on the expectation that he will never come back again, he kisses the old Inquisitor who has tortured him, and marks him for life.

In the remains of the letter, Ivo refused to apologise for his actions. He regretted Evie's death, but said he had a duty to save her from herself and ensure that *The Gospel of Eve* was kept beyond use. Its contents he felt were too dangerous – they offered false freedoms not meant for simple people. He felt that should they be disseminated they would be one more nail in the doom of the Church. Evie, he claimed, was punished for the sake of love and love alone. He also said that he'd planned to destroy the book, but to his surprise he could not. He said he thought of this as Evie's equivalent of Jesus' kiss to the Inquisitor. Every time he contemplated destroying the book he saw her, and, in the end, he'd decided that if there was anyone he might trust it with after his death, it was me. I was, he said, in my own way, someone with a gift for knowing how fragile was God's truth, and, therefore, would know what to do with the book.

It would not have been unreasonable for that letter to have left me cold, but as I took Evie's book out of its box, I wept and wept. Of all of them, Ivo had been at the mysterious heart of those months at Littlemore. Did I weep because the key to it all was gone? Perhaps. Or perhaps it was because – as Albertus said – none of us is ever simple. Ivo was capable of the monstrous, but I loved him nonetheless, as I loved them all. We were the special ones, the shining ones, and what have any of us added up to? Not a lot. Even I, for all my church achievements, live a half-life. How, then, can I not enjoy the memories I have of them? Of that first time I saw Ivo stumping towards the common-room after finishing a run. Or of that sloppy smile of his, and the way he would say, 'Come' to beckon you into his room. Of those endless afternoons when we all played ping-pong in Luxford, arguing over points and getting drunk on cocktails. Or of Evie and Charlie trying to teach me the Charleston while Piers took the piss and Richard cooked up another marvel from the strangest of ingredients. Of Albertus, presiding over seminars, like a wise, white-haired walrus. Are such memories a sin?

Albertus himself died a few weeks after I saw him. His funeral, as one might expect, was extravagant. Christchurch Cathedral was packed with the great and the good, as well as many of the students he'd shaped and taught over the decades. The choir sang 'How Lovely is thy Dwelling Place' from Brahms' *German Requiem* and there were readings and tributes delivered by at least one Head of State, as well as members of the British government. I found it all too much and left before the Commendation, preferring to remember him as I saw him that first day we'd properly met: at Luxford, when he'd greeted Evie and me with royal ceremony, as if we were going to inherit the earth. I chose then, and, I guess, I still choose to remember the fairy story unsullied, King Pellam's Land before the Plague.

In an odd way, Evie outlasted us all at Littlemore. There was, as the Principal promised, a big Memorial service in the college chapel a few months after her death. None of the others attended, but I delivered my tribute, speaking of my adventures with her in rural Oxfordshire in search of Lollardy. Gus and Miranda Kirkland looked strained, but joined in the laughter and the tears and, after the service, said that they were glad that Evie had had someone like me to share her life with. They seemed gratified when I cried at this. It was the kind of event I think Evie would have hated, but memorial services are never for the dead, only for the living, and that day, a new trust for 'struggling ordinands', 'The Evelyn Kirkland Fund' was announced. Evie lives on at Littlemore through that fund. It is, of course, a half-life and I doubt she'd be happy to be forever associated with 'struggling ordinands', but it is a life nonetheless.

One rather wonderful thing happened around the time of Evie's memorial service – news that several important libraries around the UK and Europe had received anonymous and extravagant donations of rare manuscripts. It even made the Radio 4 *One O'clock News*. Librarians from Oxford to St Petersburg were 'thrilled', 'stunned' and 'shocked' as incredible books arrived anonymously on their desks. Some, it transpired, had disappeared from the records of those same libraries between the 1930s and 1950s. Some had been written off as 'lost during the War'. Priceless copies of the *Inferno*, the *Decameron* and even an early printed *Guttenberg Bible* simply appeared out of thin air. Who could be responsible, the radio programme asked? No sufficient answer was supplied. That night, as I listened, I raised a glass of Dalwhinnie to both Albertus and Evie. They had been good and cunning servants. In those months they'd worked together, they had achieved a quiet miracle. Though the world could not know it, this was a better tribute to them than a dozen memorial services or world leaders reading slabs of Ecclesiastes at Cathedral funerals.

And what of me? I still have that biscuit box with my little things inside. Its print – of a Royal Horse Guards soldier sat on a horse, sword raised, outside a palace – is even more scratched and defaced than ever. It remains the only solid thing I have from my childhood. That tin contains my treasures. There is my beautiful Chaucer and the Hermès scarf Evie bought me, and that card of Our Lady of Tindari she sent. There is also a small cilice, one made for an arm. I look at it from time-to-time, but I daren't put it on. Some temptations run too deep. And there is a photo of Louise and me, aged about four or five. We sit next to each other in white dresses, in front of a blue background, taken I think at primary school. Lou smiles abundantly, while my smile, at best, is half-hearted. She has her left arm around me, as if preventing me from getting away. It kind of sums up our relationship. It's the only photo I have of her.

I keep one other thing in that box: Mr Chatalon. After the funeral, Gus and Miranda Kirkland asked me if there was any small keepsake of Evie's I might like. It was, I think, an absurdly generous and undeserved offer and, at first, I couldn't bear to ask for a thing. I deserved nothing from them or from Evie. In the end, I plucked up my courage and asked if I might have Mr Chatalon, expecting them to say, 'No'. After all, he would have been one of the first things they would have given Evie when she was tiny. To my surprise, they seemed glad, almost relieved when I asked for the old teddy. Miranda passed him, limp and worn, over to me as if he were a new-born, Miranda's eyes full of tears. Why did I want him? I don't know exactly, except that somehow his worn-out, absurdly loved and damaged body reminded me of Evie. Beautiful, glorious, vulnerable Evie, who had deserved love and was ruined at the hands of her so-called friends.

And now I also have what I shall always think of as 'Evie's book', that little black leather volume that, beneath *The Cummean*, contains *The Gospel of Eve*. It stands, I think, as a testimony to how remarkable, persistent and brilliant she was. It stands as a testimony to how much I failed to understand and trust her. It is, as I see it, the most remarkable book in Christendom. And, so, twenty years on from my betrayal of her, I think my job, now, is to honour her and that book. If it takes me a lifetime, I shall puzzle it out, I shall translate it and get it out into the world. Ivo once said that his motivation for wanting to keep the book away from simple minds was a love of the truth. Well, if there is going to be one good thing that might come out of the betrayals and lies of his life and mine, and of the lives of all the others, it is the truth contained in Evie's book. Contained in – forgive the pun – Evie's Gospel.

I have found that the older I get, the less I escape my past. I am ever more aware of the sins I have to work out. More and more I travel back to my childhood, to that swollen river which ends in my sister's death. Since my parents died a few years ago, it is increasingly the only dream I have. Before I left Albertus that final day, I spoke to him about Lou and the river, and about memory. I asked him if he agreed that memory is the most labile, suggestible faculty. In a moment of sudden clarity and energy, he said he knew it was. He said that memory often reforms and alters to protect us from trauma. Its flexibility is a mark of our gift for survival. That is why false memory is so common. He said, however, that I shouldn't worry, because God is truth and all shall be revealed in the fullness of time.

As I spoke to Albertus that day, I told him how troubled I was with my memories of my sister. I told him that sometimes in my dreams Lou doesn't slip down the bank and fall; sometimes she's pushed in by me. As I spoke, he was fading and falling into sleep, but I think I heard him say, 'Kitty, don't worry.' Of course, I did worry, and I worry still. If God is truth, and God judges all, there is no escape – from Lou, from Evie, from my parents or my old friends. More and more, I dream of Lou. More and more, Evie is there, sometimes watching, sometimes egging me on. Sometimes she's Lou herself. And each time the same result: A body falls. A voice, a girl's, saying my name: *Kitty ... Kitty ... what have you done?*